A BODY
IN
SEAVIEW
GRANGE

BOOKS BY DEE MACDONALD

A BODY
IN
SEAVIEW
GRANGE

DEE MACDONALD

bookouture

Published by Bookouture in 2020

An imprint of Storyfire Ltd.
Carmelite House
50 Victoria Embankment
London EC4Y 0DZ

www.bookouture.com

ISBN: 978-1-83888-214-3
eBook ISBN: 978-1-83888-213-6

CHAPTER ONE

You needed to be over sixty years of age and have deep pockets to be able to buy one of the luxury flats in Seaview Grange, up on the cliffs near Higher Tinworthy. Kate Palmer didn't qualify on age just yet, and her pockets were extremely shallow but she was nevertheless keen to see how the other half might be living.

It was a beautiful sunny early September morning and Kate felt on top of the world, having just returned from Edinburgh for the birth of her first grandson. He was the most adorable, angelic infant ever born, with the possible exception of her own two handsome, perfect sons, of course.

And now, here she was, driving up to Seaview Grange to see a lady called Edina Martinelli in Flat 4 who had recently broken her ankle and was complaining that the plaster felt too tight.

Up until now Elaine, the nurse who split the week with Kate at the medical centre in Middle Tinworthy, had been doing most of the house calls. She was also assigned to 'Assisted Living Care' which meant she'd be the designated nurse to look after the residents of not only Seaview Grange, but also The Cedars and the Moorside Nursing Homes. She was shortly going to retire and Sue, who had worked there full time for years, was offered the calls. 'Not on your life,' said Sue. 'Who wants to go visiting those decrepit old biddies? Not me, I'm staying right here. Down to you, Kate!'

Kate didn't mind at all. She loved getting out and about instead of being stuck in the treatment room all day. It was a good way to get to know people and there was normally a cup of tea or coffee on offer.

'Good luck!' Sue had called after her. 'That Martinelli woman's always complaining about something or other.'

Seaview Grange was a large, imposing grey stone double-fronted building facing the Atlantic, one of many superior residences in the Higher Tinworthy area, set in what Kate reckoned must be around an acre of gardens, and with panoramic views of the sea and coastline. It was known to some of the locals as Gwel Teg, its original title being the Cornish for 'beautiful view' but since so many of the residents were incomers that had been watered down accordingly. There were neat little windblown flower beds and garden seats dotted here and there with no one sitting on them. Kate wondered briefly what the maintenance charges might be. High, undoubtedly.

The large oak-panelled front door was ajar and led into a spacious hallway, stone-flagged and with a large royal blue centrally placed carpet. There was an impressive stone central staircase, also carpeted up the middle. An ornately carved mahogany table was situated on the right, on top of which were some bundles of mail, which the postman obviously left there for the residents to collect. What caught Kate's attention, however, was the pair of stone figures on either end: a lighthouse and a tin-mine, both intricately carved out of what appeared to be serpentine. The Cornish serpentine, found on The Lizard peninsula, was normally green or multicoloured, but these items were predominantly red, which was more unusual.

To the left was Flat 1, in the middle behind the staircase was Flat 2, and immediately on the right was Flat 3. Kate assumed Flat 4 was upstairs and, as she climbed up, she ran her fingers along the highly polished wooden bannister. Everything was immaculate: not a speck on the floor and an aroma of polish permeated the air. Didn't people walk about in here? How come it was so spotless?

When she rang the bell of Flat 4 the door was opened by a tall, slim elderly woman on elbow crutches. She was fully made up, her white hair piled on her head in an elegant chignon, and she was clad in a colourful, full-length kaftan. She wore several heavy gold chains, drop earrings (could they be *real* sapphires?) a collection of bracelets and rings galore. None of it looked cheap.

'Mrs Martinelli? I'm Kate, the practice nurse, who's taken over from Elaine. I've come to have a look at your ankle.'

'I'm *Miss* Martinelli,' the woman corrected. 'I've always retained my professional name. *Do* come in.' She hobbled ahead into the large open-plan room, furnished in traditional mahogany. What struck Kate more than the velvet sofas and elaborately draped curtains was the number of framed operatic posters on every wall: *Aida*; *La traviata*; *Carmen*; *Il trovatore*, and more.

'Oh, I see you're an opera fan,' Kate said, laying her less-than-pristine bag down on the *very* pristine cream carpet and hoping it wasn't going to leave a mark.

'*Fan!*' Edina Martinelli clutched her heaving bosom in horror, the left crutch dangling in the air. 'I'm not a *fan*, darling, I'm a *soprano!*'

'Sorry, I didn't realise you were a professional singer,' Kate said.

'Well, I've retired now of course but, in my time I sang with all the major opera companies, including D'Oyly Carte, English Opera, Covent Garden.' She stopped for breath. '*Fan*, indeed!'

'My apologies,' Kate murmured again, 'I didn't know.'

'Well, you know now. And if you were any kind of opera aficionado you'd be well aware of the roles I sang. Anyway, you're not here to discuss my career, you're here to look at my poor ankle.' She lowered herself onto a pink velvet chair and propped the ankle up on a matching footstool.

Kate bent down and examined the plaster thoroughly. 'To be honest, Miss Martinelli, it seems absolutely fine. It's exactly as it should be and I'm sure you'll get used to it.'

The woman snorted. '*Six* weeks, they said. I shall be a prisoner in here for *six* weeks with a plaster cast that's far too tight!'

'Miss Martinelli,' Kate began, 'I know it might feel tight but it really isn't—'

'I'm wearing it and I say it *is*,' Edina Martinelli interrupted. Then, in a change of tone, 'Would you like a coffee?' With that, she hobbled into the kitchen, jewellery jangling. 'Give me a minute and I'll warm up the pot. But you'll have to pour it and carry it through.'

'That's fine,' Kate said. 'Now tell me, is there anyone who can help you get down the stairs? It might cheer you up to sit in the garden and get some fresh air. It's still very warm.'

'I'm not going down *any* stairs until I am completely healed,' Edina Martinelli snapped, 'not after what happened to me.' She sighed loudly and plonked herself down on the pink chair again. 'You go and get the coffee. No milk or sugar for me.'

Kate did as she was told. 'What was the problem with the stairs?' she asked.

'What happened was that *somebody* – who could *only* have been Sharon the cleaner, although of course she denies all knowledge of it – *somebody* left the flex of the vacuum cleaner right across the top of the stairs and I did *not* see it. That's the problem, of course, I walk tall and look straight ahead, always conscious of my deportment. And the next thing I know I'm tumbling down the stairs – and there's a lot of them. It's a wonder I didn't break my neck because, you see, *somebody* wanted to kill me. I'm *so* lucky to have got away with just a broken ankle, and massive bruising, of course, but that was *not* the intention of my would-be killer. *Somebody* wishes to kill me, Nurse, mark my words!'

'It must surely have been an accident?' Kate said.

'It was *not* an accident! It certainly would *appear* to be Sharon but, unlike some of the others round here, she had no real reason to wish me dead and she would be a convenient scapegoat. I can't *begin* to tell you what some of these people are like.'

'But surely none of them would want you dead?' Kate said soothingly as she poured the coffee.

'There are several who'd want me dead! I told the police, of course, but they didn't listen. I *know* that somebody wants me dead. And I showed the police the note.'

'What note?' Kate asked.

'The note that was pushed through my door. I wouldn't call it a note exactly because it was printed from a *computer*, I think. Do you understand computers, Nurse?'

'Well, technology is hardly my strong point but I'm familiar with most of the ordinary stuff,' Kate replied.

'I can't *abide* the things. Nevertheless, I *know* if something's been printed on a computer and *this* was.'

Kate was enthralled. 'What was?'

'The note!' Edina Martinelli looked at her as if she was an imbecile. 'I *told* you, I had a note pushed through the door! I can show it to you if you're interested. The police gave it back to me and I have it in my bedroom somewhere.'

'What was written on the note, Miss Martinelli?'

'I'll tell you, Nurse, *exactly* what was written on it: "If you don't stop that noise I'm going to have to find a way to silence you!" I gave the note to the police. I *told* them I was in mortal danger but did *they* care? Not one bit! As a result I don't feel at all safe.'

Kate, fascinated, digested this for a moment. 'Who do you suspect then?'

'Probably next door. He's a writer of *awful* books! Simply *dreadful* books! But he seems to make a lot of money so I suppose someone must like reading about murder, and blood, and gore – because *that* is what he writes.'

There was obviously an awful lot more to these residents than Kate could ever have imagined. 'But surely he would just come to you and air his grievances, wouldn't he? Why on earth would he put a *note* through your door?'

'He came to the door on several occasions, but he wasn't getting anywhere. I refuse to take orders from the likes of him. The man is a philistine; he has no appreciation of music at all. He probably thought that a mysterious, anonymous note would scare me and shut me up. But he doesn't scare me and that's the reason I went to the police.'

'Surely you can't be certain it's him?' Kate said.

'But don't you *see*? He's a novelist! He uses a computer all the time. And he certainly wouldn't want anyone to prove that it's *him* by writing by hand.'

'Couldn't it have been anyone else?' Kate asked, enthralled.

'Well, I can tell you who it *couldn't* have been rather than who it *could* have been. Edgar in Number 6 is a retired vicar, you know, so it couldn't have been him. And he doesn't possess a computer. He's such a kind man, and we have dinner together often. And then there's my dear friend, Hetty, in Number 1 downstairs. She wouldn't harm a fly. And then there's the Potter twins, two ancient old ladies who live next door to Hetty. Highly unlikely it would be either of them.'

'So you have no idea who else might have written the note?' Kate asked.

Edina considered for a moment. 'Well, there's that *common* woman in Flat 3 who is insanely jealous, of course, because her husband does little jobs for me; he made these bookcases, aren't they nice?'

Kate agreed they were very nice.

'He likes to escape and come up here. I've got him interested in opera, believe it or not. She's only interested in stuffing her face with cakes. Have you seen them?'

Kate admitted she hadn't.

'Anyway, I don't want to take up any more of your time. But, believe me, *someone* out there would like to see me gone.'

'I can understand how concerned you must be after receiving a note like that, but surely falling down the stairs must have been an accident?'

Kate knew she would mull over this conversation later in the day but for now she should be concentrating on the purpose of her visit.

'How are you coping with shopping and things?' she asked, trying to remember to focus on Edina's ankle.

'Oh my friend Hetty's been wonderful. She's got me my shopping and my prescriptions and she brings up my ready meals which are delivered downstairs—' At this point the doorbell rang.

'Shall I answer it?' Kate asked, carefully placing her coffee on a coaster on the elaborately carved side table.

'If you would.'

Kate opened the door to a pleasant-looking, middle-aged man with close-cut brown hair.

'Is she *there*?' he asked and, without waiting for an answer, edged his way into the room.

'Oh, it's you, David.' Edina Martinelli spoke without enthusiasm.

'Hello, Edina. Just thought I'd call in as I was passing but, if this isn't a good time…' He glanced in Kate's direction.

'The nurse has been here to attend to my poor ankle. What do *you* want? As if I didn't know!'

The man turned round to Kate and rolled his eyes heavenward. 'She's convinced somebody's trying to do her in,' he said with a sigh as he plonked himself on the pale blue sofa opposite.

'This,' Edina Martinelli said to Kate, 'is my stepson, David Courtney. Believe me, no blood son of mine could have made such a mess of his affairs. Are you on the scrounge again, David dear?'

David dear stared at her icily. 'I'm after what is rightly mine.'

Kate was beginning to feel uncomfortable in the midst of what was plainly some sort of family row. She drained her coffee cup. 'I must go,' she said, standing up. 'I'll just rinse out my cup first.'

There was a chilly silence while she rinsed out the cup and then picked up her bag. 'I'm sure you'll get used to that cast, Miss Martinelli,' she said, pointing at the ankle, 'but I'll come back to check it in a week or so. I'll see myself out.'

As Kate closed the door behind her she heard their conversation resume, voices raised, obviously arguing. She took a deep breath and headed down the stairs, first looking carefully to ensure there was no vacuum cleaner flex positioned across the top. *Surely* that had been an accident?

Kate made her way out to the car and sat inside, with the window open, to write up her notes. She'd barely put pen to paper when she heard raised voices again. The man called David came storming out the front door, followed by a tiny old lady.

'David!' the old lady was shouting. '*Don't* let her upset you! Calm down! Come in and I'll make you a cup of tea.'

'I don't want a cup of tea, Hetty!' he shouted back. 'I just want that bitch to give me my money!'

Kate registered that this then was Edina Martinelli's great friend.

'But, David, you shouldn't drive when you're so upset!'

'Leave me alone!' he yelled as he opened the door of a silver Audi which was parked in front of Kate's red Fiat Punto. 'You're her friend – you're *always* going to be on her side!'

With that he got into the car, slammed the door and roared away, leaving the little lady standing there, looking bewildered and agitated.

For a minute Kate wondered if she should get out and comfort this Hetty, but she turned and walked rapidly back inside. As she was about to drive away Kate noticed Hetty stumble on the doorstep, only stopping herself from falling flat by colliding with the door-post and then standing for a moment, her hand on her heart, appearing shaken.

Feeling concerned, Kate switched off the ignition and walked quickly up to the door where the old lady stood, steadying herself and getting her breath back.

'Are you OK?' Kate asked anxiously.

'I'm fine, thank you,' she replied. 'So silly of me not to look where I was going. I was rather upset, you see.'

'You're sure you're all right?'

'Oh yes. When you're my age your balance isn't so good. Not that I'd have far to fall!' She giggled.

Kate reckoned that this wiry little lady wasn't much more than five feet tall.

'I've just been visiting Miss Martinelli,' Kate said, 'and I saw you come running out as I was about to leave.'

'Poor Edina!' Hetty sighed. 'She's a great friend of mine but she doesn't get on too well with David – that's her stepson. *Lovely* man though; just a clash of personalities there. Edina nearly got killed, you know; the cleaner left the flex of the vacuum cleaner stretched across the top of the stairs and down she went! *Shocking* negligence.'

'So she told me,' Kate said. 'Well, if you're sure you're OK I'll be off.'

'I'm fine. Nice meeting you,' said Hetty.

Kate got back to her car and drove away.

CHAPTER TWO

When Kate got home to her cottage on the hill in Lower Tinworthy she found her sister, Angie, downing her first gin of the evening. Any time after four o'clock was OK for Angie, and that's assuming she hadn't had a couple at lunchtime. At Angie's recent sixtieth birthday bash in The Greedy Gull, every single guest had presented her with a bottle of the stuff, so they were well stocked up.

'God, Angie, are you at it *already*?' Kate worried constantly about her sister's intake.

'Are you going to start lecturing me? I'm just feeling a bit down today and felt like a little pick-me-up.' With that Angie took a large gulp.

'Why are you feeling down?' Barney, the springer spaniel, was gazing hopefully at them both. 'Couldn't you have taken the dog for a walk and got some fresh air? That always helps to lift *my* mood.'

'Well, it doesn't do it for me.'

As far as Kate was aware, Angie had rarely, if ever, taken poor Barney for a walk. Kate sighed as she switched on the kettle.

The two sisters had pooled their resources and bought Lavender Cottage the previous year, enchanted by its nooks and crannies, the large kitchen extension, the panoramic views down to the river and to the sea. Kate, divorced twenty-eight years previously, and Angie, widowed for five years, had fond memories of idyllic childhood holidays in North Cornwall and it had seemed a brilliant idea to get away from the crowded South-East and head to the blissful peace and quiet of the South-West.

It hadn't quite worked out like that, though. The kitchen needed a new floor, the cottage needed central heating and a log-burner, which meant Kate needed a part-time job. This was the reason why she spent Mondays, Tuesdays and Wednesdays (plus occasional Thursdays) at the medical centre. And, on top of that, the sea breezes mentioned in the estate agent's blurb morphed into Atlantic gales, showering salt horizontally on the windows and dulling the panoramic views into a grey haze.

There was also the myth of a crime-free existence. Within weeks of their arrival a brutal murder had occurred up in Middle Tinworthy, during a Women's Institute meeting no less, followed by another within yards of their cottage, both of which Kate found herself involved in. But every crime has the proverbial silver lining, and in this case it was Woody Forrest.

Detective Inspector 'Woody' Forrest (she still only knew him by his nickname) had been born in California to an English father and an Italian mother. He had won a scholarship to study criminology at Oxford University some forty years previously, followed by years in the Metropolitan Police before being put out to grass in North Cornwall. Woody had admitted it had been his own choice to get away from London and crime, to enjoy a couple of peaceful years in his cottage, with his surfboard, before retiring. Instead he'd found himself in the middle of a double murder investigation, which, he said, caused some mirth among his ex-colleagues back in the Met up in London. He was still involved to some extent in the handover to the new detective inspector, Bill Robson.

Woody and Kate had both been involved in the Women's Institute murder case and they'd become close. She'd fallen for his dark brown eyes and rapidly greying, close-cut black hair, never dreaming that the feeling might be reciprocated.

And tonight they were going out to dinner at The Edge of the Moor, a gourmet restaurant in an ancient, rambling stone building that had once been a coaching inn on the edge of Bodmin Moor. It was 'their' place, in that he'd taken her there on their first date and several times since.

The evenings were becoming chilly and Kate was glad he'd reserved a table close to the roaring fire. As she studied the menu she wondered if she should mention her visit to Seaview Grange and Edina Martinelli's obsession that someone was out to kill her. She knew Woody would tell her to keep out of other people's squabbles. 'Look what happened last time' was what he'd say. Still…

'How was your day?' he asked as he studied the wine list.

'Oh, you know, quite interesting.'

'Has the population started getting colds and coughs yet, or are we still on surfboard injuries and weever-fish stings?'

Kate laughed. She decided to tell him. 'You know I'm doing a lot more home visits now that Elaine's retiring? Well, I had to make an interesting call up to Seaview Grange today.'

'The posh apartments for rich ancients?'

'That's the one. And I met a fascinating ancient by the name of Edina Martinelli.'

'Italian?' Woody asked.

'I'm not sure. She did have a slight accent but it didn't strike me as being particularly Italian. She was an opera singer in her prime, she told me, and Martinelli was her professional name.'

'Was she nice?' Woody signalled the waiter. 'How about the Chablis as we're having fish?'

'Yes, lovely. No, she wasn't all that nice. She'd broken her ankle because, she said, someone had left the vacuum cleaner flex stretched across the top of the stairs, and down she went. She's convinced someone's trying to kill her. Mind you, she's a very dramatic type of person.'

Woody rolled his eyes. 'Those recent murders have got everyone's imaginations popping. Or else, like you, she's glued to any crime drama they're airing for the hundredth time on television.' He ordered the Chablis.

'Not only that,' Kate continued, 'she'd received a threatening note warning her that, if she didn't stop, they would have to find a way to silence her.'

'Stop what?'

'Well, singing, I presume, as they wanted to silence her.'

'It seems like a pretty weak motive for murder,' Woody said.

Kate wasn't about to be put off. 'Then her stepson arrived while I was there and he seemed to want something from her which she wasn't about to give. They had a right old row.'

'Mystery solved then,' Woody said. 'He's trying to kill her off to get at whatever it is, money most likely. Let me know if he succeeds.'

Kate had known he'd make light of it and she probably shouldn't have mentioned the visit. But, for some reason, she kept thinking about Edina Martinelli and the stepson. What was his name? David? And the tiny little Hetty lady who came chasing out after him. She hoped there would be more occasions to make calls at Seaview Grange.

But then all thoughts of Seaview Grange were driven from her mind when Woody leaned across the table and said, 'I've been thinking of making a trip home.'

The wine arrived and was poured. The waiter hovered, notebook at the ready.

Kate settled for a seafood starter followed by sea bass, and Woody said, 'Same for me.'

'Home? Back to California?'

'Yeah, Santa Monica.'

'Oh, Woody! When?'

'Well, now I've more or less retired I've got all the time in the world. But, sometime over the winter I guess, most likely Christmas.

As you know I'm still involved with the handover up at the police station, but that should be all wound up by Christmas.'

Kate felt a little light go out inside her. She'd got so used to having him around and she couldn't bear to think of Christmas without him. He'd probably be gone for weeks because California wasn't exactly on the doorstep.

'It's to see my mom, really,' he said. 'She's coming up to ninety-two and I haven't seen her for a couple of years. And I should look up my brother and sister too.'

'I'll miss you,' Kate said. 'How long would you plan to be away for?'

He shrugged. 'I guess a month or so.'

A whole *month*!

'Oh,' Kate said, sipping her wine.

'I wondered' – he hesitated for a moment – 'I wondered if you'd like to come with me?'

'Wow!' Kate was taken completely off-guard. Her spirits soared for a brief moment, then plunged again. 'But I'm still working, Woody, and I'm pretty sure they wouldn't let me have a month off.'

'Have you *any* holiday owing to you?'

Kate thought for a moment. 'I've only been there eight months and I had a week off to go up to Edinburgh when little Calum was born. I might be able to scrounge a week, but never a month.'

'That's a shame because I'd like you with me,' he said quietly.

Kate sighed. Apart from getting time off, she considered her rapidly dwindling finances. 'I honestly don't think it's going to be possible,' she said sadly.

'I'll pay your fare,' he said.

Kate was so touched that she felt her eyes fill up with tears. 'That is *so* nice of you, Woody, but I wouldn't be able to get so much time off. And then there's Angie.'

'What about Angie?' he asked, sounding a little annoyed.

'Well, you know what she's like when she hits the gin. She could set the place alight.'

He placed his hand over hers. 'Kate, she's not a child. You're fifty-eight years old and she's sixty, for God's sake! Why should you feel responsible for her? It's high time she dried out and acted her age.'

'Yes, but a month…' Kate gazed at the fire. 'And then there's Barney.' She thought fondly of their springer spaniel and how he adored her and the long walks she took him on daily. 'She forgets all about him when I'm not around. She *never* takes him for walks. And now she's met this mad Irishman, Fergal, and they frequently go off somewhere for the day.'

Woody sighed. 'OK, OK, it was just an idea. But, if you change your mind…'

Kate would love to change her mind but she had to be realistic. She couldn't afford to jeopardise her three days at the medical centre. Damn, damn, damn.

They talked about other things, then. Woody spoke about his daughter in London who had a new man in her life and Kate reported the latest achievements of the precious grandson, who was without doubt going to grow up to be some sort of genius.

But, underlying their conversation, Kate kept thinking about a whole month without Woody. Who could have predicted that she'd ever feel this way about anyone again? She very much valued her independence of course and suspected Woody did too but their set-up was perfect with his cottage on the opposite hillside, facing hers, a ten-minute walk away.

They'd gone to bed together for the first time back in April when the murder investigations finally concluded and just before his so-called retirement. He was a kind, caring lover and insisted that they 'hit the sack' in his cottage, as opposed to hers. Mainly because of Angie.

'It's easier at my place,' he'd said.

After the meal, when they were curled up in bed, Kate was still deep in thought. It was a very busy surgery and arranging holidays at the best of times was a nightmare. Then again, perhaps she could get a week or two if she added on the days the surgery was closed over Christmas? She'd investigate the possibility before mentioning it to Woody, but she was not over-optimistic.

Just as she was drifting off to sleep, she was jolted awake by a dream. She was tumbling down the stairs. Wide awake again, her thoughts returned to Seaview Grange.

CHAPTER THREE

Tinworthy Medical Centre was a ramshackle place, situated in the Middle Tinworthy village – Higher Tinworthy being half a mile up the road, and Lower Tinworthy half a mile down the road. It was a one-storey concrete sprawl, painted white, with a green-tiled roof. As the population of the Tinworthys had grown over the years, so had the building with add-ons added to add-ons, mainly at the expense of car parking, which was now the main complaint and topic of conversation. It had almost become a competition amongst the patients in the waiting room as to who had had to park furthest away and who had had the most agonising hobble to get there.

Dr Andrew Ross headed the team of three doctors and, in addition, there were three nurses on duty: Sue, who worked there full-time and had done so for the last twenty years, and Elaine, who split the week with Kate.

The office and reception desk were ruled by Denise, who knew everything about everybody and put up with no nonsense in 'her' surgery. She was the old-school type of doctor's receptionist, firm but fair and unfailingly polite, even though at times it was through gritted teeth.

Kate had hardly got in the door of the surgery at 8.30 the following Monday when Denise, already at her desk and ready to do battle with anyone who upset the schedule, beckoned her over.

'Guess what? We've had a phone call expressly requesting that you should make a visit. Your new friend, Edina Martinelli, appears to be at death's door: vomiting and diarrhoea, and insists on seeing *you*. Obviously, she can't come to the surgery.' Here Denise sighed deeply.

Ten minutes later Kate was back in her red Fiat Punto and heading towards Seaview Grange, hoping against hope that whatever tummy bug Edina Martinelli might have, it would not be infectious.

As she entered the hallway the first person she encountered was a plump little middle-aged blonde with a vacuum cleaner, busily attacking the royal blue carpet. On seeing Kate she switched the machine off.

'I hope you've come to see Miss Martinelli in Flat 4? I've been so worried about her.'

'Oh dear, is she very poorly?' Kate asked.

'She seems that way to me. Come and see for yourself. I'm Sharon, by the way, and I do the cleaning. I'll come with you and let you in,' said the blonde, digging an enormous bunch of keys from the pocket of her overall. 'She says she can't get out of bed.'

Kate sensed genuine compassion emanating from Sharon which she thought surprising considering that Edina Martinelli had more or less accused her of attempted murder.

'She's got some kind of bug,' Sharon went on, 'but I think it's more serious than that.' She led the way upstairs and unlocked the door of Flat 4. 'Let me know how you get on and if you need me to do anything for her.'

Kate thanked her and went in, then navigated her way round the velvet sofas to the open door which presumably led to the bedrooms. 'Miss Martinelli!' she called. 'I'm Kate, the nurse, come to see you again.'

'I'm *here*!' croaked a weak voice from inside the first door she came to.

Kate entered a darkened space with the unmistakable stench of illness to find Edina Martinelli propped up in an imposing four-poster bed which filled most of the room. The woman was ill without doubt, waxen and wan against the pillows.

Kate was quite shaken at the change in her appearance. 'Oh, Miss Martinelli! You do look under the weather! How long have you been feeling like this?'

'Twenty-four ghastly hours,' Edina replied, wiping her brow. 'And I have nothing left inside me, *nothing*! I want to be sick and there's nothing there, and I have these griping pains. Ohhh…' She doubled up and let out a low moan.

'I'm going to open up the curtains for a moment,' Kate said, edging her way round the bed towards the window, 'so I can examine you.'

Kate checked her pulse and blood pressure. There was no doubt that this wasn't just an ordinary tummy bug; she was very ill, which was emphasised by the fact that her pulse was abnormally slow and missing the odd beat.

'Have you eaten anything unusual in the last few days, Miss Martinelli?'

The woman groaned and gripped her stomach. When the pain appeared to pass she said, 'No, I've eaten nothing different from usual.'

'And what about your medication, Miss Martinelli? I see from your notes that you're on digoxin. Do you think you might have taken more than you should have done?'

'No, most certainly not.' In spite of her obvious pain she was quite indignant. 'I'm always extremely careful. I'm sure this is just a bug and will go away. Some medicine is all I need.'

'Miss Martinelli,' Kate said patiently, checking her pulse again, 'I think we need to send you to hospital.'

'*No!*' Edina Martinelli shouted, then gasped with the effort. 'No hospital! Absolutely not! Just get me some medicine!' She breathed heavily. 'My dear friend Hetty downstairs is away in Bournemouth at the moment, and she would normally look after me and now I must rely on you and Sharon. She's the *cleaner*.' Even in her weakened state there was disapproval in her voice. 'I'm not at all sure after the stairs incident that I trust her.'

Kate renewed the half-empty jug on the bedside table with water and gave her something which she hoped, but doubted, would settle her tummy.

'I'm going to come back later, Miss Martinelli,' she said, 'and if you're no better then it's hospital, and *that's* that!'

'No hospital,' Edina repeated. 'I shall be all right so you can go now. And close the curtains again, please.'

Kate felt very uneasy as she let herself out of the flat and headed downstairs. She found Sharon in a room which led off the hall and which turned out to be the residents' sitting room. 'They come in here if they want a bit of company,' Sharon said, indicating half a dozen assorted armchairs and an enormous television. 'How is the old girl?'

'She's not at all well,' Kate said, 'and she should really be in hospital, but she won't entertain the idea. I'm going to try to come back later but, in the meantime, if you think she's getting worse, would you please ring me?' Kate gave Sharon her phone number. 'But if you're *really* worried then phone for an ambulance straight away.' She watched, fascinated, as the cleaner entered the number into her bright pink mobile phone. Where had she got a phone like *that*?

Sharon looked concerned. 'I can't spend all day checking on her cos I got my work to do. But I promise I'll pop in as often as I can,' she added.

Kate spent the remainder of the morning worrying about the old woman. When she had her lunch break at one o'clock she approached Dr Ross's room in the hope that he didn't have a patient with him. Fortunately, he didn't.

'Oh hi, Kate,' he said, getting up from his desk. 'I was just thinking about getting myself a sandwich.'

Andrew Ross was a tall, lean Scotsman with kindly blue eyes who had a soft spot for Kate due to their shared experiences during the murder investigations in the spring.

'Andrew, I'm awfully worried about Edina Martinelli up at Seaview Grange,' Kate said, then proceeded to tell him of her concerns about the pulse rate and Edina's refusal to go into hospital.

He looked thoughtful for a moment. 'Tell you what, how about I come up with you and have a look at her? I can eat my sandwich in the car.'

Kate felt a flood of relief; what a lovely man he was!

Within minutes they were driving up to Seaview Grange in his old Jaguar but, as they approached, flashing lights could be seen ahead.

'What on earth…?' Kate leaned forward in her seat.

'Looks like the medics have beaten us to it,' said the doctor as he pulled up at the gate. The ambulance was parked at the front door, and a stretcher was being loaded in by two young paramedics. He leaped out of the car and bounded across, Kate right behind him, catching only a glimpse of Edina Martinelli, who appeared to be unconscious. The doctor chatted briefly to the paramedics before they roared off, lights flashing and sirens blaring.

He turned to Kate. 'Apparently, she's in a coma, so you were right to be worried.'

'I must see Sharon,' Kate said, 'because she would have called for the ambulance.' She walked into the hallway, ahead of the doctor, where some shocked-looking people were huddled together and all talking at once. They stopped and turned round when they saw Kate and the doctor.

'You're too late,' a fat bald man said.

Sharon, still in her overalls, came forward. 'I'm sorry I didn't ring you, Nurse, but I checked on her like you said and, to be honest, I thought she was dead and I got a helluva shock. Don't think I'll ever get over it!' The others looked at her admiringly, and Sharon was plainly enjoying her brief heroic status. Alongside Sharon was the extremely obese man accompanied by an equally well-padded woman whom Kate suspected was the jealous wife Edina Martinelli had referred to. And, by way of contrast, standing back slightly, was a gaunt gangly man with long grey hair and piercing dark eyes.

'At least it'll be quiet now until she comes back,' said the fat woman. She pointed to the door on the right, which was Flat 3, according to the sign. 'We live in there,' she said. 'The doctor knows us but we haven't met before, Nurse, have we? I'm Gloria Pratt, and this is my husband, Ollie.'

Ollie extended a hand. 'I help Miss Martinelli out with odd jobs now and again.'

'Yes, my Ollie can tell you, that woman could screech away from mornin' to night, couldn't she, Ollie? And poor Mr Crow here' – she indicated the gangly man – 'lived right through the wall from her upstairs and could hear her all the time, couldn't you, Mr Crow?'

Mr Crow nodded but said nothing.

'Mr Crow here is a writer and needs peace and quiet,' Gloria went on, 'but you don't get it, do you, Mr Crow?'

This, then, was the man who Edina Martinelli had suspected of posting the poison pen letter through her door.

Mr Crow turned to Kate, extending a bony hand. 'Cornelius Crow,' he informed her in a deep voice. 'Dear Edina does like to air her vocal cords on a regular basis. "Use it or lose it" she's constantly telling us.'

'Hetty will be shocked,' said Sharon, pointing across the hall to Flat 1. 'She's Edina's best friend, but she's away in Bournemouth at the moment looking after her sister who's poorly. I haven't got a phone number for her so I can't let her know.'

Andrew Ross turned to Kate. 'We may as well go back,' he said, 'and I'll phone the hospital later this afternoon to see how she is.'

As they seated themselves in the car, Kate said, 'Wasn't that Crow fellow weird! Miss Martinelli told me he writes horror and crime stuff.'

'Yes, that's right,' the doctor said with a grin, 'horror mainly, with lots of murders.'

'My God, doesn't he look the part!' Kate exclaimed. 'Like someone out of a Hammer Horror film!'

When Edina Martinelli had first mentioned that she'd suspected Cornelius Crow, Kate thought she was accusing him merely because he was a crime writer and that she was being somewhat fanciful and a little overdramatic. But, having seen the man, now she was not so sure.

CHAPTER FOUR

The afternoon was so hectic that Kate barely had time to think about anything other than the patients in front of her. It was only when she was finally leaving at 5 p.m. that she saw Andrew Ross deep in conversation with Denise at the reception desk. When he saw Kate he beckoned her over.

'Bad news, I'm afraid,' he said sadly, laying his hand on Kate's shoulder. 'Edina Martinelli died this afternoon at twenty-five minutes past three.'

For a moment Kate was speechless.

'There's going to be a post-mortem,' he continued, 'because apparently they suspect some sort of poisoning. I've checked all her records here and we've never prescribed her anything other than the digoxin which she's been on for years, the occasional laxative and some antihistamine.'

'When will they be doing the post-mortem?' Kate asked.

'In the next day or two, and normally the result takes a week or so,' he replied. 'I've asked the consultant to get in touch with me as soon as he hears anything.' For a moment he looked troubled. He cleared his throat before speaking. 'I spoke to her consultant and, given that this came about so suddenly, and factoring in her abnormal heart rate, there's concern about how much digoxin she was on.'

'Will *we* be in any trouble?' Kate asked.

'Let's hope not,' Dr Ross said, but he looked distinctly worried.

Kate sighed. 'It's hard to believe she's gone when I saw her just this morning,' she said. 'I should have ignored her protestations and called for the ambulance there and then, shouldn't I?'

'No, Kate, I doubt it would have made any difference at that stage.' The doctor smiled. 'I suggest you go home and have a couple of glasses of wine and put it out of your mind.'

The last thing Kate would be able to do was put it out of her mind. She could only recall Edina informing her that someone wanted to kill her. Had that someone finally succeeded?

When Kate got home she kicked off her shoes and made herself a cup of coffee. She'd leave the wine for later.

'You're looking very morose,' Angie commented when she came in.

'Oh, we've had an unexpected death,' Kate said as she gulped her coffee.

'Surely people are popping off all the time?'

'Hmm. This one seems just a little suspicious to me.'

Angie stopped in her tracks and turned to glare at her sister. 'Don't tell me you're super-sleuthing again! Haven't you done enough detective work since we got here? Not everyone who pops their clogs is a murder victim, for God's sake!'

'It's just that this woman was convinced someone wanted to kill her. Someone had pushed a note through her door recently, threatening her because they didn't much like her singing. She'd already fallen down the stairs and now there's a chance she's been poisoned.'

Angie rolled her eyes heavenwards. 'Perhaps she wasn't looking where she was going? Perhaps she ate something dodgy?'

'I'm not at all sure about that,' Kate replied.

*

After an early supper it was still light enough to give the dog a short walk which gave Kate an excuse to call on Woody. He might of course be out, but it was worth a chance, she thought, as she crossed the old stone bridge over the River Pol. Then she had to call back Barney, who was already running up towards the path leading to Penhallion cliff. 'We're not going up there tonight!' she shouted at him and, looking dejected, the dog turned back and followed her along the lane to Woody's cottage.

'Hey, I was just about to call you,' Woody said, opening the door with his mobile in his hand. 'Wondered if you fancied going out for a drink?' He stood back to let her in. 'Or we could have a drink here?'

'That would be great,' Kate said, heading into the sitting room, 'because I really need to talk to you about something.' The dog promptly settled himself in front of the stove.

Woody raised a questioning eyebrow. 'And what might that be?' he asked as he followed them in. 'Wine? Gin? Scotch?'

'Wine would be lovely,' Kate replied, taking off her coat and collapsing onto the settee. 'I've had quite a day!'

A couple of minutes later Woody reappeared with a bottle of Malbec and two glasses. 'Relax!' he ordered, handing her a glass. 'Get yourself on the outside of that!'

Kate took a grateful sip. 'I just want to get your opinion on something.'

'Like what?' He sat down next to her and put his arm round her shoulders.

'Remember I told you about Edina Martinelli up at Seaview Grange? The woman who broke her ankle after falling down the stairs and was convinced that someone was trying to kill her?'

He nodded. 'What's she done now?'

'She's died. This afternoon. And the hospital think it might be something to do with the medication we prescribed her. What if she was poisoned by her drugs?'

Woody took a deep breath. 'Are they going to do an autopsy?'

'Yes, they are, so Dr Ross said.'

'Well, you'll find out the results sooner or later. But she probably just ate something dodgy.'

'Eating something dodgy rarely has such dramatic results,' Kate said. 'She was convinced someone wanted to kill her after getting that note, and then she had that fall down the stairs. What if someone *was* trying to kill her? What if she was poisoned?'

'Oh Kate,' he said. 'It's highly unlikely she was poisoned. Most likely she tripped down the stairs in the first place because she wasn't looking where she was going and blamed it on the vacuum cleaner or whatever. And people *do* die from severe food poisoning every day.'

'I have a *feeling* about this,' Kate said, 'because it's all too much of a coincidence. And apparently, she got on the other residents' nerves because of her endless singing. And, according to some of them, her voice had gone long ago.'

'Maybe so, but murder's a bit *extreme*, wouldn't you say?'

Kate ignored him. 'And then there was the stepson I told you about – remember?'

'Yes, yes, but don't take it all so seriously. You'll know soon enough when the autopsy results come through.' Woody gulped some wine. 'Why did I ever get involved with such a darned persistent woman?'

Kate laughed, feeling relaxed for the first time that day. 'I don't know why, but I'm really glad you did!'

CHAPTER FIVE

Two days after Edina's final departure from Seaview Grange, Kate was asked to attend to the newly replaced knee of the Reverend Edgar Ellis who lived in Flat 6.

'We know how much you like making house calls,' Denise said.

Even so, with the rain coming in horizontally, as it frequently did in North Cornwall, it would have been a relief to have a day in the treatment room, tending to the medical problems of the more mobile inhabitants of Higher, Middle and Lower Tinworthy. Still, it was an ideal opportunity to meet more of the residents of Seaview Grange.

Kate hummed to herself as she drove, windscreen wipers going frantically, up – via the rarefied heights of Higher Tinworthy – and parked outside the windswept Grange. She thought of the last time she'd been up here when poor Edina had been taken away in the ambulance.

Kate wandered into the large hallway and there were the two well-nourished Pratts and the lugubrious Cornelius Crow chatting to Sharon again. They stopped and turned when they saw Kate.

'I've come to see the Reverend Edgar Ellis in Flat 6,' Kate said.

'Oh, *him*!' Gloria Pratt said dismissively.

'Upstairs, door on the right,' said Sharon. 'He'll still be in shock, I expect, poor old soul. He's shut himself away the last couple of days since Edina was taken because he was besotted with her, wasn't he?' She looked at the others, who nodded.

As Kate made her way upstairs, she could hear that animated conversation had resumed in the hallway. 'What do you *really* think happened to Edina Martinelli, Mr Crow?' The voice belonged to Gloria Pratt. 'Do you *honestly* think she could have died of natural causes? You know all about murder after all, don't you, Mr Crow?'

'True, I've carried out extensive research into the subject,' Cornelius droned. 'In a case like this, one could suspect poisoning.'

'Let's hope no one suspects *us*,' Sharon said with feeling.

'More like the surgery overprescribed. They could well be in trouble,' said Cornelius Crow.

The door to Flat 6 was ajar, so Kate called, 'Cooee! I'm the practice nurse come to have a look at your knee.'

She could hear a great deal of nose-blowing going on from inside before a tall, sad-looking old man, leaning on a stick, pulled the door fully open.

'Have I come at a bad time?' Kate asked.

The Reverend Edgar Ellis stared blankly at her for a moment before standing to one side. 'It can't be helped, you'd better come in,' he said, sniffing.

Kate found herself in a large open-plan living area. There was a cumbersome sofa of oak and leather, and a couple of tartan-covered armchairs. Two walls were lined ceiling to floor with bookshelves, stuffed with leather-bound volumes, the odd ornament fighting for space amongst the tomes. Every available surface was covered with newspapers, magazines and discarded correspondence.

'Forgive my manners,' he said, holding out his hand. 'Edgar Ellis.'

She shook his outstretched hand. 'Kate Palmer.'

Edgar Ellis was tall, skinny with untidy white hair and a drip on the end of his long, bony nose. He regarded Kate for a minute through watery blue eyes which he dabbed gently.

'We haven't met before,' he said, 'but I've heard about you.' He sniffed. 'You're the nurse who helped to solve the murder case back in the spring, aren't you?'

'I do seem to have a knack of being in the wrong place at the wrong time.'

He nodded. 'Please excuse my state of grief but I'm recovering from the most *tremendous* shock. Edina was a dear, dear friend.'

'I'm sorry to have come at a bad time, Reverend,' Kate said, 'but I really need to check the state of your stitches after your knee replacement. I see you're managing to walk about.'

'With difficulty,' he said.

'Have you had any physiotherapy yet?' Kate asked.

'Oh yes,' he replied, 'but the man's a *sadist*. He had me in agony.'

He limped back across the room, leaning heavily on his stick, and sat down carefully on the raised seat of a straight-backed armchair and rolled up the leg of his trousers. 'I understand from Sharon, our cleaner, that you were the last person to speak to dear Edina before she died. It would help to know a little more about *how* she died.'

'I'm sorry, Reverend, I don't know, and anyway I can't disclose personal matters about patients.'

'Even when they're dead?'

'Even when they're dead,' Kate said.

He nodded solemnly. 'Edina and I became very close over the past few years. *Beautiful* woman! *Wonderful* voice! Sang at Covent Garden, you know.'

'Yes, she told me about her operatic career,' Kate said, examining the long scar running down his knee as she removed the dressing.

'I should have *known*!' His voice wobbled. 'I hadn't seen her for a few days but I didn't *think*!' He blew his nose again lustily. 'I've been concentrating on my knee, you see, whereas normally I'd have knocked on her door to see if she needed any shopping.

But, being incapacitated, I haven't been doing that and I shall *never* forgive myself.'

'You mustn't blame yourself in any way; there's nothing you could have done,' Kate said, checking the stitches. 'The wound has healed well.'

But the Reverend wasn't in the least bit interested in his knee.

'She was *such* a beautiful woman! So talented! The loveliest voice – like a nightingale. Such a waste of life!' Tears began to roll freely down his cheeks.

Kate patted his hand. 'Would you like me to make you a cup of tea?'

He drew a shuddering breath. 'Thank you.'

Kate made her way into an extremely untidy kitchen. There were dirty dishes in the sink and a couple of unwashed saucepans which she decided to soak in soapy water. It was unclear what he'd been eating but there were several empty baked beans tins in the top of his pedal-bin. He plainly did not go in for recycling. The mugs, which featured patterns of spring flower bouquets, didn't look too clean either, so Kate gave them a little scrub while the kettle boiled.

'Milk and sugar, Reverend?' she called through.

'Just milk, my dear. You're so kind! And *please* call me Edgar.'

'Is there anyone at all I can ask to be with you?' Kate asked as she set down the tea on the table beside him. 'You really shouldn't be alone when you're this upset.'

'No, there's no one,' he said, reaching for the mug.

'You're not married?'

'I was, but unfortunately my dear wife passed away shortly before we were due to move down here. It wasn't long after I gave up my parish. She died very suddenly after a short illness. But we had forty-six years together so I could not complain when God saw fit to take her.'

'You still wanted to move to Cornwall nevertheless?'

'Yes, my late wife and I used to come down here on holiday, you see. She was the one who actually bought this flat because she'd inherited some money.'

'The same as my sister and me. We had lots of holidays down here.'

'You haven't been living here very long, have you?' the Reverend asked.

'No, Angie and I bought Lavender Cottage down in Lower Tinworthy and moved in at the beginning of February. We love it here although it's been an eventful few months. Where was your old parish?' Kate wanted to distract him from his misery.

'Oh, the Cotswolds,' he said.

'The Cotswolds are lovely,' Kate said. 'I have a cousin who lives in Little Something-or-Other near Cheltenham. I can never remember the name.'

'Not Little *Barrington*?'

Kate was surprised that he sounded anxious; all signs of his grief appeared to have gone.

'I don't think so. I have to look it up each time I send her a Christmas card.'

Did she imagine it or did he look relieved? Perhaps he hadn't been a very popular vicar?

'You can imagine how distressing it is for me to have poor Edina dying too.' He mopped his eyes again. 'It brings my wife's death back.'

Kate had the distinct impression he was trying to steer the conversation away from the subject of his old parish. 'I'm so sorry,' she said. 'Are you sure there's no one I can call? Do you have a family?'

'No, we were never blessed with children.' He stared out the window with a faraway look in his eyes. 'We both devoted our lives to the community.'

'You must be lonely now.'

'Well, I am lonely at times, but that's no excuse for me to monopolise your time, Nurse. I mustn't be keeping you from your important duties.' He put down the mug and got to his feet. As he escorted her to the door, he said, 'I try to spread God's word to my neighbours, of course, and also to help in practical ways.' His eyes misted again. 'I shall never forgive myself for not knocking at Edina's door.'

Kate thought it best to try to steer him away from the subject of Edina Martinelli. 'Well, look after that knee and try to do a little more walking now,' she said.

As she was about to take her leave he grabbed her wrist. 'Edina was convinced someone wanted to kill her, you know. I rather fear they may have succeeded because I'm not at all sure that she died of natural causes.'

'Why do you say that?' Kate asked, intrigued.

'Firstly, because she was a very healthy lady but, most of all, nearly everyone in this building, apart from myself and her dear friend, Hetty, *hated* her.'

'Hated her? That's a very strong accusation,' Kate said.

'Strong but true,' he replied. 'You mark my words.'

I will, Kate thought, *I will.*

CHAPTER SIX

When she descended back into the hallway she found the four residents still there chatting. Cornelius Crow, she noted, was wearing a cape and looked like he might have just flown in from Transylvania.

'How is he?' Sharon asked, inclining her head upwards.

'Oh, his knee is doing well,' Kate said, unwilling to get bogged down in what appeared to be an ongoing gossip session.

'No, not his *knee*!' Gloria Pratt said impatiently. 'How's *he*? *Edgar?* He was mad about Edina, wasn't he, Ollie?'

'He was,' Ollie confirmed, 'but it was unrequ…' He struggled for a moment. 'But she didn't fancy *him*.'

'Unrequited love,' Cornelius supplied.

'That's it,' agreed Ollie.

'Well, at least now it should be quieter,' Sharon added as Kate edged past.

'Nowhere quieter than the grave,' droned Cornelius Crow.

Kate nodded, grimaced and finally made it out the door.

When she got to her car a large Audi pulled up alongside and David Courtney emerged. Kate hesitated for a moment, feeling she should convey some sympathy to Edina Martinelli's stepson.

'I'm so sorry about your stepmother,' she said.

He stopped in his tracks. 'Well,' he said, 'it's kind of you to say so but *I'm* not particularly sorry about my stepmother.'

'Oh,' Kate said, recalling the argument they were having when she first went to visit Edina. 'I know it's not quite the same as losing your natural mother…'

'Apparently, my natural mother died not long after I was born, and my father wasted no time in finding someone else,' he said. 'So, one way or the other, I've not had much luck with mothers.'

'No,' Kate agreed as he headed towards the door, 'but, if there's anything I can do…'

'Thanks,' he said shortly and gave a brief wave before disappearing inside.

As she drove away Kate felt incredibly sorry for David Courtney. To never have known your own mother, and then to have a stepmother who you didn't get on with – how awful!

And, try as she might, she could not imagine Edina Martinelli being particularly maternal.

'There are some characters up there at the Grange,' Kate informed her sister when she got home in the late afternoon. 'There's the ancient vicar with a new knee who, apparently, was in love with Edina, the deceased, but she didn't fancy him. He used to live somewhere called Little Barrington, and I have a feeling our cousin Pam lives in Little Something-or-Other, doesn't she? There is the chubby old couple who don't look like the normal well-heeled residents, and a cadaverous old man who looks like something out of a horror film and who's apparently a writer. And Edina sang all day and drove all the other residents mad. You couldn't make it up!'

'Yeah, right,' Angie said. 'Is it too early for a gin?'

'For God's sake!' Kate consulted her watch. 'It's only five o'clock!'

'Well, it's six o'clock in most of the rest of Europe and I'm feeling very European today.'

Kate sighed as she gazed out the window down to the valley, at the shops and restaurants which lined the banks of the River Pol as it wound its way to the sea, which could be seen clearly as it crashed its way onto the beach.

'Perhaps I'll pop down to The Greedy Gull,' Angie said.

Des, the landlord, who knew a good customer when he saw one, always had one hand on the gin bottle and the other on a glass the moment she walked in the door.

'What about your masterpieces out in the summerhouse?' Kate asked.

After years as a not-very-successful actress, Angie had decided to be an artist and had commandeered the pretty summerhouse for this purpose. It now had to be called 'the studio'. She'd spent most days daubing paint on large canvases and had even befriended the owner of the local gallery and persuaded him to display some of her work. She had two canvases on display there, neither of which had sold and Kate suspected she was losing interest. And, now Fergal was on the scene, she spent a lot of time phoning him, getting ready for his visits, talking about him, and her time in the 'studio' had rapidly diminished.

'So are we going to have a gin then?' Angie asked.

Kate sighed. 'Oh go on then!'

It was one of those occasions where if you couldn't beat them you might as well join them.

Five days later, while she was gazing down at the beach after work, watching two little boys wrestling over a bodyboard, her phone rang.

'Hello, Kate,' said Andrew Ross, 'I wanted to let you know that we've had the results of the post-mortem. Edina Martinelli died of a massive myocardial infarction, which was almost certainly caused by digoxin toxicity. She was pumped full of the stuff.'

'Oh my God!' Kate was so stunned for a moment she didn't know what to say.

'Did you get any impression that she might have wanted to take her own life? Was she depressed or anything?'

'Absolutely not – quite the opposite,' Kate replied. 'But, Andrew, she was *convinced* that someone was out to kill her.'

'Well, that's interesting but now the surgery's in the firing line because it could be construed as medical negligence. The report has been handed over to the coroner and it looks like the police will be involved.'

'Oh heavens!' Kate was horrified. 'Does that mean we might end up in court?'

'Almost certainly.'

Kate's mind was in turmoil. She knew she had checked Edina's pulse and blood pressure correctly and she knew that Edina had been prescribed digoxin for her heart. Could she have overdosed accidentally? That didn't seem likely; she'd been on the drug for some years. But, she thought, perhaps someone wanted to make it look like she had died of an accidental overdose? If so, that 'someone' was the killer. And the killer must have *known* she was on the drug. Who could have known that? Would she have told everyone? Most unlikely. Kate knew that Edgar Ellis and Cornelius Crow collected her prescriptions for her as did her friend, Hetty. And David Courtney might possibly know. But the Pratts? And the Potter twins who she hadn't yet met? But Kate was only too aware that old people loved talking about their ailments and medication, so it was possible that any of them could have known. All these thoughts raced around in her head as she walked up the hill to Woody's house.

'Oh, Woody,' she said as he hugged her. 'You'll never guess…'

'I don't need to guess,' Woody said. 'I've been working up there today and heard what was going on. It's now very much a police matter. But can I say something?'

'Yes, what?'

'Do *not* get involved, Kate. I know you only too well. You will, though, need to give a statement to Bill Robson about what Edina said to you about someone wanting to kill her. And probably mention the stepson. But nothing else, do you hear? You do *not* want to get involved in this.'

'But I *am* involved, Woody. Andrew Ross has spoken of medical negligence and I was the last person from the surgery to see her. I'm really, really worried that I might be in trouble but I'm certain I did everything I should. And, knowing that Edina was convinced somebody wanted to kill her, isn't it possible that someone administered an overdose of digoxin to her?' As she uttered the words Kate now knew there was no way she *couldn't* be involved and that she'd find any excuse to visit Seaview Grange again. And the first chance she got, she intended to check whether any of the other residents of the Grange were prescribed digoxin, because if the person who wanted to kill Edina *had* poisoned her, they needed to have access to a large amount of the drug.

Woody sighed. 'Why are you *always* around when murders happen, Kate?'

'Yes, it does rather seem to be my mission in life since I've come to live down here. But it's not my fault.'

'Do you really think one of the oldies could have killed her?' Woody asked.

'I intend to find out. I can't wait to get back there and suss out some more of the residents!'

'Kate,' he said, sounding all serious, 'be careful. Dear Lord, it's only a few months ago that you were nearly a murder victim yourself! And entirely due to your nosiness!'

'Natural curiosity,' Kate corrected, but nonetheless she shivered as she recalled her experience. 'Anyway, I helped to solve the case.'

'Yes, you helped to solve the case and nearly got yourself killed in the process. I think you should consider changing your reading matter and try to wean yourself off Agatha Christie and P.D. James. And you should stop watching all those crime shows and whodunnits on TV, Kate. I know it fascinates you but sometimes I think you've become too fixated with it all.'

'I can't help it,' Kate admitted. 'I just love trying to unravel the mysteries!'

Furthermore, there was a repeat of *Midsomer Murders* on TV this evening, and she planned on watching it.

Kate knew Woody worried about her and that he had her best interests at heart. But she had found herself becoming quite addicted to real-life investigating, after the murders last spring. It was exciting and exhilarating and, at times, of course, extremely dangerous – as she knew to her cost. It hadn't put her off though and, looking back, she had to admit she was rather good at it.

And on this occasion it wasn't as if she'd gone around *looking* for trouble. On the contrary, she just happened, purely on account of her job, to have met not only the victim of a poisoning, but several of the suspects as well. She had become involved, like it or not. And she *liked* it. And because Edina's murder was committed in this manner – poisoning by medication – she felt a greater responsibility than she had on the previous occasion when she'd only been one person amongst a large gathering at the Women's Institute. Not only that, but her reputation, and the surgery's, could be at stake this time.

Or perhaps she was just plain nosy.

Kate mulled, over and over again, her visits to Edina Martinelli. She knew that Edina's prescription was reviewed every few months, that she was never over-prescribed and that Edina thought someone wanted to kill her. She also knew she had to pay a visit to Bill Robson.

'He's a busy man,' said the self-important-sounding constable on the phone. 'Is it important?'

'Yes, it is,' Kate replied, 'that's why I'm phoning. And it's probably very relevant to the case he's currently investigating.'

With much sighing and paper-rustling the constable finally came up with a date and a time. 'Thursday morning, ten thirty?'

'I'll be there,' Kate said.

Detective Inspector Bill Robson had come down to Cornwall from Wolverhampton, according to Woody, in the hope – as had Woody himself – of a few quiet years prior to retirement. He was in his fifties, short, stocky, balding and unsmiling.

'How may I help you, Mrs Palmer?'

'Well, I'm a nurse at the medical—'

'I know who you are,' he interrupted. 'Your surgery is under investigation at the moment for possible medical negligence.'

'I *know* that!' Kate felt her hackles rising. 'And I can assure you that neither myself, nor anyone at our surgery, have ever been negligent.'

'We'll be the judge of that,' he snapped, picking up a folder and shuffling the contents around. 'My officers are currently checking with Dr Ross.' He glanced at the clock on the wall.

'I feel I need to remind you,' Kate continued, 'Edina Martinelli was convinced that someone wanted to kill her. She'd had a threatening note pushed through her door, someone had stretched a flex across the top of the stairs to trip her up and it was pure luck that she wasn't killed then. And, when I first visited her, I met her stepson, David Courtney, and I know they were arguing about something.'

'We will bear it in mind.' He glanced at his watch this time. 'So, if there's nothing else?'

'But there *is*!' Kate was becoming increasingly frustrated. 'Please believe me when I say that it is entirely possible that someone could have poisoned her.'

Robson stood up. 'Mrs Palmer, I understand that you're a friend of ex-Detective Inspector Forrest and that you've been involved in some amateur detective work during the past year, but please do *not* tell me how to do my job. You are plainly concerned about your own, which is why you've come here. I very much hope we do not find the medical centre is the guilty party in this matter, but time will tell.' With that, he stood up, file in hand, and headed towards the door, holding it open. The interview was at an end.

'Well, don't say I didn't warn you,' Kate said, barely suppressing her fury as she marched out past him. What a humourless, nasty little man he was!

CHAPTER SEVEN

Two days later Kate went through the medical records of all the residents of Seaview Grange to ascertain whether any of them were on digoxin. Nobody was – so she'd drawn a complete blank in the first stage of her investigation. As she walked back into reception it seemed that fate wanted to lend her a hand when Denise said, 'We've just had another request for someone to make a visit up at Seaview Grange, Kate. Would you be able to call in on Daisy Potter this afternoon?' Denise went on to inform Kate that Violet and Daisy Potter were eighty-six-year-old spinster twins who lived in Flat 2. Violet had rung up the medical centre to say that she was very concerned about poor dear Daisy, who had dreadful stomach cramps and couldn't possibly get as far as the surgery because she kept having to go to the toilet all the time. She then proceeded to give a detailed account of Daisy's bowel movements.

'I think this one's *definitely* yours,' Kate's fellow nurse, Sue, informed her with a wink.

Kate, on arrival at Seaview Grange, stood in the hall and studied the doors of the three downstairs flats. There was no sign of Sharon the cleaner on this occasion. Number 2 was in the centre, alongside the door to the communal lounge which no one appeared to use. Kate noticed the still immaculate royal blue carpeting and the arrangement of fresh flowers on the mahogany table in the hallway. She rang the bell at Flat 2 where, at her approach, there was a cacophony of barking from within.

A thin, stooped old lady with sparse white hair opened the door, accompanied by an irate black pug.

'Oh, it's *you*, dear,' she said, opening the door wide. 'Come in, come in! I'm Violet.' She turned to the dog. '*Do* be quiet, Jasper!'

Kate followed her into yet another open-plan living area, this one a sea of chintz. The two sofas were covered in pink roses and blue wisteria respectively, honeysuckle scaled the curtains, two easy chairs were covered in pink velvet, and all on a carpet of pastel blue. The pug, still yapping, settled himself on one of the pink chairs.

'Oh, *Jasper*!' The old lady shook her head. 'He's very spoilt. Pay no attention.'

Kate reckoned this old house must have been converted into flats by knocking down some walls and erecting others. She liked the high ceilings, cornices and central roses with their hanging lights.

'Poor dear Daisy's just gone to the loo again but she'll be back in a minute,' Violet said. 'All very worrying after what happened to Edina. Do sit down, dear. Would you like a cup of tea?'

'That's very kind, Miss Potter, but—'

'No trouble at all,' interrupted Violet. 'I'll just put the kettle on.'

As she hobbled into the kitchen area another door opened and in walked an identical old woman, who could only be Daisy.

'Hello, Nurse,' she said as Kate stood up. 'I'm having an *awful* time of it.' Daisy sat down on the chair opposite. 'I've been getting these pains and diarrhoea ever since they took poor Edina away. Sharon's told us all about Edina's terrible tummy when she was taken to hospital. Do you suppose someone's trying to poison us all?'

'No, I'm sure that's not the case,' Kate said. 'Just a coincidence.'

Kate got Daisy to stretch out while she examined her tummy and checked her over but nothing appeared to be abnormal. The dog yapped some more.

'Tell me,' Kate said. 'Are you a nervous sort of a person, Miss Potter?'

'Oh, call me Daisy, dear.'

Violet, who was now slowly approaching with a wobbly tray of tea and biscuits, said, 'Yes, Daisy *is* a little nervous at times, aren't you, Daisy dear?'

Daisy nodded sadly. 'I've always had a delicate tummy.'

'Perhaps Miss Martinelli's death has affected you?' Kate suggested.

'Oh, it has,' Daisy agreed. 'That someone died so suddenly like – someone who lived right above us…' She shuddered. The pug had finally shut up, stretched out on the chair and fallen asleep.

'And she'd been in there, like *that*, for two days, wasn't she, Daisy?' Violet put in. 'I'm relieved she died in hospital and not in there. Sharon said there was a terrible smell—'

'Oh, don't *talk* about it, Violet,' said Daisy clutching her stomach.

'It wouldn't stop us moving up there though, would it, Daisy?'

'No, it wouldn't.' Daisy turned to Kate. 'That's the flat *we* wanted, you see. Upstairs, and on the front. But Edina beat us to it.'

'We were very upset at the time, weren't we, Daisy?' Violet sniffed. 'We did ask Edina if she'd be prepared to swap, but she wasn't having any of it.'

'No, she wasn't,' Daisy confirmed. 'But we didn't hold it against her.'

'Not really,' said Violet. She didn't look altogether certain. 'But we had a lovely policewoman come round yesterday, didn't we, Daisy? Asking us all these questions, like on the telly.'

'Did you?' They hadn't wasted any time, Kate thought. 'Did they interview everyone?'

'Oh yes, I believe so,' said Daisy. 'But she was such a nice lady. We made her a cup of tea. And offered her a biscuit.'

'And we told her that we didn't mind Edina's singing too much, not like some of the others.' Violet sniffed. 'Live and let live, we say.'

'That's what we always say,' confirmed Daisy.

Kate sipped her cup of tea. 'What sort of things were they asking you?' she enquired as innocently as she could.

'Oh, they were asking some strange questions, weren't they, Daisy?'

'Really? Like what?'

'They asked if she ever got depressed and we said no, never. Well, not that we know anyway.'

'Well, that's very interesting. What else did they ask?'

'Well, I seem to remember they did ask if we knew of anyone who she might have upset recently,' Violet said. 'But we couldn't think of a soul, could we, Daisy?'

'No, not a soul,' said Daisy.

'Well, now you need something to settle that tummy of yours, Miss Po—, Daisy.' Kate wrote out a prescription. 'Are you able to get to the chemist's?'

'Oh, Cornelius will fetch it for us,' said Violet.

'Cornelius is very kind,' Daisy confirmed.

'He goes for long walks, you see. He says it's to counteract sitting at his computer for most of the day. He writes books, you know,' Violet said.

'I've met Mr Crow a couple of times,' Kate said, remembering the tall, creepy-looking man.

'Oh yes, Cornelius lives directly above us, doesn't he, Violet?'

Violet nodded assent. 'Directly above us, between Edina – God rest her soul – and the Reverend. He's recently had his knee replaced you know.'

'Yes, I've met the Reverend too,' Kate said.

'He's a real gentleman,' said Daisy. She leaned forward. 'He was in love with Edina, you know.'

'That, of course, is just *rumour*,' Violet said, 'but he's a *lovely* man. And Cornelius is a lovely man too.'

'If a little strange,' added Daisy.

Kate drained her cup. 'Strange? In what way?'

'Well,' said Violet, 'he looks at you kind of funny sometimes, doesn't he, Daisy?'

'Yes, he has a funny look at times.'

'Probably because he writes all that murder stuff,' Violet went on. 'All that nasty killing and things! Must affect you.'

Kate accepted a second cup of tea because she was keen to discover more about these ageing oddball residents. 'I also met another couple, Gloria and, er, what's his name, when I was here,' she prompted.

'Oh,' said Daisy, 'that'll be the Pratts, Ollie and Gloria. Nice enough, I suppose.' She sniffed.

'They won some money,' Violet said. 'Was it on the pools, Daisy?'

'No, dear, I think it might have been some sort of lottery. They were in a little flat somewhere on the estate and then, after their win, up they came here.'

Violet nodded. 'I don't want to sound snobbish,' she said, turning to Kate, 'but they're a little bit…'

'*Common*,' Daisy supplied. 'And all they do from morning to night is *eat*. They didn't get into that shape by accident.'

'Two heart attacks waiting to happen,' Violet confirmed.

'Oh dear,' said Kate, sipping her tea and refusing a Jaffa Cake. 'And who lives in Flat 1?'

'That's dear Hetty,' replied Violet. 'Hetty Patterson. Hetty's a little younger than us, don't you think, Daisy?'

'I do believe she's only eighty-one,' Daisy confirmed.

'Respectable lady. Retired schoolteacher. She's in Bournemouth at the moment tending to her poor sister,' Violet said, looking sadly out the window. 'I do believe the sister has some nasty terminal disease, and Hetty takes herself off every few weeks to take care of her. Is the sister's name Julia, Daisy?'

Daisy thought for a moment. 'No, I think it might actually be Judith. Anyway, Hetty chose a good time to be away with all *this* going on.'

'I think she's due back after the weekend,' said Violet, 'and what a *shock* she's going to get! She was a great friend of Edina's, you know.'

'And have you two ladies lived here long?' Kate asked as she laid down her cup and began to pack away her things.

'Oh, ever since the house was converted into flats,' Violet replied, 'and that must be five years or so now, isn't it, Daisy?'

'Thereabouts,' said Daisy, 'because we retired in 2014, didn't we?'

'Yes, 2014,' said Violet, 'that's when we retired.'

'My goodness,' Kate said, 'you retired very late in life, didn't you?'

'Oh, we loved our work, didn't we, Violet?' Daisy's eyes shone for a moment. 'We had a shop, you know, down in Middle Tinworthy. Potters the Draper's, ladies' clothing.'

'*Quality* ladies' clothing,' Violet corrected. 'Lovely twin-sets, beautiful nylons, pure silk vests and panties.'

'All the Tinworthy ladies bought their knickers from us, didn't they, Violet?'

'Oh yes, we couldn't sell enough of those panties, the ones with the lace tops.'

'And the cotton gussets,' added Daisy.

'It's a boutique now,' Violet said sadly. 'They sell those silly crop-tops, or whatever you call them, and mini-skirts. *Tiny* mini-skirts.'

'Pussy pelmets,' Daisy confirmed. 'That's what they call them.'

'Well, this has been most interesting,' Kate said, turning towards the door, 'but I really must go. Thank you so much for the tea and the chat.'

At this Jasper, awakened from his slumbers, leaped onto the floor and resumed barking.

'*Naughty boy!*' scolded Daisy. She turned to Kate. 'It's lovely to have a visitor.' She appeared to have made a rapid recovery as they both accompanied Kate to the door. As they opened it and Kate went out, Violet said, *sotto voce,* 'We think poor dear Edina might have been poisoned.'

'Really?' Kate asked. 'Why do you think that?'

'Well, we reckon it was that stepson of hers who did it. He was always visiting her and asking for money, wasn't he, Daisy? Apparently, his business wasn't doing too well.'

'And she wouldn't give it to him, would she? We know because we could hear them rowing when we were out in the garden, couldn't we, Violet?'

'Yes, well, the nurse doesn't really need to know that,' Violet said hurriedly.

Kate, stepping out into the hall, said, 'Bye, ladies, and do get in touch if the tummy continues to bother you, Daisy.'

'Oh I shall,' said Daisy, grabbing the pug by the collar, and both ladies waved as Kate headed for the front door.

CHAPTER EIGHT

When Kate arrived at the door she almost collided with a small, bald, bespectacled man carrying a large package.

'Ah,' he said, 'do you live here?'

'No,' Kate replied, 'just visiting.'

'Well,' he said, edging past her and depositing the package on the hall table between the two serpentine carvings, 'that's the Reverend fed for the week.'

Kate looked out at the little green van parked by the main gate. It had lines of daisies painted along the side, above which was written 'Fresh-as-a-Daisy! Fernfield Farm Foods!'

Then, as he turned back towards the front door he said, 'Goodness only knows how long it'll be before it gets collected.' He glanced back at the table. 'They're chilled and they're supposed to be put straight in the fridge or the freezer, you know, but I'm not allowed to deliver to the individual flats. I come at the same time on the same day every week so they should know that by now.'

Kate walked back towards the table. 'Don't worry,' she said, 'I know the Reverend so I'll take these up to him. As a matter of interest did you used to bring meals for Edina Martinelli?'

The little man stopped at the door. 'Yeah, of course I did, and sometimes they'd sit on that table for ages. I happen to know that because I delivered the wrong ones once and, when I came back a couple of hours later, there they were, still sitting on the table where I'd left them!'

'How interesting!' Kate said truthfully, her mind full of new possibilities. *No, no*, she thought to herself, *that's ridiculous! You're clutching at straws, Kate Palmer!*

'You should try them,' he went on. 'They'd be right handy for a working lady like yourself.' With that he headed towards his daisy-dappled van.

'I'll bear it in mind,' she called after him as he waved and drove off.

Kate studied the package which consisted of seven ready meals, one on top of the other, in plastic containers, each covered in clingfilm, and finished off with a slide-over cardboard sleeve with a picture of the contents. She could only see cottage pie sitting on the top, and wondered if the vicar might have been so bold as to order anything more exotic such as lasagne or moussaka, perhaps.

As she was about to pick it up an anxious little voice called out, 'Everything all right?'

Sharon was coming down the stairs brandishing a mop and a pail.

'Oh yes,' explained Kate. 'I was visiting the Potters and, as I was leaving, bumped into the chap who delivers the ready meals. These are for Edgar Ellis so I thought I'd take them up to him, since I'm told that these meals can sit there on the table for ages.'

'You're right,' Sharon said. 'I've often gone home by the time he comes and these folks are never in a hurry to pick up their mail or parcels. When I am here I deliver them myself. Anyway, I'll take these up to the vicar.'

Kate hesitated. 'Sharon, I don't suppose I could have a quick peek inside Edina Martinelli's flat for a brief moment? I've got a feeling I may have left a thermometer in there when I visited her just before she died. I can't find it anywhere.'

'I'm not really supposed to let anyone in,' Sharon said, chewing her lip, 'but I suppose it's all right, you being a nurse and all… I did give the place a tidy-up but I didn't see it.'

'It's quite small,' Kate said, 'so you could easily have overlooked it. I'd just like to make sure I didn't leave it in her bedroom.'

Sharon thought for a moment. 'Well, I suppose there's no harm,' she said. 'I'll open the door for you and you can let yourself out because the door locks automatically. I'd come in with you but I'll give this lot to the Rev and then I'm going home for my tea.'

'That's very kind, Sharon. I shan't take long.'

Sharon laid down the mop and pail and, digging the bunch of keys out from her apron pocket, picked up the box of meals and headed back upstairs again. Kate followed behind.

It's only a hunch, of course, but it's worth a try.

As Sharon unlocked the door she said, 'David Courtney's the only one who's been in there apart from me. I think he needed to get some of her papers or something. But I ain't touched anything.'

'Thanks so much,' Kate said as she went inside.

'No problem,' said Sharon as she headed towards Edgar Ellis's door with his weekly dinners.

Kate stood for a moment inside the door. There was a stale smell in the air and the place was in darkness, due to all the curtains having been pulled across. She walked quietly into the kitchen, conscious of the fact that Cornelius Crow was directly next door and might hear her every move.

She had a quick look in the bin which had, of course, been emptied. There'd be little point in checking the bins outside because they'd almost certainly have been emptied at least once since Edina's death. What had she expected? It was a crazy idea to begin with.

Kate was still chiding herself as she opened the door of the built-in fridge. There was nothing whatsoever in there. Nothing. Someone had obviously cleared it out.

The freezer section was underneath and it had not been emptied. There was a drawer half-full of vegetables and fruit, a drawer with some packets of mince and chops, and a drawer containing two ready meals from 'Fresh-as-a-Daisy! Fernfield Farm Foods'.

Kate removed them from the freezer and carried them across to the window. She opened up the blind and studied the meals: one cannelloni, one shepherd's pie. She wished she'd brought a magnifying glass, but her reading glasses would have to do.

She turned the containers over and over and it took several minutes before Kate found what she was looking for. She saw it first in the plastic base of the shepherd's pie.

A series of tiny pinpricks.

She examined the cannelloni again and it took another couple of minutes before she was able to discern another row of minuscule pinpricks in that too.

Kate took photos with her phone in the hope that, if she enlarged them, the pinpricks would be visible. She then placed both meals back in the freezer and let herself out of the flat.

CHAPTER NINE

Kate wasn't sure how Woody might react to the idea of her snooping around in Edina Martinelli's flat. He'd most likely go on and on again about not getting involved, but she was desperate to tell him of her discovery.

She took a deep breath. 'I think I've found out how the poison was administered.'

Woody stared at her over the rim of his glass. 'What has Miss Marple deduced *this* time?'

Kate decided to ignore his mocking tone. She told him about her meeting the man from Fernfield Farm Foods as she was leaving the Potters', and how he commented on the length of time the meals could remain on the table before they were collected. 'And then I made a visit to Edina's flat,' she said.

'Oh yes? And how did you manage to get in there?'

'Well, I had to tell a tiny white lie,' Kate admitted.

'And…?'

She told him all. 'I've taken photos, but the pinpricks are so tiny they hardly show up,' she said.

He was silent for a moment.

'So,' he said eventually, 'you reckon someone injected digoxin into the meals while they were awaiting collection on the hall table?'

'Yes, digoxin or some form of digitalis. That's what I think,' Kate confirmed.

'You should have gone straight to Bill Robson,' he said. 'This could be important.'

'I wanted to tell you first,' Kate said. 'And I don't like that man.'

He smiled. 'You were very naughty going in there under false pretences, you know. Bill's likely to ask you about that.'

'Then I can tell him that I went in to look for my thermometer,' she said.

'And you thought it might be in the *freezer*?'

Kate grimaced. 'I suppose I'd just have to remind him about my suspicions then.'

She hesitated. 'I honestly don't want to set eyes on him again. Couldn't *you* tell him, Woody?'

Woody shook his head. 'No, Kate, it has to come from you. Would you like me to come with you? I'm not working up there tomorrow, but if you need my support…'

She shook her head. 'I know you mean that kindly, but if I must go, then I think it best that I don't involve you.'

'Promise me you'll go to the police station first thing in the morning?'

'I will,' Kate promised.

'So who did you say you were visiting up there today?'

'Daisy and Violet Potter,' Kate replied. 'They were *such* sweet old ladies, absolutely identical! And, would you believe, they used to have a draper's shop in Middle Tinworthy where, they assured me, all the local ladies bought their knickers.'

'A *draper's*?' Woody looked bewildered. 'Remind me what *that* is?'

'They were shops that sold mainly ladies' clothing in the days before you were allowed to browse around, and there was a lady behind every counter waiting to find out what you wanted and to serve you.'

'So, women's clothing outlets?'

'Something like that. You don't hear the word used much now.'

'You sure don't. I've heard of knickers, though!'

'It's Demelza's Boutique now.' As Kate gazed into the flames she wondered if she should inform him that one of the old ladies referred to the stepson and his supposed quest for money. Perhaps not; he'd only tell her not to get involved. But she *was* involved! And the twins obviously resented Edina getting the flat they wanted. But surely not enough to kill her?

Kate looked round the book-lined room. She had never seen so many books outside of a library before and wondered if he'd read every single one of them. Woody had two walls of his sitting room shelved from floor to ceiling, groaning under the weight of books, not to mention the bookcases on the upstairs landing and in his bedroom. It was a masculine sort of house with few ornaments and lots of pictures of boats on every spare wall surface. It was comfortable and homely, but hardly *Homes and Gardens*.

Kate suddenly decided she *would* tell him what the Potter twins had said.

'And they reckon that Edina Martinelli was having no end of problems with her greedy stepson. They were earwigging from the garden.'

'Don't tell me they're amateur sleuths too!' Woody raised an eyebrow as he took hold of Kate's hand. 'What *is* it with you women?'

'No, no, but apparently they could hear the stepson rowing with her on a regular basis and, as we guessed, he wanted money. They rowed a lot because she wasn't obliging.'

'Where have I heard *that* before!' Woody exclaimed. 'And that doesn't make him a killer. That's assuming we *are* now looking for a killer.'

'But it *could*. And then there's that Cornelius Crow! I mean, the very name is spooky! He's really creepy and he writes murder novels full of blood and gore apparently. Perhaps he knows all about poisons too.'

'That doesn't make him a killer either,' Woody retorted. 'Just as likely to be one of your old ladies who'd got a grudge against her. If you ever have to do some super-sleuthing again then you can't just come up with random theories. You've got to work on means – *how* they managed to do it, on motive – *why* they wanted to do it, and then, *when* would they have had the *opportunity* to do it. Kate, I appreciate you're trying to protect your job and the surgery, but we have no real proof that there's a killer around.'

'I'm trying to be methodical and, if my suspicions are correct, then I've discovered *how* the person did it and also how they had the opportunity. I'm convinced one of them is a killer! But the residents are all so *weird*, apart from the Potter twins, so it makes it difficult to narrow down the choice of suspects. Don't forget there's the old vicar as well who was besotted with Edina, but the feelings were not reciprocated. Perhaps he was driven mad with desire and couldn't live with the rejection?'

'How do you know his love was unrequited?'

'Well, that's what the very chubby couple in Flat 3 reckoned.'

'The chubby couple?'

'The Pratts, who, according to the ladies, had won money on the lottery or something, and upgraded themselves from a flat on the estate. The twins, who are a wee bit snobby, think they are a tad *common*. Not my words,' she said as Woody raised an eyebrow. 'Ollie, the husband, did lots of small jobs for Edina and she rewarded him with CDs of opera, which made Gloria, his wife, jealous as can be. She's not a very nice woman but I have to admit that I find it hard to believe she had enough motive.'

Woody laughed. 'I'm surprised you haven't got all their birth dates, heights, waist measurements and hobbies yet.'

Kate grinned. 'Give me time! The only resident I don't know much about yet is the little lady in Flat 1, but she's been away and missed all the drama.'

'To change the subject,' Woody said as he refilled their glasses, 'how's that crazy sister of yours getting on with her beau?'

'Oh, you mean Fergal?'

Fergal was *very* Irish, very friendly, and worked for a firm in Plymouth who supplied postcards and local paraphernalia to tourist shops. In fact, that's how he met her – he literally picked her up when she tripped and fell flat on the pavement right outside the shop he was delivering to. Kate hadn't told Woody that, some months previously, Angie had got completely plastered on her own in The Greedy Gull and Kate had been summoned to take her home. The person who gallantly came forward to help Kate get Angie onto her feet was none other than Fergal, a fact of which Angie was completely unaware. So, in fact, he'd picked her up twice.

Fergal was a free spirit. He appeared to be very fond of Angie but one weekend he'd appear and the next weekend he wouldn't. It drove Angie mad.

'At least he seems a good influence,' Kate said, 'and keeps her out of The Greedy Gull. Pity he lives in Plymouth; if he lived nearer they'd probably see each other more often.'

Woody sighed. 'Poor Angie.'

'She takes after our dad. "The alcoholic gene" is what my mother called it. Mind you,' Kate said as she drained her glass, 'the way I'm knocking back this wine, who am I to talk?'

'It is a great wine,' Woody said, holding up the bottle and scrutinising the label. 'Considering it's only French and not Californian, it's pretty good. I guess maybe we've taught the French a thing or two!'

Kate laughed. 'Very decent of you to consider drinking it.'

'I may even be persuaded to open another bottle of the stuff. What can we celebrate? Your great discovery? Or you becoming a grandmother? Me retiring? Or supposed to be. A day without rain?'

They clinked glasses.

'Now, Kate, shall we take this bottle upstairs with us and go to bed?'

'Sometimes you come up with just the right solution.' Kate smiled.

CHAPTER TEN

The next day Kate presented herself at the police station in Launceston at half past nine. Detective Inspector Bill Robson looked his usual dour self. He had a considerable paunch, which he massaged continually with one hand.

'Ah, Mrs Palmer,' he said when Kate was shown in, 'we meet again. Do take a seat. Woody Forrest told me you'd be calling. Nasty business, this, at Seaview Grange.'

'Yes, it is,' Kate agreed. 'I've got to know most of the residents due to my visits there as a nurse from time to time. And I think I've discovered some interesting facts.'

'Hmm,' said Bill, shuffling some pieces of paper around.

Kate told him again of her visit to Edina prior to her becoming ill, and reminded him about how convinced Edina was that someone was trying to kill her by causing her to trip down the stairs.

'Well, of course,' he said with a sniff, 'it's easy enough to trip down the stairs.'

'It's a lot easier when an electric flex has been positioned across the top,' Kate pointed out.

He continued to stroke his belly. Did the man have an itch, Kate wondered, or was it some sort of method to activate his brain?

'I know from my own visit there,' Kate continued, 'that Edina Martinelli's stepson was frequently calling on her asking for money. And that was verified by the Potter sisters, who have heard them arguing on the subject.'

'What exactly did *you* hear the stepson say?' he asked.

Kate recounted David Courtney's visit, his unenthusiastic welcome and how they waited until she was outside the door before they began to argue. Kate told him she could hear their raised voices through the door, but not what they were saying. She described how he left shortly afterwards, obviously in a temper, while Miss Hetty Patterson, in Flat 1, came running after him, begging him to calm down.

He removed his hand from his stomach and scratched his head instead. 'Now why would she do that?'

Kate shrugged. 'I've no idea.'

He was now twiddling a piece of rolled-up paper.

'And yesterday,' she went on, 'as I was leaving after my visit to the two old ladies, the twins in Flat 2 that I told you about, I met the man who delivers ready meals. He told me that these meals should be put straight away into the fridge or the freezer, but that the residents there, including Edina, were never in any hurry to pick them up. So they could remain on the hall table for some time.'

'And that's relevant?'

'Very relevant.'

'Enlighten me.'

'I happened to be in Edina Martinelli's flat…'

'So you were interfering with what may be a crime scene! Why were you in there?'

'Because I thought I might have left a thermometer there, and guess what?'

'I can't imagine.'

Kate didn't much like the tone of his voice. 'In the freezer—'

'What do you mean, in the *freezer*?' he barked. 'Why would you leave a thermometer in a *freezer*?'

'No, no,' Kate said, getting flustered, 'of *course* I didn't! But I got this idea when I heard about how these meals were sometimes left on the table.'

'What idea was that exactly?'

Kate didn't particularly like the way this conversation was going. She didn't like the sarcasm she could hear in his voice either.

'I got the idea that the meals might have been tampered with. So I looked to see if any of them were left in the fridge.'

'And of course they *weren't*,' Bill Robson said smugly, smothering a yawn.

'No, of course they weren't. But two of them had been transferred to the freezer and no one has yet emptied out the freezer. And, after examining them carefully, I found tiny pinpricks in each, like the needle of a syringe might make.'

'Well, well, well,' he said. 'Now you're going to ask if we can analyse them, aren't you?'

'Yes, I am.'

'Forgive me for asking,' he said, 'but why are you so interested in this? It still seems to be a fairly straightforward case of an overdose, probably either wrongly prescribed from your surgery, or because she'd been storing the stuff up for some time.'

'She's been prescribed digoxin for years, for her heart,' Kate protested, 'and she was always careful with the dosage. Really she did *not* want to die.'

He was studying her intently. 'You were involved in the murders here back in the spring, were you not?'

'Yes, but only because I was in the wrong place at the wrong time. Or the right time, depending on how you look at it.'

'Does it not seem strange that it's only since you came to live down here that these murders have taken place?' He was studying her intently now.

Kate gasped. 'What are you *insinuating*?'

'I *never* insinuate, Mrs Palmer. I'm just considering the possibility that you might have developed a taste for all the attention you received at that time. Maybe you'd *like* this to be murder, Mrs

Palmer? Or perhaps you realise it was the *surgery's* fault and you're trying to shift the blame away from them? Because they most likely have overprescribed this drug. Perhaps you want to cover up for them? If I were looking at all the possibilities, Mrs Palmer, I might be thinking that it was you that injected digoxin into those meals, for the sake of saving your surgery's reputation.'

Kate stood up. 'I came up here to try to help you to solve this crime. And it *is* a crime! I've met this lady, and she was certain someone was trying to kill her. Now they've succeeded and all I'm asking you to do is examine the two meals in the freezer. And I don't like your attitude one little bit!'

'I can't say I'm over-impressed with your amateur meddling either. I suggest you concentrate on your nursing, Mrs Palmer.'

'And I suggest you check on the evidence, Detective Inspector Robson!'

Kate was so angry she knew she had to get out of the place before she either burst with fury or with tears.

What a despicable man! Kate headed towards her car almost blinded with tears of anger. How could he insinuate such a thing! And why wasn't he doing his job thoroughly and examining every single lead? All he seemed intent on doing was passing the blame onto the surgery and making her the scapegoat. As she got into the driving seat she offered up a silent prayer of thanks that it had been Woody who had been in charge when she first arrived here.

Because, for sure, she was not going to enjoy any communication with Bill Robson.

CHAPTER ELEVEN

On the drive home Kate realised she was driving far too fast because she was so incensed at DI Robson's insinuations. She needed to calm down so she pulled in to the layby, just below Higher Tinworthy, from where there was a magnificent panorama of the ocean and miles of coastline. Woody had introduced her to this spot which, in summer, was crammed with tourists' cars but, thankfully, today there were none. She took deep breaths, admired the view and began to feel her pulse slow down and her mind begin to clear. Once she felt sufficiently recovered, she would phone Woody. At least he *listened* to her. Even if he did sometimes tease, his remarks were never nasty like Bill Robson's.

It was a cool, sunny day with good visibility and the sea was a beautiful turquoise colour with drifts of sea-green towards the shore. If it wasn't for the icy wind outside it could pass for the Caribbean. Well, almost.

She phoned Woody.

'I'm up in the layby,' she said, 'trying to calm down.'

'Why, what's happened?' he asked.

'What's happened is my interview with Bill Robson,' Kate replied. 'What a despicable man!'

'Surely he's not *that* bad, Kate?'

'He bloody well is!' Kate related an account of her conversation with the new detective inspector. 'And, Woody, he made some snide remark about the murders having only been committed since *I* arrived down here! The cheek of the man! And he's desperate to pass the buck for Edina's poisoning to us at the medical centre and more or less accused us of not controlling her dosage. I think the man is too lazy to do his job. He seems determined to blame Edina's death on medical negligence. Either that or simply put it down to the fact that she finished herself off! But, Woody, I *know* she didn't want to die!'

Woody was silent for a moment. Then he asked, 'Did you tell him about the meals?'

'Yes, I did, but he doesn't even seem to think it necessary to test them. And do you know what? He's quite fit to say that I made those holes myself. Next thing you know I'll be the chief suspect!' Kate was aware that her voice had been rising higher and higher.

'Kate, the first thing you need to do is calm down. Go home, take the dog for a walk or something. I have to go up there today so I'll have a word with Bill Robson. He *is* still concentrating on suicide or, I'm sorry to say, a mistake at the surgery. But the least he can do is check those meals to see if they contain digoxin. I'll see that he does. And' – he paused, but she could tell he was smiling – 'I'll give you a very good character reference!'

When Kate arrived home she was welcomed by an ecstatic Barney. The first thing she was going to have to do was take him for a walk. Kate always felt guilty because she'd been away overnight and out for most of the morning. She worried about Barney, in spite of the fact that the dog was supposed to be Angie's. Where was Angie anyway? Still in bed, Kate guessed. She couldn't always be trusted to let Barney out for a late-night pee before she went to bed, and she was rarely up early enough to do likewise in the morning. The result was frequently a puddle on the kitchen floor, an apologetic-looking dog and a row with Angie. On one occasion Angie, who, as usual, had had one too many, did remember to let Barney out but then forgot to let him in again, leaving the dog outside all night. Kate reckoned it was worse than having an unpredictable teenager in the house because at least you could blame it all on hormones as opposed to gin.

On this occasion there was no puddle and Kate decided to have a quick cup of tea before setting out with Barney for a walk up to Penhallion cliff opposite, on the north side of Woody's house, which was easier terrain than the steep climb to the cliff walk above Lavender Cottage that eventually led to Seaview Grange, if you walked and climbed long enough. As she drank her tea, she felt herself finally beginning to relax.

Kate loved their kitchen, a large extension which had been added on at the rear by the previous owners. It was light and airy with Shaker units and French doors to the back garden. There was a wide arch leading to the sitting room, which overlooked the sea at the front. It had taken them a little time to get used to the three steps which separated the two rooms. On one occasion Angie and her glass of gin went flying across the kitchen floor but, fortunately, both Angie and the glass remained intact by some stroke of good luck.

Kate drained her cup of tea, feeling much calmer, and set off with Barney. As they climbed the path her thoughts kept returning to the unfortunate Edina Martinelli. Whoever had poisoned her hadn't done it by halves as they'd taken the trouble to inject every meal. It could therefore be assumed that the person who administered it had wanted her well and truly dead.

The wind was chilly but there was hardly a cloud in the sky on this beautiful autumn day. When they reached the top Kate, as always, stopped to admire the stunning views in every direction. Looking out across the ocean she could see a container ship on the horizon heading north, probably to Avonmouth, full of shiny new cars from the Far East. Looking south the dramatic coastline was visible as far as Trevose Head, and to the north she could decipher

Hartland Point up in Devon and the silhouette of Lundy Island in the Bristol Channel. The sea washed rhythmically on the rocks beneath and the gulls, as always, wheeled and screamed overhead. While Barney investigated every tuft of grass and hollow, Kate remained deep in thought.

This whole Edina Martinelli business fascinated her. Who *was* this woman anyway? Might she be Italian, as her name suggested? She had a stepson so she must have been married at least once. And what about her singing career? If she'd sung at Covent Garden then she must have had a good voice. If she'd been successful then probably she could be googled. Kate decided that, as soon as she got home, she'd get her laptop out.

She'd now reached the wooden seat, anchored to a concrete base, which faced the Atlantic at the highest point of the cliff, and sat down to get her breath back. Since coming to Cornwall this seat had been a pivotal point of her life and it had taken weeks for her to face coming back here again after a dramatic incident some months previously.

She had the remainder of the day to herself. She'd see Woody again tomorrow. The good thing about their relationship was that they both felt the same way in that, much as they loved being together, they needed time apart and their own personal space. Kate knew there was no way she could exist full-time amid Woody's chaotic collections of books and boats any more than he could survive in the tidier, feminine environment of Lavender Cottage, complete with Angie. And particularly not with Angie. Woody was fond enough of Angie but didn't pretend to understand her.

Growing up, people remarked diplomatically that Angie was the 'pretty one' and Kate the 'sensible one'. Nevertheless, prettiness had not brought Angie much self-confidence or contentment. On the contrary, she always seemed to be striving for something or someone she couldn't have; 'chasing after rainbows', their mother had put it. At sixty years of age Angie was still chasing after those rainbows.

Now Fergal was on the scene. But Fergal was in a world of his own and, on one occasion, actually 'forgot' it was Saturday and left a furious Angie, high and dry, all dressed up with nowhere to go.

Kate walked the dog for nearly an hour but, when she got back, she found the kitchen still empty. She put on the kettle, got out her laptop and googled 'Edina Martinelli'.

Edina Martinelli was born plain Edna Martin in Bognor Regis in 1940. There followed brief details of her schooling, of her singing lessons and winning 'Soprano of the Year' in 1962. Then there were some years with the D'Oyly Carte Opera Company, the English National Opera and finally to Covent Garden where her one starring role was as Leonora in *Il trovatore* in which, of course, she poisoned *herself*. She married twice, the first time to a fellow opera singer, Maurice Le Fevre, from 1959 to 1964, which ended in divorce. She then married Roger Courtney in 1966. She had no children of her own, only David Courtney, her stepson. Miss Martinelli retired from public performances in 1999.

Kate was about to switch off her laptop when she thought about this Roger Courtney. Had he been the person who brought Edina down to Cornwall? There was no harm in googling him to find out. And there he was, Roger Courtney of Courtney & Son Motors, with a large showroom in Exeter, and so that was most probably the reason why Edina had ended up in the South-West. He'd died in 2010. Was the stepson still running the motor business? Hadn't the twins said the business was struggling? Was that the reason he was desperate for money? She wondered then if the Potter twins might have been right. Would he have had enough motivation to murder his stepmother and could he have had the opportunity to poison her? Perhaps it was time to investigate David Courtney.

*

As Kate closed her laptop she felt re-energised by the information she'd just discovered. The thought of investigating David Courtney had given her a new focus – who needed Bill Robson? At that moment Angie shuffled into the kitchen in her dressing-gown and sat down morosely at the kitchen table.

'Good afternoon!' Kate said cheerfully. 'Cup of tea?'

'Why are you always so bloody cheerful?' Angie groaned. 'Oh, need I ask – a night with the wonderful Woody? And *I'm* having coffee.' With that she stood up and stuck a pod in the coffee machine.

Kate sighed. 'And why are you always so grumpy? What have you got to be miserable about on a nice day like this?'

'I *know*, I *know*, there are children starving all over the planet and drinking filthy water, I *know*. I know there are homeless people on the streets and I know there are people dying of dreadful diseases. I know, I *know*. I should be thankful for what I've got, blah, blah, blah.'

'Well,' Kate said, 'can you crack your face into some sort of a smile then? What's biting you anyway – or need I *ask*?'

'No, you needn't ask. It's that bloody Fergal. He was supposed to ring me last night to make plans for tonight and tomorrow.'

'And he hasn't?'

'Bloody right he hasn't.' Angie took a gulp of her coffee.

'Have you tried calling him?'

'Yeah, he's not answering. Straight onto voicemail.'

'Well,' Kate soothed, racking her brain for a comforting remark, 'perhaps something's cropped up at work or…'

'For God's sake, Kate! He only flogs postcards, he's not a bloody brain surgeon! And he always carries his phone on him *everywhere*.'

'Maybe he's lost it?'

'There is such a thing as a landline, you know. No.' Angie stood up and gazed out the window. 'I have to accept that he's not *exactly* reliable. I'm beginning to have my doubts.'

'About what?'

'About *him*. Do you think he could be married?'

'Unlikely.' Kate stared at Angie in astonishment. 'Why on earth do you say that?'

Angie shrugged. 'Dunno. He's too enigmatic. I mean, I'll probably not hear from him all weekend and then next week he'll surface like nothing's happened.'

'Nothing *has* happened.'

'No, well, you know what I mean. Do you fancy a trip to Plymouth?'

Kate poured boiling water over her teabag. 'Plymouth? What on earth for? Don't tell me you're heading for The Gin Factory?'

Angie grinned. 'No, although that's not such a bad idea. No, I mean to see where he lives. Let's face it, we've been going out for months and he always finds some excuse for us *not* to go to Plymouth. We always go out around here. Doesn't that sound a bit dodgy to you?'

'Hmm,' Kate murmured, unconvinced.

'I thought we could maybe do some shopping and lunch and then have a stroll around where he's supposed to be living.'

'Have you got his address?'

'Not all of it, but it's a flat somewhere in the Barbican and I think it's called Raleigh something-or-other. We could go tomorrow if you haven't made plans with Wonderboy.'

'I'm afraid we *have* made plans.'

'Oh bugger. Never mind, I might go myself anyway.'

Kate took a deep breath. 'Don't let this get to you, Angie. There's probably a logical explanation and, if not, there's plenty more fish in the sea.'

'You *would* say that, wouldn't you, now you're all tied up with Wonderboy. Everything works out for *you*. And there aren't that many half-decent fish in the sea, because I've *looked*.' She sniffed.

'After all, Fergal's very *presentable*, and he's got his own hair, teeth and hips. They haven't *all* got the full quota, you know.'

Kate didn't want to get into an argument; she'd heard all this before. Yes, she'd been lucky to meet Woody but, over the years, she'd not always had a great deal of success when it came to romance. Angie was the pretty one, the actress, with a husband who adored her and put up with her dalliances. She was not accustomed to feeling insecure in her relationships with the opposite sex. But she'd met her match with Fergal.

CHAPTER TWELVE

On Monday, when Kate reported for duty, she noticed that her first patient was Mr Oliver Pratt, of Seaview Grange. This could be another opportunity to find out more about the residents perhaps.

'What can I do for you, Mr Pratt?' Kate asked.

'Oh, call me Ollie. We *have* met before, if you remember?' He plonked his enormous bottom on one of the metal chairs.

'Oh yes, I do remember,' said Kate. 'How are things up at the Grange?'

'Very tense,' Ollie replied, wiping the sweat from his brow. 'Edina's passing has affected us all. You've heard, I suppose, that she had some sort of poisoning?'

'Yes, I've heard,' Kate said briefly. 'Now, what seems to be the trouble, Ollie?'

'I'm having palpitations,' he replied, 'and I've never had palpitations in my life before, *never*. Last night I'm just sitting there with one eye on some rubbish Gloria likes to watch on the telly, and then my old ticker starts banging away, faster and faster and faster. And for nearly an hour! I thought I was going to *die*.'

'Let's check you over then,' Kate said, and proceeded to give him a thorough examination. 'Everything seems pretty normal, Ollie, although your blood pressure's on the high side, but I see you're on medication for that. Have you ever considered losing a little weight?'

Ollie sniffed. 'Well, I know I'm a little on the tubby side…'

'Would you step on the scales, please?' Kate registered his weight. 'I have to tell you that you're obese, close to being morbidly obese.

And that's affecting your heart as well as everything else. Why don't you and your wife consider joining a weight-loss group? Or I can give you some diet sheets if you'd prefer?'

Ollie frowned. 'To be honest, Nurse, I think these palpitations are due to *stress*. Did you know that I used to do lots of jobs for Edina? I made her some bookcases and she was really pleased with them. She even got me interested in opera! I've never been to an opera in my life but, after listening to her singing some of that stuff, I've got really keen. She lent me some CDs, you know: *La Bohème*; *La traviata*; *Madame Butterfly*! Drives poor Gloria mad! I don't mind telling you, Nurse, I'm *devastated*. And, to make matters worse, dear little Hetty gets back from Bournemouth tonight and I dread telling her. She *loved* Edina, you know; they were best mates.' He tapped his nose and narrowed his eyes. 'I'll tell you something else – *somebody* at the Grange had it in for Edina, you mark my words.'

'Well, we can only hope that the police get round to doing their job,' Kate said, still smarting from her interview with Bill Robson.

'I reckon it's the old vicar,' said Ollie as he got up to go. 'After all, it makes sense after the way his wife died.'

Before Kate got the chance to ask what he meant he was out the door.

The number of suspects who might have wanted to murder Edina was growing. The Potter twins were convinced David Courtney had something to do with it. There was general agreement that Cornelius Crow had been driven mad by her singing, and now Ollie Pratt had pointed the finger at Edgar Ellis. *It's time to make my list*, Kate thought when she got home in the late afternoon. They were all suspects, no doubt about that. She put David Courtney at the top of her list, then Cornelius Crow, then Edgar Ellis. It was unlikely to be Ollie Pratt, but she wrote down his name next, along with Gloria. Then there were the two old Potter twins. Even more unlikely, but they were residents so down on the list they must go. And Hetty Patterson, who wasn't even *there*, but she was a resident. Who else? Of course! Sharon Starkey, the cleaner, and her husband, who turned out to be the gardener/handyman. What was his name?

And what was it Woody had said? Something like means, reason and opportunity? Why had Ollie Pratt singled out poor Edgar Ellis? He appeared to be a rather harmless character. Why would he *want* to kill a woman he was plainly besotted with? Perhaps it was time to try to find out a little more about the Reverend. It was a long shot but maybe a phone call to her cousin, Pam, might shine some light on the situation. But first of all she'd check the map to see if Pam lived anywhere near Little Barrington. According to Google, Little Perrinton, where Pam lived, was no more than ten miles or so from Little Barrington so she *might* be familiar with the area. She was due to give Pam a call anyway because she hadn't spoken to her cousin for months. Pam was a widow, and a merry one at that, so chances were she wouldn't be in. She'd had a succession of men friends who were always very well-heeled, and thus Pam was an expert on exotic locations and upmarket cruises.

On this occasion, however, Pam was at home.

'*Who?*' Pam asked.

'Kate. Your *cousin!*'

'Oh, hi, Kate! You just caught me! I'm packing for a cruise round Cambodia and Vietnam, with Frank. Was I with Frank when we spoke last?'

Kate couldn't recall the names of Pam's various male friends. 'Very nice, too,' she murmured.

'Yes, I'm looking forward to it. Everything OK at your end?'

'Yes, fine. We've settled in well down here.' She described the house and the village and confirmed that Angie was fine. 'I was wondering if you could give me some information. I'm interested in finding out a little more about an old chap who lives down here. It's in connection with a recent incident,' Kate said casually. 'He hails from a place called Little Barrington which, I see from the map, isn't too far from you?'

'An *incident*? Whatever do you mean?'

'Well, one of my patients died and there's a possibility she was murdered. One of her next-door neighbours hails from Little Barrington and I thought I'd ask you if you might know him, although I realise that's a long shot.'

'A murder! Oh my God! Aren't you afraid? There could be a killer on the loose!'

'That's a possibility, Pam, but I can't stand back and do nothing.'

'Well, be careful, for goodness' sake! As regards Little Barrington? It's about twelve miles from here. Who is this person you want to know about?'

'He's an old retired vicar who had the parish there.'

There was a silence. 'Edgar-the-Lecher?'

'*What?*'

'Edgar-the-Lecher Ellis was the vicar there for years. I don't suppose it's *him*, is it?'

'Yes, it is. What do you mean, Edgar-the-Lecher?'

'He made the national press! But you probably didn't see it. He was certainly famous, or *infamous* rather, round here!'

Kate was dumbfounded for a moment. 'But *why?*'

'Why? Because he had it off with most of the women in the choir and then, glory of glories, managed to get the organist pregnant.'

It took a few seconds again for Kate to find her voice. '*Edgar Ellis?*'

'I shouldn't think there's *two* of them. Tall, skinny, long nose, not exactly God's gift to women, but that didn't stop him.'

'Unbelievable!' Kate found it impossible to visualise him as some kind of Lothario.

'Rumour has it he poisoned his wife,' Pam went on, 'but apparently that was down to the local takeaway. Health and Safety closed the place down after that. So, he's down in your neck of the woods now, is he? Better put a padlock on your knickers! Surely they don't suspect old Edgar, do they?'

'No, no, he's not a suspect. But he is a patient of mine so I was interested.'

Kate could only think of the old man with the drip on the end of his nose. And his devotion to Edina, *who'd died of poisoning too*! It seemed too similar to just be a coincidence.

'Well, he's no angel,' Pam said, 'dog collar or not.'

'This has been a most interesting conversation, Pam. Thanks for that information!'

'Let me know what happens, *after* I get back from my cruise!'

After Kate came off the phone she realised that her main suspect, David Courtney, was now second on her list, *after* Edgar Ellis. But *why* would Edgar have wanted to kill Edina? It didn't make any sense.

'Today I found out something which may interest you,' Kate said casually into the phone.

'Go on,' said Woody, 'I'm holding my breath.'

'My cousin Pam lives very close to the village in the Cotswolds where the Reverend Edgar Ellis once presided over the local congregation.' Kate paused.

'I can't hold my breath much longer.'

'I spoke to her on the phone today and she told me a few interesting facts. Apparently, he was a real Lothario, spreading it about among the lady members of the choir – at least I'm *assuming* they were all ladies. And he got the organist *pregnant*! Got himself into the papers as well!'

'Well, good for him! That must have livened things up at the Sunday services!'

'But that's not all. His wife died of food poisoning shortly before they were due to move down here. *Food poisoning!*'

There was silence for a moment. 'Really?'

'They'd had a dodgy takeaway, apparently,' Kate went on.

'Oh.'

She could hear the disappointment in his voice. 'But that doesn't mean that it *was* the takeaway that killed her, does it?'

'How did the takeaway come out of this incident? Did anyone investigate?'

'Well, Health and Safety closed the place down but—'

'Kate,' he interrupted, 'calm down! The woman very probably *did* eat a dodgy meal. You've just said yourself it had to be closed down.'

'I still think this is important,' Kate said. 'It could be very convenient to blame a takeaway when you've poisoned someone, particularly if the place hasn't got a very good reputation anyway.'

'OK, Kate, I'll make a note of it, just in case.'

'Will you tell Bill Robson, or shall I? I don't suppose for a moment he's looked into Edgar Ellis's past.'

'I'll tell him. But I don't think you should read too much into the takeaway meal and the food poisoning,' Woody said.

'Well, I've elevated him to the top of my list, *above* David Courtney,' Kate informed him.

'You may need several sheets of A4 before this case is wound up,' said Woody.

'Well, at least I'm trying to do *something*, even if one day I think I'm making progress and the next day I don't. I mean, what's Robson come up with? Nothing that we know of!

Do you suppose he's got anyone on *his* list of suspects – apart from me?'

CHAPTER THIRTEEN

Kate had now met all the residents of Seaview Grange, even Hetty, the lady in Flat 1 who she'd met fleetingly on her first visit to Edina. Apparently, she'd been very friendly with Edina, so perhaps she could throw some light on the situation and have an idea as to who could have committed such a deed. But the little lady was proving to be very elusive and was rarely around when Kate was visiting the Grange. When Kate had mentioned this to Sharon, Sharon had said, 'Oh, Hetty keeps herself to herself. Funny old bird.' Funny old bird or not, Kate thought, she was the only person who'd been really close to Edina. So, now what? Kate's mind was going round in circles. And getting nowhere fast.

What she needed to do was think of something else. She could see Angie at work in her 'studio', having spent the weekend on her own. She had suddenly been inspired to paint again and Kate wondered if this was some sort of delaying tactic because she feared what she might find (for example, a wife) if she went to Plymouth. Then the elusive Fergal had finally rung up, full of apologies. He'd had to work overtime, he was very tired and yes, he should have phoned earlier but… Kate couldn't remember all the excuses. She couldn't make him out at all, particularly as he was such a charmer and seemed very fond of Angie.

She decided she'd make lasagne for supper and then discovered that there was no grated nutmeg with which to make the bechamel sauce. She could get back into the car and head for the supermarket or she could walk down to the village and chance her luck at Bobby's

Best Buys. Bobby prided himself on stocking 'everything you could need' – provided it wasn't too exotic. There was a fifty-fifty chance Bobby would not have nutmeg but Barney needed a walk and Kate needed to get on with her lasagne.

She fastened the lead onto Barney's collar and set off down the winding lane, past a couple of cottages, bungalows and The Greedy Gull before reaching the river. Bobby's was one of a straggle of shops and tea-rooms on the other side of the Pol and, as they crossed the ancient stone bridge, Kate looked over the side at the water level, which was high due to the rapidly incoming tide. The few remaining holidaymakers down on the beach were hurriedly gathering up their windbreaks and retreating to avoid the oncoming waves which would shortly cover most of the sand.

Bobby's did a roaring trade in bodyboards, buckets and spades and all manner of highly coloured necessities to satisfy holidaying families. He'd probably keep them on display until the end of the month before adorning the window with all the Halloween paraphernalia.

The shop suffered from lack of light, which only came in via the front display window. This was always packed with 'Bobby's Specials' which, depending on the season, varied from Christmas trees and festoons of tinsel in winter, she'd been told, to plastic paddling pools (displayed upright) in high summer. The interior was therefore gloomy and lit only by a single strip light. Bobby, who was in his late sixties, was short, tubby, bald and sported a bristling moustache. He always wore a striped apron, butcher style, and he had an opinion on absolutely everything, which could anchor you there for hours or until another customer came in.

Today Bobby was explaining patiently to an elderly lady in a voluminous floral gown that yes, indeed, his prices were a tiny bit higher than Tesco and Lidl and the rest, but that was because he was a one-off, in the middle of nowhere, and every single item had to be delivered by road from Plymouth or Truro, so it was a holy wonder that he was able to stay open at *all*. 'And, in the winter,' he concluded, 'there's only a handful of locals buying *anythin'*, because the tourists have gone and all them second-home owners have gone back to London or wherever. Ain't that right, Mrs Palmer?' He nodded at Kate.

'Oh yes indeed,' Kate agreed as the woman pushed past her, an orange in her hand and a face like thunder.

'Bloody woman!' Bobby said after she'd slammed the door behind her. 'She comes in here, buys *one* bloody orange and then has a go at me about my prices. Oranges don't grow on bloody trees round here. Them people 'aven't a clue! Now, what can I do for you?'

Kate was looking round the shelves in the hopes of seeing some little jars of herbs and spices. 'I wondered if you had any nutmeg?'

'Nutmeg,' repeated Bobby.

'Yes, you know, the spice? Comes in a little jar usually.'

Bobby frowned. 'I got some spices *somewhere*. Perhaps they're out the back. Hold on a sec.' With that he disappeared into the murky depths of the storeroom at the rear of the shop and reappeared a couple of minutes later with a jar of mixed spice.

'Will this do?' he asked hopefully.

'Sorry, Bobby, but I really needed nutmeg.'

Bobby pushed his spectacles up his nose and scrutinised the jar closely. 'There'll likely be nutmeg in there *somewhere*,' he said.

'Well, never mind, it's not important,' Kate said. Then, to soften the blow, she said, 'But I'll take half a dozen of your newly laid eggs, please.'

Bobby tossed the mixed spice onto the nearest shelf and, as he carefully inserted the eggs into the box, said, 'I hear there's an old girl died of poisoning up at Seaview.'

'Yes, I believe so,' Kate said as she got out her purse to pay for the eggs. 'Do you know any of them up there?'

'Only Stan. Funny lot up there,' Bobby said dismissively. 'Stan Starkey's a mate of mine and we often have a pint together in The Tinners.' He was referring to The Tinners Arms, an ancient pub up in Middle Tinworthy where the older locals preferred to drink and for whom The Greedy Gull in Lower Tinworthy was considered to be 'too bloody touristy'.

'Stan's the gardener and handyman up there, does everythin' what needs doin'. His missus is the cleaner, and they can tell you some stories!' He snorted. 'The police came up there and took some stuff out of the old woman's freezer. You don't need to be bloody Sherlock to work out what their thinkin' was! Anyway, Stan's had a word with his mate on the *Post*, so I expect some of the press will soon be nosin' around.'

'Oh really?' Kate said as she picked up her eggs.

'Yeah, and the old girl what was poisoned and drove them all nuts with 'er screechin'. Got a funny name, foreign like.' He looked at Kate. 'Not a foreigner like yourself but a *proper* one.' He referred to the fact that anyone who hailed from the other side of the River Tamar, which separated Cornwall from Devon and the rest of England, was considered alien. But not quite as alien as anyone from across the Channel. 'Well, if it turns out to be dodgy we'll see what this new detective bloke's gonna be like. Maybe your mate, Woody Forrest, will sort it out in the meantime?'

Just as Kate was thinking up a suitable comment, in walked a large noisy family. Taking this as her cue to leave, she said, 'Well, I'd better be off.' She'd have liked to extract some more informa-tion out of Bobby but, bearing in mind his reputation for gossip, decided it was, on this occasion, better to keep her nose out of it, publicly at least. But she knew now that she had to devise some way to meet Stan Starkey, Sharon's husband. There was a very good chance he might know something that the others didn't – or wouldn't – divulge.

As she untied Barney from where he was tethered to the post outside, Kate decided she'd forget about making lasagne. She'd do spaghetti bolognese instead.

CHAPTER FOURTEEN

'I've got some news for you,' Woody said as he stepped inside the door of Lavender Cottage.

'Good news or bad news?' Kate asked.

'Both,' Woody replied. 'The good news is that you were right. The bad news is that the meals *were* found to have been tampered with, pumped full of digoxin, meaning we now definitely have a murder inquiry on our hands. You were right, Kate! And I think I've convinced your friend, Bill Robson, that it wasn't *you* who did it!'

'I should hope you did!' Kate retorted. 'And, if he'd listened to me in the first place, he could have started this investigation a week ago.'

'This is serious police business, Kate. They are going to be going through Edina's flat with a fine-tooth comb, questioning everyone, searching everywhere. You must keep well out of it now. I *know* you don't like Robson, but he *is* in charge. Not only that, your life could be in danger – again. You should know *never* to get on the wrong side of a killer. And, once again, a killer is who we're looking for.'

'Yes, I *know*.' Even so, Kate felt a tiny frisson of delight that all her hunches had been right. Not that she need ever expect any kind of apology from that wretched detective inspector of course.

'The press will be back, no doubt,' Woody warned, 'because the police station have had a call from the *Post* asking if it's true that there's been another murder in Tinworthy. God knows how they found out so quickly.'

'I can tell you that. According to Bobby in the shop, Stan Starkey got in touch with his mate on the *Post*,' Kate said.

'And they've only just recovered since the last load of crimes!' said Woody. 'At least this one was a tad more subtle,' he added, obviously recalling the crudity of the previous methods of killing. 'Now, promise me you're going to behave yourself? Kate, you could get yourself killed this time. Please leave it to the police.'

Because Kate had been so directly involved at the time of the previous murders, she wasn't altogether surprised to find a couple of reporters in the lane the following morning, a few yards from the cottage.

'They're out there like vultures,' Angie said. 'What do you suppose the group name for reporters is? A posse? A gaggle? A clutch?'

'A pest,' Kate muttered as she prepared to go to work. When she opened the door of her car they both accosted her.

'More murder in Tinworthy!' one of them exclaimed. 'Any idea what's happening, Mrs Palmer?'

'None at all,' Kate replied shortly. 'Nothing to do with me.'

'Stan Starkey tells us you were the last person to talk to her,' one of them said. 'And I thought you were friendly with the inspector,' he persisted, 'so thought you might have heard something.'

'Detective Inspector Forrest is retiring, as you must be well aware,' Kate said, 'and I know no more than you do so there's no point in hanging about round here. I suggest you contact the police in Launceston.'

There followed some grunts of dissent before they finally shuffled off down the lane. Kate sighed and wondered if they'd discovered where Woody lived and were heading over there.

She arrived at the medical centre a little early to find Dr Ross standing outside the door. 'Just thought I'd get a breath of fresh air,' he said, 'before the rush begins and everyone comes in convinced they've been poisoned. There were three of them yesterday, clutching their bellies.'

'Yes, I had a couple yesterday too,' Kate said.

'I read an article not long ago,' he said, 'about a poisoner – I think it was in France – who decided to kill off all the old people in his village. So let's hope that hasn't given anyone round here any ideas.'

'I'm sure it's a one-off,' Kate said, mentally crossing her fingers.

'Well, let's hope so,' Andrew Ross said with a grin, 'or there'll be a few flats available up there at Seaview Grange!'

Although Kate realised he was joking and knew this to be a highly unlikely scenario, she also knew she'd think about it every time someone elderly came in with tummy problems.

Gossip was rife in Tinworthy; Edina was probably *foreign* after all, the villagers said. Kate had been in Cornwall long enough to know that anyone not born in the county was regarded as foreign and therefore suspect. In addition, Edina had been a singer and who knew what transpired backstage in the opera world? Opera heroines were no strangers to being poisoned either, falling dramatically to the floor in the final act. And she was *bound* to have had lovers in the past, they said, and you know how unpredictable and passionate these people could be. You certainly couldn't blame the husband on this occasion, could you, when he'd been pushing up the daisies for years? There was the stepson of course, and it was well known that they didn't get on. It was bound to be something to do with either love or money, they said, which is what people normally got excited about.

A couple of days after her chat with Andrew, Kate met another resident of Seaview Grange: the one she was particularly keen to meet. It was during one of her daily walks with Barney; occasionally she liked to hike up the hill to Middle Tinworthy and stroll in the woods behind the old church. On this occasion she'd actually managed to persuade Angie to accompany her. And it was there that she came across a stocky, dark-haired man walking a French bulldog and a small black pug. Kate felt sure she'd seen the pug before and, as Barney sniffed round the pug, it started yapping.

'Bloody animal!' said the man.

'Ugh, noisy thing!' Angie remarked under her breath.

'Have you had it long?' Kate asked politely, indicating the pug, which continued to yap.

'It ain't *mine*!' he said. 'I'm walkin' it for a couple of old girls up where I work.' He nodded his head vaguely in the direction of Upper Tinworthy. 'Hate the thing – yaps all the time.' He grinned. 'I bring it down through the woods so nobody sees me with the bloody creature!'

Kate laughed. 'It wouldn't belong to the Potter ladies, would it?'

He sniffed. 'They friends of yours?'

'No, but I'm a nurse and I had occasion to visit them recently.'

He studied her for a moment. 'Would you be that nurse what got mixed up in them murders back in the spring?'

'That's me,' Kate admitted.

'She gets mixed up with everything,' Angie put in as she stooped down to stroke the bulldog.

'Well, you don't want to get mixed up with this one! Somebody had it in for Edina Martinelli you know, but you'd be spoilt for choice.'

'I would?'

He held out a grubby hand. 'Stan Starkey's the name.'

'Kate Palmer.' She shook his hand. 'And this is my sister, Angie.'

Stan Starkey at last! She'd been wondering how to meet this man. 'I work up there, see, and me missus does the cleanin'. She was the one who called the ambulance.' He sniffed loudly. 'Bloody place! Only good thing about it is the little house they gave us, what used to be the stables. It's separate, at the back of the house, away from all them old codgers.'

'I don't fancy your job though,' Angie said. 'All those *old* people...'

'God, Angie, you're sixty! *You* could be living up there!' Kate was annoyed at Angie's comment. 'That remark is ageist!'

'No, it's not,' Angie argued. 'I just don't fancy his job, OK?'

Stan laughed. 'I'm outside most of the time; it's Sharon who has to deal with them residents. I only go in there if somethin' needs fixin'.'

Kate sighed. 'I met your wife briefly,' she said, 'because she let me into Edina's flat when I called recently.'

She wondered what else she could say to get him back to the subject of the old codgers when he said, 'At least there's one less of them now!'

'Yes, very unfortunate,' Kate said.

'Are you kiddin'?' He rolled his eyes upwards. 'Blessed relief, more like! You ever heard her warblin'?'

Kate shook her head.

'No? Thought not. The racket she made would curdle the milk, drove everyone mad. I wouldn't be surprised if they all clubbed together to get that stuff and finish her off.' He paused for a second. 'But we got a good idea who done it. There's this weird writer bloke who lives in the next-door flat to Edina Martinelli, and he's had to listen to her just through the wall. He writes all that crime stuff.'

'Cornelius Crow?'

'That's him. Looks like somethin' out of a horror film. And he's an expert on finishin' people off in his books. And I don't blame him, mind.'

'That's very interesting, Stan,' Kate said truthfully, thinking of her list.

There was no stopping Stan now. 'Did you meet the tubbies?' he asked.

'The tubbies?' He too appeared to be somewhat deficient in political correctness.

'Yeah, the Pratts in Flat 3. And she, Gloria's her name, *hated* Edina. Now you're goin' to ask me why? Well, I'll *tell* you why. Her husband, Ollie, was forever hangin' round Edina, doin' little jobs for her and that. And it was because he fancied her rotten. She gave him all of them records and things, opera stuff you know? Played it from mornin' to night, drove Gloria mad, it did, particularly when he tried singin' along!' He guffawed. 'Gloria was jealous, see.' He bent down and attached the lead to the pug. 'Well, I'd best be goin'; can't stand around here chattin' all day, still got the grass to cut. Been nice meetin' you.'

'Nice meeting you too,' Kate said.

'Next time you're up there come in and have a cup of tea. You can have a look at the wife while you're at it. She has asthma really bad.'

'I'll bear it in mind,' Kate said.

'Not on your life,' murmured Angie when he was out of earshot.

When Kate got home she consulted the nine names on her list again. At the top were the stepson, David, and the Reverend Edgar Ellis, who was reputed to be a randy devil but loved Edina, and whose late wife had died of food poisoning. At the moment he appeared to be the most likely candidate. Food poisoning was not altogether uncommon, but rarely did anyone die from it.

And now Stan had mentioned Cornelius Crow. Kate was conscious of the fact that Woody said it was unfair to be listing the macabre Cornelius purely because he wrote books on the subject. Then again, he must have had to do a fair amount of research on the various methods of annihilating his characters. And, if he had to listen to Edina's warbling at close quarters, perhaps he'd reached the end of his tether.

Then there was Ollie Pratt's wife, Gloria. Neither Ollie nor Gloria had struck her as being likely opera enthusiasts, but Ollie had obviously been converted. There was no way that elegant, cultured Edina was likely to have fancied Ollie, but she, like many ladies living on their own, would have been grateful for someone to do odd jobs. As his reward she would have introduced him to the beauty of operatic music as opposed to rewarding him by any other method and he might have become besotted, not only with Edina herself, but by the world she'd inhabited and the music he'd never troubled to listen to before. This could have made Gloria jealous – her husband in a world of which she was not a part and unable to appreciate. She may well have *felt* like doing away with Edina but how could she have carried the boxes into the flat and doctored the meals without Ollie seeing her? However, Kate remembered from her notes that Gloria was a diabetic so she *would* have had syringes available. And Kate also knew, from all the whodunnits she'd read and watched, that poison was more likely to be a woman's weapon of choice.

So that left the Potter twins: two old ladies with no apparent motive other than they hadn't got the flat they'd wanted. There was also Hetty. Should she remove these three from The List and concentrate on the Starkeys, who were an unknown quantity? Firstly, there was Sharon who had, after all, been suspected of tripping Edina down the stairs. And what about Stan himself; perhaps he'd aided and abetted his wife to position the cord across the top of the stairs? Perhaps it had been his idea in the first place? All credible. They certainly had the means and the opportunity but what possible motive could they have?

Still top of the list as far as Kate was concerned was David Courtney. She needed to do some investigating there. In fact, now that the weather was turning a little cooler, she really needed a couple of new sweaters and there was nowhere in Tinworthy selling anything other than the dreaded crop-tops and pussy-pelmets. Where shopping was concerned the choices were always Exeter, Plymouth or Truro and, on this occasion, Kate decided it would be a good idea to head for Exeter. Exeter would fit the bill not only for sweaters, but to take a look at Courtney & Son Motors.

CHAPTER FIFTEEN

It had been a successful day, Kate reckoned, as she finally headed home from Exeter. She'd found two sweaters that she liked, in itself a miracle, in the right size and at the right price, which was even more of a miracle. As she drove out from the city centre she turned into the enormous Marsh Barton Trading Estate where the Courtney garage was situated. After getting totally lost twice, and ending up in three different cul-de-sacs, she'd almost given up before she finally located Courtney & Son, a shabby one-storey building with a selection of second-hand cars outside. It was wedged between two large, shiny main dealerships for brand-new cars, which was unfortunate to say the least, since its shabbiness was emphasised by its glamorous neighbours.

Kate wondered if she dared look, on the pretence of searching for a second-hand car, but was afraid David Courtney might come out and recognise her. It was surely worth a try, though, since there was no reason why she *wouldn't* be looking for a used car. Everyone knew nurses were not well paid and so it would be a normal thing to do.

Kate hesitated for only a moment then decided to get out and browse. After all what was the point of coming all this way and then not investigating properly? She wandered along the lines of cars, feigning interest in a five-year-old Ford Focus and an eight-year-old Honda Civic, all the time keeping an eye on the shabby-looking office. Eventually the door opened and out sauntered David Courtney in jeans and a leather jacket. He stopped outside the door and lit a cigarette.

'Need any help?' he asked without enthusiasm as he strolled across to where she was standing. Then, running his fingers along the roof of the Ford, said, 'Hang on a minute, don't I *know* you?'

'We met at Seaview Grange, I seem to recall,' Kate said casually. 'I'm just browsing, trying to get an idea of what it might cost for me to change my car.'

After several deep drags on his cigarette he asked, 'What car have you got?'

'Oh, a Fiat Punto,' Kate replied.

He sniffed. 'Nice car, we could do part-exchange.'

'Well, I haven't decided yet whether to keep it or sell it,' Kate said hastily, 'but I thought this looked like a good place to look for a bargain.'

He took another deep drag of his cigarette and, tilting back his head, blew the smoke skyward. 'Don't you live in Tinworthy?'

'Yes, I do,' Kate said. 'I was shopping in Exeter and this is on my way home.'

He narrowed his eyes and ground out the cigarette under the heel of his shoe. 'I remember you now; you were the nurse who visited my stepmother when she had her leg in plaster and I've seen you around a few times since. They told me she's been poisoned.'

'Yes, I had heard,' Kate replied.

'She was a tight-fisted old bitch,' he said, 'but it wasn't me who poisoned her. The police haven't wasted any time in sniffing around here and I told them – she upset a lot of people so they'd be spoilt for choice. Just for starters Old Crow next door hated her guts. Mind you, he had to listen to her screeching away every day. And Gloria Pratt's an evil cow – wouldn't put it past her. Your surgery hasn't come out of this smelling of roses either.'

Kate decided to ignore his insinuation. 'I'm sure they'll soon find the killer,' she said without conviction.

'In the meantime, can I sell you a car?'

Kate was struck by how callous he was about the woman who must have brought him up even if she hadn't been the ideal stepmother. 'I'm only browsing,' she said. 'I shall probably leave it now until the spring.'

'Don't leave it too long,' said David Courtney. 'I'm expecting to close down here shortly and move the business to better premises.'

'Oh?' Kate was surprised. 'Why is that?'

'Too much competition round here, and I'm thinking of going in for classic cars.'

Kate glanced at the big shiny showrooms on either side.

'This has been most interesting,' she said truthfully, 'but I really haven't decided what to do yet.'

David Courtney nodded and wandered back towards the office.

Kate, pleased that she'd taken the trouble to stop off, got into her Fiat Punto and headed home. This piece of research had at least appeared to confirm that David Courtney expected to inherit some money. He plainly needed funds – funds that Edina undoubtedly had.

The first thing Kate saw as she drove up to Lavender Cottage was Fergal's grubby old black BMW parked alongside Angie's car in front of their garage. As far as she was aware Angie wasn't expecting him today but, if there was one thing you could be certain about with Fergal, it was his unpredictability. And, if nothing else, it should put a smile on her sister's face.

She found the two of them huddled over a mountain of brochures on the coffee table in the sitting room.

'Oh hi, Kate!' Fergal glanced up as Kate came in.

'Good afternoon, Fergal, and to what do we owe the pleasure?'

He beamed. 'Well, I was just stocking up in the gift shops in Boscastle and I thought to myself now that I'm up here on the north coast why don't I just pop in to see the lovely Angela?'

The lovely Angela glanced at Kate's carrier bags and asked, 'What have you been buying?'

'Oh, just a couple of jumpers,' Kate said, sitting down wearily.

'Now how about I make you a cup of tea?' Fergal asked, getting to his feet.

'Well, that's very decent of you, Fergal,' Kate said.

As Fergal filled the kettle, humming away to himself, Angie leaned forward and whispered, 'Fergal wants to stay here tonight – you don't mind, do you?'

'Yes, that's OK,' Kate replied. 'You're a big girl now. Just don't keep me awake half the night.'

Angie grinned. 'As if.'

Kate wasn't sure if she minded or not. When she was with Woody she always slept at his house, partly out of consideration for Angie, and partly because she liked to be alone with him. Why Angie didn't sleep at Fergal's now and again was a moot point. Did Fergal *really* have a flat in Plymouth's Barbican?

'What are you looking at there?' Kate asked, indicating the brochures.

'Oh, just some travel stuff. Didn't I tell you we fancied being away for Christmas?' Angie asked casually.

Kate's spirits plunged as she imagined herself spending Christmas here on her own – first Woody, now Angie.

'Where are you thinking of going?' she asked when she regained her composure.

'Somewhere hot,' Angie said. 'Don't think we can stretch to the Maldives or the Seychelles though, so we'll probably settle for Lanzarote.'

'Oh,' Kate remarked, 'won't these trips be all the more expensive over Christmas?'

Angie nodded. 'There's some special deals though. Why are you looking like that? Aren't you spending Christmas with Wonderboy?'

'Woody plans to be in America,' Kate said, gazing out at the sea and the thousands of miles that would separate them.

'Oh well, at least you'll have the dog for company,' Angie said dismissively.

Fergal carefully navigated the steps up from the kitchen with a mug of tea in each hand, one for Kate, one for Angie. Kate found him very likeable, very humorous, but somewhat enigmatic because there was something about the Irishman that didn't quite add up. Perhaps she should be investigating Fergal rather than the possible murder of an old opera singer.

Meanwhile Fergal, back with his brochures, was saying, 'How about Barbados, Angela? There's a friend of my brother who lives out there, so he might be a useful contact.'

'That would be more expensive than the Canaries, though,' Angie said.

'But we only need to put down the deposit now,' Fergal went on.

'What were you planning to use for money?' Angie asked a little sharply.

'Well, I'll have the money by Christmas, for sure,' said Fergal. 'I'm just a bit short at the moment but I'll have enough for the deposit by the end of the month.'

'These offers could be gone by then,' Angie said. 'But don't worry because I can handle the deposits.'

'You're a saint, Angela, that's what you are,' said Fergal.

You're a mug, Angie, that's what you are, thought Kate, as she noticed a flicker of doubt cross her sister's face. Then she thought about the prospect of Christmas here alone with the dog. She might be welcome up in Scotland with Tom, Jane and the new baby, but she'd only just *been*, for goodness' sake, so it might not endear her overmuch to her daughter-in-law. Her other son, Jack, lived in Brisbane, so no chance of popping out there for a few days. And, if Angie was away, and she managed to get time off to go anywhere, then what about Barney? He'd have to go into kennels. More worry, more expense. She'd need to work something out in the three months before Christmas.

CHAPTER SIXTEEN

Kate was still mulling over holidays, dogs and kennels the next day as she walked Barney up onto Penhallion cliff. She passed a couple of hikers in their sturdy boots and many-pocketed rucksacks on her way but then, as she headed towards the seat where she normally rested to get her breath back, she saw him. A tall, dark, caped figure, topped with a wide-brimmed black hat, was heading in her direction.

For a moment it reminded her of the advertisements for Sandeman port and the black-caped figures which dotted many an Iberian hillside. Or, worse, Count Dracula! The man from Transylvania! She told herself not to be ridiculous but her heart was definitely beating faster than it normally would, even after the climb.

Then the strange figure stood stock-still by the seat, looking out over the sea, with his black cape billowing out behind in the wind. Such dramatic personae did not, as a rule, go swanning along the Cornish coastal path and Kate was not only fascinated but also a little afraid. As she neared he turned and stared at her with those unforgettable dark eyes.

Cornelius Crow!

What on earth was he doing up here, poised like an enormous black bat (or, indeed, a crow)? Kate would not have been entirely surprised if he'd stretched his arms out and taken off, over the cliffs, out to sea.

He continued to stare as she got closer and, feeling somewhat disconcerted, Kate looked around to see if there was anyone else nearby. There wasn't. Even the dog had ceased romping around and was walking slowly behind her, his tail perfectly still.

'Good afternoon,' Cornelius said sonorously, his eyes never leaving hers.

'Good afternoon,' Kate replied, hoping her voice didn't sound shaky.

'We've met somewhere before,' he droned.

'I'm a nurse,' Kate began, 'I—'

'I remember you,' he interrupted. 'You arrived the day Madame Martinelli was removed from Seaview Grange. And you came back to see Edgar.'

'Yes, that was me.' Kate sat down on the seat, half hoping he'd go away and half hoping he wouldn't. This was surely a golden opportunity to do a little detective work.

At this point he wrapped his cape around him and sat down at the far end of the seat, staring out to sea again.

Kate cleared her throat. 'I wondered if things had got back to normal up at the Grange yet?'

'*Normal!*' he bellowed, and turned to stare at her some more. 'Nothing is *normal* in Seaview. There are bad vibrations in that house, and people are not what they seem.'

Kate gulped. 'In what way?'

'In *every* way!' This man was wasted in Tinworthy; he should have been strutting across the stage of the Old Vic. There was silence for a moment and then he said, 'They are *all* potential killers! We all are! I am, you are! I spend my life studying crime, madam. We kill not only for self-preservation but also for jealousy, anger, love, and money, of course.'

'So why do you think Edina Martinelli was poisoned?' Kate asked.

He scowled. 'For all the reasons I've just given you.' He spoke slowly and distinctly, as if talking to an imbecile. 'For anger, love, jealousy, money.'

'Well, that's pretty general,' Kate remarked, feeling disappointed at his reaction.

There was silence for a minute and then he said, 'I could have killed her myself on many occasions, purely out of anger. Pent-up rage at her utter lack of consideration for the other residents, particularly *me*. If you wish to make a noise all day you should live somewhere remote, like the middle of a field. Don't you agree?'

'That would seem a considerate thing to do,' Kate concurred.

'But she was *not* considerate; all she wanted was an audience. She didn't give a damn if her caterwauling disturbed us or not. I didn't kill her, but I was tempted to on many an occasion. After all, I spend my life writing about the various methods for disposing of people.'

What a bizarre man, Kate thought. She shivered and glanced down at Barney, who was sitting quietly at her feet, occasionally giving her a beseeching look.

'I've never yet pushed any of my victims over a cliff,' he continued chattily, 'so I thought I'd come up here and do some research. I might use this method in future.' He stood up and strode over to the very edge of the three-hundred-foot drop. Kate could hardly bear to look at this strange figure, his cloak billowing dramatically behind him again, with only a few centimetres from a certain death. For sure he didn't suffer from vertigo.

'Very satisfactory,' he said after a minute staring straight down. 'Lots of ledges and sharp rocks on which a body might bounce on and off. But you would know about that, wouldn't you? You're the nurse who was involved in our famous crimes, aren't you? Of course, being a writer of murder fiction I took a very close interest in the case.'

Kate was haunted by the memory of her own narrow escape at this very spot last April. But somehow this man seemed, for the moment anyway, even more disturbing than that. She shivered again. She wanted to move away; he was giving her the creeps.

Cornelius Crow did not sit down again. 'We are *all* murderers, *all* of us. We *all* wished Edina dead. We are *all* guilty.' He jammed his hat more securely on his head. 'Good day.' With that he strode away in the direction from which he'd come, his cape flowing behind him.

Kate sat very still for a few minutes, dazed by this somewhat surreal encounter. Had he actually *admitted* to having killed Edina? Not exactly; but the police had already interviewed all the residents of Seaview Grange anyway, so what on earth had they made of *him*? Kate didn't think she'd ever met such a weird character.

Woody was not particularly bowled over with Kate's impression of Cornelius Crow when they met for a drink that evening at The Greedy Gull.

'Yes, he's a weirdo, but that doesn't make him a killer,' he said.

'He admitted to having been driven mad by Edina's warbling,' Kate said, 'and he openly admitted that, at times, he'd have liked to kill her.'

'I gather most of the residents felt the same way,' Woody said. He tapped his nose. 'It's the quiet ones you have to watch.' He sighed. 'I certainly shouldn't encourage you to go nosing around, but it's the caretaker and his wife who interest me.'

'Really?' Kate put down her drink and leaned forward. 'Why do you say that?'

'Well, Stan Starkey's a bit of a rough diamond, and his wife has access to everyone's apartment so she'd have plenty of opportunities to doctor Edina's food, don't you think? And it's now common knowledge that someone previously tried to annihilate Edina Martinelli by stretching the vacuum cleaner flex across the top of the stairs. So, who's most likely to be using a vacuum cleaner? Cornelius Crow? The ancient twins? The overweight Pratts? The old girl who was away at the time of the murder? All unlikely, Kate, don't you agree? And the only outside visitor she *appears* to have had in the last few weeks is the stepson.'

'I had a look at Courtney's garage when I was in Exeter,' Kate admitted. 'I made out I was looking for another car and guess who came out of the office? None other than David Courtney himself. He remembered me and made some remark about how the police were "sniffing around", as he put it, but it wasn't *him* who'd killed her, he said. Even more interesting, he said he was planning to change premises and go upmarket and start selling classic cars. He's obviously confident he's going to be getting some money.'

'OK, super-sleuth! So the stepson's no longer short of cash. He's most likely the chief suspect at the moment. But that incident with the vacuum cleaner flex still points at the Starkeys, as far as I'm concerned. The wife in particular, who probably doesn't want to admit to leaving the vacuum cleaner plugged in.' He took Kate's hand. 'But I shouldn't be encouraging you! Please remember what happened last time, Kate, and stay well out of it.'

'But I don't believe Sharon had anything to do with this. She's a nice woman, a caring person.'

'She could still be a killer. You're far too trusting, Kate.'

'But I'm usually right about who *didn't* do it!' Kate thought for a moment. 'I remember Stan Starkey mentioning his wife's asthma, so I'll find an excuse to be "just passing" and I can offer my professional services.'

Woody sighed. 'OK, but just be careful. People are not always what they seem.'

CHAPTER SEVENTEEN

In fact, she didn't need an excuse. The garden mower had given up the ghost and Kate had heard that Stan Starkey was a dab hand at mending most mowers. She decided to take Barney on his daily walk up via the steep path from behind their cottage, which she normally avoided because of the hundred steps that had to be climbed to get to the top. There was then another twenty minutes of steep walking before she reached the flatter ground, with the views to Trevose Head. It was breathtaking in more ways than one. And there, on the crest of the cliff, was Seaview Grange.

There was no one around as she passed by the first time, but both Kate and Barney enjoyed the change of scenery, the moorland views and the opportunity to see the back of Seaview Grange, which had been built in a T-shape, with a wing extending out in the middle at the rear. Kate worked out that this wing housed Flats 2 and 5, the Potter sisters downstairs and Cornelius Crow upstairs. Taking care not to step into any camouflaged rabbit holes, of which she'd been warned there were many, Kate descended from the edge of the moorland to the path that led back to the road and skirted past the Grange.

And her luck was in; from behind she could see Stan Starkey working on the engine of a car at the side of the house. Hoping he'd stay there until she and Barney could stroll nonchalantly past at the front, Kate increased her pace, an ecstatic Barney running and barking alongside. Then, regaining her composure in time to stroll past Seaview Grange, Kate was relieved to see Stan still fiddling with the engine of what looked like an old Ford Capri. She coughed discreetly, hoping he'd look round, which he did.

'Nice day!' she called. Would he recognise her?

He shielded his eyes with his hand. 'Ah!' he said. 'The nurse with the springer spaniel!'

'That's me,' Kate confirmed.

He wiped his hands on an oily rag and walked towards the front wall. 'What brings you up here?'

'I hear you mend lawnmowers? Mine's playing up a bit and I wondered if you could take a look at it.'

'If you bring it up I can give a look it over.'

'That would be great,' Kate said.

'You look a bit puffed,' he said, 'you must be ready for a cup of tea. Sharon normally brews up at this time.'

'That's very kind but I hate to bother you…'

'No bother!' he said cheerfully. 'Maybe you could have a chat to Sharon about her asthma? I keep nagging her to go to the surgery because it seems to have got worse lately, but she won't go.'

'I'd be glad to,' Kate said as she walked up the drive with Stan leading the way.

'We're round the back in what used to be the old stables,' Stan explained.

Kate was impressed with the old one-storey grey stone building which appeared to have been sympathetically converted, alongside which was a prolific vegetable plot.

'When I ain't mowin' and weedin' I'm lookin' after them vegetables,' Stan informed her as he pushed open the white-painted wooden door, which led directly into the kitchen. 'Look who I found, Sharon!' he yelled.

Sharon, standing ironing in the long low-beamed kitchen, said, 'You must be mind-readers, I was just fancyin' a cup of tea.'

The bull terrier, who'd been dozing in his basket in a corner, growled at the sight of Barney. He gave a half-hearted bark and then must have decided Barney presented no real threat, and closed his eyes again. Barney, unconvinced, cowered against Kate's legs.

Sharon, peering at Kate through the blonde curls which had fallen over her forehead, said, 'Oh, hello, what are you doin' up here? I nearly came down to you lot to get some of them sedative pills or somethin' cos I ain't sleepin' well with all this kerfuffle goin' on about Edina been poisoned and that.'

'Very understandable,' Kate muttered.

'Anyway, now you're here I'll put the kettle on.'

With that she filled up an old red enamel kettle from the butler sink and placed it on top of the ancient Aga.

Kate looked around at the dated Formica-covered units and worktops, and at the tiles depicting lurid carrots, tomatoes, leeks and peppers. It had plainly been fitted at least fifty years ago, she reckoned, probably as servants' quarters. But the room seemed warm and friendly and Kate would have been happy to down her tea there, but Stan was already beckoning her to follow him through into another low-ceilinged room, complete with beams, a slate floor and an open fireplace with a log-burning stove. There were a couple of very saggy sofas upholstered in an old Sanderson fabric which Kate remembered from her youth. It was also a friendly room and Kate could see that when the log-burner was lit, which it wasn't, it would be a very cosy retreat.

'Sit down, sit down,' ordered her host, removing a copy of the *Sporting Life*, which had shed its pages all over one of the sofas. Kate sank down into its depths, and wondered if she'd ever get up again without the aid of a crane. Barney sat close to her feet. Just then the bull terrier came through and sniffed him suspiciously, while Barney sat absolutely still, with only his tail thumping slowly and warily.

Sharon appeared with a tray loaded with teapot, mugs, milk, sugar, teaspoons and a box of biscuits. Kate's mug, which featured a picture of Princess Diana, contained the nicest tea she could ever remember drinking.

'We don't use them teabags,' Stan informed her after she'd commented. 'We always has proper tea, don't we, Shar?"

It was years since Kate had drunk 'proper tea' and her opinion of the Starkeys was already soaring skywards. Sharon, sitting opposite, offered the box of biscuits. Kate declined politely while each of her hosts tucked into a macaroon.

She cleared her throat. 'I imagine you've been pestered by the police and press?'

'Yeah, but they got their jobs to do, don't they?' said Sharon, wiping crumbs from her mouth.

'That's true,' Kate agreed, 'but it must still feel like an intrusion.'

'Well, we can't complain. It was Stan's fault really for ringin' up his mate at the *Post* in the first place.' She smiled at her husband, who was sitting alongside and shuffling about in the tin searching for a desirable biscuit. 'But we can cope, don't we, Stan?'

'We got nothin' to hide,' he said. 'I don't know who poisoned the old cow, and I don't much care, but it wasn't us.'

Kate felt the need for a prompt. 'The first time I met Edina Martinelli was when she broke her ankle falling down the stairs.'

'Yeah, that's somethin' else!' said Sharon, helping herself to another macaroon. 'Everyone pointed the finger at *me*! As if I'd leave a bloody flex across the top of the stairs!'

'But someone presumably *did*?' Kate persisted.

'Yeah, *someone* did. My fault I suppose for not puttin' the bloody machine back in the cupboard, although I was pretty sure I did.'

'Who do you think it might have been?' Kate asked, sipping her tea slowly in an effort to prolong her stay.

'Could be *any* of them.' Stan sighed as he finally unearthed a custard cream. 'Most of them old gits would've been glad to see her gone. At least we were far enough away that we couldn't hear her screeching, thank God.'

'That Gloria Pratt's a vicious piece of work,' Sharon put in for good measure. 'She was jealous cos her old man was forever runnin' up there to change a lightbulb, mend a fuse, build a shelf, any bloody excuse. Madam called, up he went with the speed of light. Potty about her he was.' She paused. 'He was right out of his depth, mind you, wasn't he, Stan?' Stan nodded. 'Tryin' to make out he was interested in all that opera stuff! Nearly drove Gloria mad!'

'Mad enough for her to want to kill Edina?' Kate asked.

'Who knows?' said Sharon. 'But I wouldn't put it past her, she's got a real temper on her.'

'Like I said before, my money's on Cornelius Crow,' Stan said. 'He's an expert on finishin' people off; got nothin' else to do all day while he's writin' them stories. Sure you won't have a biscuit?' He waved the tin in Kate's direction. Then, to Sharon, he asked, 'Why did you get all them ginger things? You know neither of us like them.' He looked hopefully back at Kate. 'You sure you won't have one of them?'

Kate shook her head. 'No, thanks. But what about your asthma, Sharon?'

Sharon shook her head. 'Don't tell me he's been bothering you with all that? I'm fine most of the time.'

'What about when you're not fine? Have you been using your inhaler as often as you should?'

Sharon shook her head. 'I always take my blue one when I have an attack.'

'And what about your brown one?' Kate asked.

'Well, I take it sometimes, but the prescription is expensive having both of them.'

'Sharon, it's really important you take your brown inhaler regularly, because that's the preventor and it'll stop you having so many attacks.' Kate got her phone out. 'I'm making you an appointment for next Friday, OK? In the meantime, remember to take your brown inhaler regularly, as prescribed.'

'Thanks,' said Sharon. 'I did keep meaning to go down there but… you know…'

'Well, you have an appointment now,' Kate said, 'and we must be on our way.' She patted a drowsy Barney. 'Thanks so much for the tea.'

'Any time,' said Sharon.

Kate waved goodbye and headed back towards the main gate, keen to mull over the conversation they'd had. Somehow or other she didn't think that the Starkeys were killers but, as she knew to her cost, you could never tell.

She was just turning out of the gate when a tiny figure came rushing out the front door.

'Excuse me!' she called. Kate turned and recognised the woman as Hetty, who'd rushed out after David Courtney when she'd visited previously.

'Can I help you?' she asked.

'I need to talk to you,' said the little woman. 'Can you come in for a minute?'

'I'd love to talk to you,' Kate said truthfully, 'but I really need to be getting home, and so does the dog. Could I come back tomorrow?'

'Yes please. I need to talk to someone not connected to *here.*' She looked up at Kate with tears in her eyes. 'Edina was my best friend. I can't believe *anyone* would do this to her, and I can't forgive myself for being away when she died.'

'I'll come tomorrow,' Kate promised.

CHAPTER EIGHTEEN

During the summer Angie had bought herself a second-hand Mercedes Smart car. It was tiny and it was practical; Angie was neither. Nonetheless she loved it.

'I'm fed up of car-sharing,' she'd said to Kate, 'because *you've* always got it.'

'Well, it *is* my car,' Kate had replied reasonably enough, 'and I do have to go to work.'

Angie of course promised never to go *near* the car if she'd as much as sniffed at the gin bottle.

When she got home from the Starkeys' there was no sign of Angie or the Smart. Since her cereal bowl was still lying in the sink Kate assumed she'd been out for most of the day.

As she was filling the kettle to make some tea, Kate reckoned she'd now met all the residents of Seaview Grange, however briefly. She would meet Hetty Patterson again properly tomorrow. When she dug out The List she remembered that she'd placed the Potter sisters and Hetty right at the bottom as very unlikely suspects, but suspects nevertheless. She somehow doubted that the Starkeys should be on her list either because she couldn't imagine what their motive might have been. Still, better leave them on there for the time being.

As Kate drank her tea she heard the sound of a car drawing up outside and minutes later Angie came in via the kitchen door while Barney barked his usual enthusiastic welcome.

'Phew!' said Angie as she removed her coat. 'What a day!'

'Why? Where have you been?'

'I've been to Plymouth,' Angie replied, 'and I'm now in dire need of some liquid refreshment.' With that she headed straight for the gin.

'Were you shopping?' Kate asked.

'No, I was doing what *you're* always doing – *investigating.*'

'Investigating what?' Kate asked.

'Investigating Fergal, that's what. I had to know why he never takes me to his place in Plymouth. And he never seems to have much money.'

'And are you any the wiser?'

'Oh yes,' Angie said as she sat down and poured tonic into her gin.

Kate waited. 'Well? And what did you find out?'

'I've found out that he does *not* have a flat in the Barbican, Raleigh Park he called it. I went to the Barbican, had a good snoop round, asked everybody I met, but nobody had ever heard of Raleigh Park.'

'So?'

'So I spoke to an old boy who was selling newspapers and he said, "Raleigh Park? That's not round here, that's on the other side of Saltash." I thought he was talking rubbish but, as it was on my way home, I thought there was no harm in having a look, and guess what?'

Kate shook her head. 'No idea. What?'

'It's a *caravan* park! And a shabby one at that. But there was a little office so I went and asked this ancient toothless old crone if they had a Fergal Connolly living there.' She took a large slug of gin. 'And they did. Number 26, she said, but she doubted he'd be there because he'd be doing one of his jobs.'

'*One* of his jobs?' Kate echoed.

'That's what she said. So off I went in search of number 26. Although it was a scruffy site there were some big vans there, mobile homes or whatever, but number 26 was *tiny*.'

'Was he there?'

'No, he wasn't, and all the blinds were down so I couldn't see in the windows. But I got talking to a neighbour who said he'd got about three different jobs and today was the day he normally went minicab driving. No word at all about flogging postcards and stuff.'

Kate sighed. She'd had doubts about Fergal ever since they'd had the conversation about the proposed holiday, and she knew Angie had too. 'Oh, Angie, I really don't know what to say except that, for some reason, he may have fallen on hard times and perhaps he's trying to get his life back together? He was obviously ashamed of his little caravan and that's why he never took you to Plymouth.'

Angie took another large gulp of her drink. 'What do I do now?'

'You don't *do* anything,' Kate replied, 'You just ask him what it's all about. I mean he's a really nice guy and you're obviously fond of him, so give him the benefit of the doubt. But tread carefully.'

'Do you think there's anything else he's not telling me?'

'I've no idea, Angie. You'll have to ask. And you'll have to decide if it matters if he's as poor as a church mouse.'

Angie thought for a moment. 'I just wish he'd been honest with me.'

'Well, don't torture yourself about it, *ask* him,' Kate said, 'and don't go booking holidays if he hasn't got any money. When are you seeing him again?'

'Tomorrow.'

'Tomorrow is another day, to quote Scarlett O'Hara.'

There was now a chill to the early morning air but no frost as yet. Frost didn't usually hit the far South-West until November or December and, occasionally, even later. The closer you were to the sea the less likely you were to see frost or snow, which got melted by the salty air. Back in February Kate had been amazed to find the ground white in Middle and Higher Tinworthy when there was none down by the sea in their village.

No time had been arranged for her meeting with Hetty. She had seemed so distressed and desperate to talk about her dead friend and Kate hoped she could offer some small measure of comfort. She also hoped to glean some information about Hetty's friendship with Edina, but knew she had to tread carefully.

At half past four, feeling a little tense, she knocked on the door of Flat 1.

'Come in, Nurse,' said Hetty as she opened the door.

'Please – call me Kate.' She took a deep breath.

Hetty led the way into an immaculate lounge decorated, like the Potter sisters', with lots of chintz. She also appeared to have a passion for Lladró figurines, of which there were many, all positioned centrally on highly polished side tables.

'Sit down, my dear,' said Hetty, 'and I'll just get the kettle on for some coffee.'

Kate settled herself in an armchair adorned with orange and gold chrysanthemums. As Hetty scuttled in and out of the kitchen, Kate was able to study her properly for the first time. She couldn't have been more than five feet tall, Kate reckoned, with short white hair, no make-up, and clad in a sensible pink twin-set and tweed skirt, beneath which were a pair of surprisingly sturdy little legs encased in dark brown stockings, and on her feet some sensible lace-up brogues.

'Here we are,' Hetty said, laying down a tray on the mahogany coffee table.

Kate noted she was not wearing a wedding ring and wondered if she'd ever been married.

As Hetty poured coffee into the dainty china cups she said, 'I'll let you help yourself to milk and sugar.'

Kate hadn't balanced a china cup and saucer for a long time and it felt strange to be drinking coffee out of anything other than a mug.

'I want to talk to you about my dear friend Edina,' Hetty went on. 'You'll have heard all sorts of rubbish from the others.' She nodded towards the door. 'But *they* didn't know her like I did. She was my dearest friend.'

'You must be very sad,' Kate said.

Hetty nodded. 'I shall never forgive myself for being away while poor Edina was so very ill, but I had to be with my dear sister. She has terminal cancer, you see. I've been going up to Bournemouth as often as I can.'

'That's very understandable,' Kate murmured as she sipped her coffee and placed the cup very carefully back onto the saucer.

'I shall lose my sister soon as well,' Hetty sighed, removing a white lace-edged handkerchief from her sleeve and dabbing her eyes, 'but at least that's *expected*. This' – she pointed at the ceiling to what was Edina's flat upstairs – 'has come completely out of the blue.'

'Have you lived here long, Miss Patterson?'

'You may call me Hetty. I've lived here ever since the house was converted into flats, five, six years ago. I was headmistress at a girls' school near Bodmin, you know, and I bought a little cottage when I retired. But this is much more manageable and I don't have to worry about maintenance or cleaning. I moved in shortly after Edina did and we became friends straight away.'

An unlikely pair, thought Kate, studying prim little Hetty in her twinset and thick stockings and comparing her to the dramatic and flamboyant Edina with her kaftan and her jangling jewellery.

Hetty was gazing out the window. 'She had the most beautiful voice, you know. *Beautiful!* But what do these ignorant people know?' She nodded towards the door again. 'Always complaining, and *one* of them' – here she leaned forward – '*poisoned my friend Edina.*' She paused to let this sink in. 'I believe it was you who alerted the police. Well, the sooner they make an arrest the better.'

'I hardly dare ask,' Kate said, 'but do you have any idea who might have done it?'

'As far as I can see there are three likely suspects. There's that horrible Ollie Pratt who was always hanging around, ingratiating himself, with that ugly, jealous wife of his. I wouldn't put it past *her*. And that ghastly author upstairs with those menacing eyes! Have you met him yet?' Here Kate nodded. 'Well, you might have come to your own conclusion. And then there's Sharon Starkey, who's the only person who'd be likely to drape the vacuum cleaner flex across the stairs or whatever she did. Poor Edina broke her ankle but I feel sure she was meant to break her neck.'

Hetty was breathing heavily.

'What about the stepson who everyone says wanted money from her?' Kate couldn't resist asking, and waited with interest for Hetty's response.

'A *charming* man! I grant you he has some money problems but he would never do such a thing. *Never!*'

Kate wondered how she could be so sure. He hadn't appeared to be particularly charming as far as she was concerned.

'Just because they used to row about money occasionally doesn't mean that he was planning to *kill* her,' Hetty continued. 'But these people out there are *looking* for someone to blame to protect themselves. You mark my words, look no further than Gloria Pratt, or Sharon Starkey, or Cornelius Crow. You tell your detective friend that when you next see him.'

Kate was taken aback. 'My detective friend?'

'Yes, that American, whatever his name is.'

'Hetty, my American detective friend has retired from the police force and is *not* involved in this inquiry. And I have no influence on this case whatsoever,' Kate added, 'but I have no doubt that the police will solve it all in their own good time.'

'I salute your optimism,' Hetty said curtly.

Kate decided it was time to escape. 'Well, that was delicious coffee but I should be on my way, Hetty.'

'I wanted to ask you if you have any idea when there's likely to be a funeral?' Hetty asked as they both got to their feet.

'No idea at all,' Kate replied. 'You must check with the police or maybe Edina's stepson if she hasn't any near relatives.'

Hetty sniffed as she opened the door. 'Well, thank you for calling in. It's been interesting meeting you.'

Was it interesting? Kate pondered their conversation as she walked back to her car. Hetty had seemed adamant that David Courtney wasn't involved so, yes, that was interesting. Had Kate misjudged him? After all, she didn't really *know* the man. Perhaps she'd been too harsh.

There was no doubt, however, that they really were a strange lot at Seaview Grange.

CHAPTER NINETEEN

Denise, who organised holidays as well as manning reception, reckoned Kate had about ten days owing to her which, added to the surgery being closed for the public holidays at Christmas and New Year, meant Kate could probably stretch her holiday to at least two weeks. But it all depended on Sue, who, as the senior nurse, got first preference. As Sue had three teenagers at home the chances were she'd want to be with them over the festive season.

'Leave it with me,' Denise said next day, 'and I'll try to sort something out.'

When Kate mentioned about going to the States with Woody, Denise got excited. 'I mean,' she said, 'you could go over there and get *married!*'

'*Married?*' Kate spluttered. 'I am *not* going over there to get married!'

'OK, OK, keep your hair on! But it's so *easy* over there in Nevada and places, isn't it? You just turn up at one of these little chapels and next thing you know, hey, you're married! They have all these fancy themed weddings' – Denise had a wistful faraway look in her eyes – 'with Elvis Presley lookalikes and everything!' This was a completely unexpected side to Denise's character, who always came across as the no-nonsense type.

'Denise, we are *not* getting married! He's going over to see his old mum and thought it would be nice if I went along too.'

'He'll want his mum's approval, I expect.' Denise was unstoppable now. 'If his ma approves he'll whisk you off to one of those wedding chapels!'

'Denise,' Kate said loudly, 'this man is sixty-one years of age and he has no more intention of getting married again than I do. We're in the twenty-first century, remember? I value my independence, and so does he. We've got the ideal relationship and we aren't about to change it. All I want is a couple of weeks in sunny California – so, is there any chance I can have some leave?'

Denise sniffed. 'I'll have to check with Sue later.'

Kate grinned. 'You do that.'

'I should know soon how much leave, if any, I can take,' Kate informed Woody as they sat with their drinks in The Greedy Gull that evening. She decided it was not a good idea to relate the rest of her conversation with Denise.

'I'll arrange my dates as soon as I know yours,' Woody said helpfully, sipping his pint of bitter. 'It would be real fun to show you around my neck of the woods.'

The pub was half empty this evening. Most of the visitors had gone home, the nights were drawing in and Des, the landlord, had swapped his T-shirt and shorts for a jumper and jeans. He was leaning on the bar drawing up plans for darts matches and pub quizzes, which was a sure sign winter was on the way.

'I've lots to tell you,' Kate said.

'You do? Fire away!' he said with a wry smile.

'I got myself an invitation into the Starkeys' a couple of days ago – they live in what used to be the stables. It's well away from the main building so there was no way they could have heard Edina's warbling from there, but they didn't like her much for all that. And Sharon vehemently denied having stretched that cord across the top of the stairs; in fact, she couldn't even recall having left the vacuum cleaner out. Their money is on Cornelius Crow or Gloria Pratt.'

Woody sighed. 'Poor Cornelius! Just because he looks and acts a bit weird! I'm guessing that's all a big act anyway to match the crime stuff he writes – probably helps to sell his books.'

'And Gloria,' Kate repeated.

'That seems unlikely,' Woody said. 'If her husband was driving her mad with his operatic arias why didn't she kill *him*? Apart from anything else I should have thought it would have been a whole lot easier.'

'And then yesterday,' Kate continued, 'I had coffee with Hetty Patterson. Now I *know* she wasn't there at the time but she was very friendly with Edina and she too thinks it could be Cornelius or Gloria – or Sharon. But what was most interesting was that, when I mentioned the stepson, she strongly defended him. She said he was charming and would *never* do such a thing.'

'Now, that *is* interesting,' said Woody thoughtfully. 'Maybe she fancies him?'

'Don't be ridiculous! She's over eighty! And then of course there's the old vicar upstairs,' Kate said. 'Edgar, that is. He idolised Edina but she didn't fancy him. Perhaps he'd had enough of being rejected? And he told me that he often got her shopping and deliveries for her so he *could* have doctored the meals, couldn't he? And remember *I* was the one who found out that his wife died of food poisoning.'

Woody grinned. 'Perhaps we should arrest the lot of them and stick them *all* in jail!'

'I get the impression that you are still not taking me seriously,' Kate said, draining her wine glass.

'So, who's left?' Woody asked. 'Is anyone *not* likely to be the killer? Hetty, probably, since she wasn't there, and the twins. Now, what sort of a motive might these two old gals have?'

Kate shrugged. 'Only that they got fed up with her singing like everyone else. And, of course, they were miffed that she got the better flat. Violet, in particular, still seemed annoyed.'

Woody laughed. 'Better stick both of them in jail with the others, just to be on the safe side!'

'I'm only trying to help,' Kate said, becoming cross.

'Yeah, I appreciate that, Kate, but you'd do well to leave it to the police. You see we – they – act on facts and not on guesswork, and there's bound to be a clue sooner or later.'

'I'm doing my best to find the clues,' Kate said.

'I *know* you are,' he soothed, patting her hand.

Kate bristled. He was being patronising and belittling her efforts. Much as she adored him, Woody was irritating her now. Perhaps she wouldn't bother about trying to get that leave. He could go to California on his own.

At that very moment Angie and Fergal came into the pub. They waved, got their drinks and took themselves off to a quiet corner.

'*He's* got some explaining to do,' Kate said to no one in particular.

It was now two weeks since Edina's death and Kate hoped that the police were making more headway than she was, but doubted it. As she left work, her thoughts turned to Angie. What *was* Fergal playing at? She hadn't had the opportunity to ask her sister what had happened yesterday, but when she got home that was overshadowed by a phone call Angie had just received.

'Apparently, Maman is on her last legs,' Angie said. 'That was Paul, my brother-in-law, on the phone.'

Maman was Angie's ancient mother-in-law who was French, and had been living as a recluse in Essonne, near Paris, for the past forty years. She must be at least ninety, Kate reckoned.

'The old *vache* is eighty-nine,' Angie continued, 'and Paul says she's only got a few days left.'

Maman had married an Englishman some sixty-five years earlier and decamped, much against her will, to leafy Surrey. She'd had two sons, Paul, who was the older, and George, Angie's late husband. When her own husband had died, Maman shot back to France and rarely crossed the Channel again. Angie and George had made an annual pilgrimage to visit her, but since George's death Angie had only visited her once as far as Kate could remember. Angie's son, Jeremy, lived and worked in Sweden and had made the trip with his Swedish wife and two boys every couple of years, not so much on account of Maman's great charm but more on account of her very considerable bank balance.

'Will you go over there?' Kate asked.

Angie wrinkled her nose. 'Not much point if she's at death's door but I'll have to go to the funeral, I suppose. Why do all these dramas happen at once?'

'Talking of which…' Kate looked at her.

'Yes, Fergal,' said Angie. 'Oh Kate, he's absolutely *broke*! You know his wife emptied their bank account and then went off to the States? This was back in Ireland, of course, and at the same time some friend had advised him to invest what little money he had left in some fancy scheme or other which, wouldn't you know, crashed. He'd lost everything but, fortunately, he had no kids, so no ties, and he decided to head for London – which he *hated*. So he took to the road and ended up in Plymouth which, for some reason, he liked. Says he needs to be close to the sea.'

'So what happened in Plymouth?'

'He got a job valeting cars, and found some cheap lodgings somewhere, which he described as a flea-infested slum. Then he heard that this company were looking for salespeople to flog their cards and things. He's got the gift of the gab, as you know, so he was offered the job. And, even better, although it was part-time, it came with a car. Then he heard about Raleigh Park where he could buy a cheap caravan on the never-never, and that's what he's doing. He's continued with the odd day of car valeting, and spent all his free time familiarising himself with Plymouth and the surrounding area so he can do some minicab driving when he doesn't have anything else on. He works his fingers to the bone, you know.'

'Why didn't he tell you all this when you first met him?' Kate asked.

'He was afraid I wouldn't want to go out with him. He seems to think we're rather *refined* ladies' – here she snorted – 'because we've got a nice cottage and all that, and he was afraid I'd think he was a layabout.'

'Well, he certainly *doesn't* sit around, does he?'

'No, he doesn't. He's got three jobs and often he gets offered an extra day doing valeting or minicabbing and that's when he doesn't show up here at the weekend.'

'He should, of course, have *told* you all this when you first met him,' Kate remarked.

'Yes, I suppose he should but, like I told you, he thought it would put me off him.'

'And *has* it put you off him?' Kate asked.

'Not really,' Angie said. 'I actually admire him for trying to get back on his feet. And, let's face it, he's very fanciable!'

Kate grinned. 'So, that's all right then?'

'Yes, here's hoping,' said Angie.

Nevertheless, shortly afterwards, Angie came off her phone and swore under her breath. 'Fergal can't come up this weekend because he's been offered some minicabbing and he can't afford to turn it down.'

'Doesn't he get paid enough for doing his selling?' Kate asked.

'Yes, but a lot of it's on commission and he's trying to get some money together. And pay for the caravan, of course.'

'Then maybe you should spend the weekend at his caravan?' Kate suggested. 'At least you'd be together when he's finished work.'

There was silence for a moment.

Then Angie cleared her throat. 'I wondered,' she said slowly, 'if maybe he could move in here for a little while?'

'Move in *here*?' Kate asked in horror. 'Most definitely *not*! What about all the jobs he does? And you know what we agreed when we bought this place: that male friends were welcome and OK for an occasional night if we ever got friendly with anyone of the opposite sex again. But moving *in*? No, Angie.'

'Not even for a few weeks?' Angie whined.

'And *then* what? Where might he be going? It could turn into months, *years* even – no way!'

'I *knew* you wouldn't agree,' Angie snapped.

'So why did you ask then?'

Angie didn't reply but stomped into the kitchen where Kate could hear her breathing heavily as she noisily poured herself a gin.

Later she related the incident to Woody on her phone. 'Was I being mean?' she asked anxiously.

'Not at all,' he replied. 'After all, you hardly know the guy and he might be there forever – squatters' rights or something.'

'Talking about guys I hardly know, how's Bill Robson getting on with his detective work? No word of an arrest yet then?'

'Not yet,' Woody admitted.

'Hmm,' Kate said. 'He's taking his time. After all, it's been two weeks now.'

Woody laughed. 'OK, I admit he's a little lacking in charisma but he's very efficient, believe it or not. I know he missed those meals in the freezer and the constable who searched Edina's flat is in trouble because he should of course have checked it out. And who would have been looking for pinholes in the packaging except you? But Bill's worked on some big stuff up in the Midlands, always gets his man. Or woman.'

'So he's unlikely to be fazed by an old lady full of digoxin?'

'He's probably only fazed because he thought he could see out the next few years until retirement dealing with the odd bicycle thief or sheep rustler.'

'Like someone else I know.'

'No idea who *that* could be! Anything else exciting happening across the valley there?'

'No, life goes on much as usual,' she said, listening to Angie crashing around in the kitchen.

The next day, Kate, having worked an extra shift and feeling weary, emerged from the treatment room, keen to get home, when she saw two small white-topped ladies in the waiting room.

'Oh, hello, Nurse!' one of them exclaimed. Was it Violet or Daisy? 'We've just been in for our flu jabs and we're about to order a taxi to take us home.'

'I can give you a lift,' Kate said. 'It's no distance.'

'Oh, how *lovely*! Thank you, dear!' They looked delighted.

Kate wasn't certain who was who. As she shepherded them to her car one of them said, 'I hope you'll have time for a cup of tea?'

'That's most kind of you but I really must be getting home,' Kate said, checking to make sure they were strapped in, one in the front, one in the back. They chatted away about everything and anything on the few minutes' drive up through Higher Tinworthy on the way to Seaview, by which time Kate had worked out that Violet was sitting next to her in the green coat, and Daisy in the back was clad in beige.

As she dropped them off Kate saw Sharon running towards the car.

'Is that you, Nurse Kate?' Looking harassed, Sharon wiped her brow. 'We've a bit of an emergency here, can you come in for a minute?'

Kate was beginning to wonder if she was *ever* going to get home. She sighed. But there was something about Sharon's manner that alerted her. She bade farewell to the Potters in the hallway and followed Sharon upstairs, running to keep up.

'It's Edgar Ellis,' Sharon said when she regained her breath. 'I think he's overdosed.'

CHAPTER TWENTY

'*What?*' Kate was astounded as they rushed into Flat 6. 'Edgar?'

'Yes – Edgar. A parcel arrived for him and I took it to his door but no reply. So I let myself in.'

The Reverend Edgar Ellis was sprawled across his sofa with a bottle of Scotch on the side table, along with a couple of empty paracetamol foils. Kate took his pulse and checked his breathing. She took out her phone. 'We need an ambulance,' she said, dialling 999. 'Shake him and keep talking to him. We need to get him conscious enough to be sick.'

Sharon obeyed. 'Edgar, Edgar, wake up!' she yelled as she shook him by the shoulders. 'Silly man!'

He remained comatose.

'They're on the way,' Kate said, putting down her phone. 'Let's just try getting him to his feet, Sharon. Sometimes that does it.'

He was a heavy man and it took all of their combined strength to haul him up onto his feet, only for him to crumple back down onto the sofa again.

'Keep yelling at him!' As she spoke she had a sudden thought. 'I wonder if he left a note somewhere?'

Sharon was checking the table alongside when, lifting up the bottle of Scotch, she found it.

'Look!' she cried. It was neatly folded under the bottle of Scotch, a piece of white notepaper. When she unfolded it Kate read aloud, deciphering his spidery writing:

'*If it wasn't for me she'd still be alive. I can't live with the guilt any longer. Edgar Ellis.*'

Sharon looked over Kate's shoulder. 'Oh my God,' she said. 'Well, at least we *know* now who it was.' She stared at Edgar's prostrate body. 'Who'd have thought it?'

Already the sirens could be heard in the distance, then becoming louder and louder as, with much crunching and spraying of gravel, the ambulance arrived at the front door of Seaview Grange.

Alerted by the noise, all the residents had assembled in the hallway to witness the Reverend Edgar Ellis being stretchered out into the ambulance.

Ollie Pratt was last on the scene. 'Who is it *this* time?'

Kate spoke to one of the paramedics and handed him the empty foils and the half-empty bottle of Scotch. He thanked her, nodded and jumped into the back with Edgar, while the other leaped back into the driving seat and they roared away, gravel flying again.

Sharon, who was standing by the door, burst into tears. Kate gave her a hug.

'We did what we could, Sharon. Thank God you went in there.'

Sharon wiped her eyes as everyone crowded around. 'That's the *second* time I've found somebody like that,' she said, crying some more.

'What was wrong with *him*?' Gloria Pratt asked as she waddled back into the hall.

Kate met Sharon's eye and put her finger to her lips. 'He appears to have passed out,' she said.

'Probably poisoned,' boomed Cornelius Crow. He sounded hopeful.

'We have no idea,' Kate said, wondering if she could make her escape.

Little Hetty looked badly shaken. 'Who'll be next?' she asked, her voice wavering.

'Do you think he'll *die*?' Violet Potter, followed closely by Daisy, had pushed her way to the front.

'I hope not,' Kate said. She glanced at Sharon, who was still distraught. 'Come on, Sharon, you need to go home. I'll walk you round. Where's Stan?'

'He's gone to Launceston to get one of the mowers mended,' Sharon replied, dabbing her eyes again.

'Funny thing that it's always *you* what finds them,' said Gloria nastily. There was a murmur of disapproval from the others as they turned to stare at Gloria. 'Well,' she continued, in defence mode, 'I *suppose* it's coincidence.'

Sharon stopped weeping. 'How *dare* you, Gloria Pratt! What a thing to say! You *know* I have everyone's keys. How many times have I let myself into your place to do your cleaning or deliver a parcel? How many *times*?' Her voice was rising to a crescendo.

'Yes, well,' said Gloria, backing down.

Ollie put an arm round his wife. 'Calm yourself, love.'

'Sod off!' snapped Gloria, roughly pushing his arm away. '*Somebody* here is guilty of trying to finish us all off!' With that she strode into Flat 3 and slammed the door behind her.

Ollie looked round at all the stunned faces and, for the first time, Kate felt sorry for him. 'Sorry about that,' he said. 'She gets a bit upset.'

Ignoring this understatement, Kate said, 'You should all go and brew yourselves a nice cup of tea. I'm sure Sharon will let you know just as soon as we hear from the hospital. Have you a notice board anywhere?'

'Yes, in the residents' lounge,' Sharon said. 'I'll put a note up there the moment we hear from the hospital.' She turned to Kate. 'You'll let me know, won't you, if you hear anything before I do?'

'Of course I will,' Kate said, looking round at all the anxious faces. They weren't to know that the Reverend had brought this on himself, and she wasn't about to tell them. She checked to make sure she still had Sharon's number. She knew too that she must contact the police in light of what appeared to be a suicide note. And which might, or might not, solve the case. She called the police station.

Kate accompanied Sharon, still visibly upset, back to The Stables.

'They all think I've got something to do with it,' she said, dabbing her eyes as she opened the door. 'I'm the one with the keys, I'm the one who finds them.' She deposited the keys and her bright pink mobile phone on the table.

'Sharon,' Kate said as they entered the kitchen, 'Edgar Ellis tried to take his own life and you, hopefully, have saved him.'

Sharon nodded as she filled the kettle. 'They all drive me barmy but I'd never hurt any of them,' she said.

'I know you wouldn't. Sit down and let me make the tea.' Kate pulled out a chair from the kitchen table and Sharon sat down shakily.

'It's just that I keep *finding* them,' she said.

'Just as well you do,' Kate said firmly as she poured boiling water into the pot. 'At least Edina had a chance and Edgar will hopefully be fine once they pump him out.'

'Do you suppose he really did kill Edina?' Sharon asked.

'Difficult to say. Milk? Sugar?'

Sharon nodded. 'What did he mean by saying that if it wasn't for him she'd still be alive? The police will want to interview him, won't they?'

'I think he blamed himself for not checking on Edina more often,' Kate replied. 'He mentioned it to me once.'

'They'll be questioning us all again, I guess. I'm going to think twice before I let myself into any of them flats again, I can tell you! Next thing you know I'll find that old bat Cornelius hanging from a hook in his ceiling! Isn't that what bats do?'

Kate giggled. 'Has he got a hook in his ceiling?'

'Not that I've noticed.' They caught each other's eye and burst out laughing in a release of emotion.

'That's better,' said Kate. 'Now, relax! Old Edgar will probably survive and then he can explain why he did what he did.'

'Well, he scared the daylights out of me.' Sharon sipped her tea. 'But I'm OK now.'

As Kate walked back to her car she thought about Sharon. She came across as a caring type of person and, furthermore, if she'd been the killer, then surely she wouldn't have been so anxious to save Edgar's life? Because, if he were dead – having left what could be construed as an admission of killing – then no one would suspect her.

When Kate rang the hospital for the fourth time that evening she was informed that the vicar had come round and was on the road to recovery. He'd be kept in overnight for observation, and the police were already at his bedside. She rang Sharon straight away to impart the news.

An hour later, just as Kate was hoping to have an early night, Bill Robson knocked on the door.

'I'm sorry to call so late,' he said, not sounding sorry at all, 'but I've been up to Seaview to have a look at this suicide note.'

'I left it on the table,' Kate said, as she reluctantly let him in. 'I gave the empty foils and the half-bottle of Scotch to the paramedics so they'd know how much he'd taken. Sharon found the note, which was under the bottle. But I didn't touch anything else.'

'Yes, quite,' said Robson. 'Thank you for phoning us so promptly. Could you just run through what happened from the time you arrived up there?' He got his recorder out just as Woody arrived at the door.

Woody squeezed Kate's arm. 'What's this I hear?' he asked gently.

'Mrs Palmer is about to make a statement,' said Robson sternly.

'OK, don't mind me – I'll make myself a coffee,' Woody said, smiling at Kate. 'And earwig from the kitchen.'

Kate recounted everything she could recall from the time she dropped the Potter sisters off at their doorway, following a frantic Sharon upstairs, phoning for an ambulance and trying in vain to bring Edgar Ellis round. She said that, as it was a suspected suicide, she'd thought there might be a note. And there it was.

'He appears to be taking the blame for Miss Martinelli's death,' Robson remarked as he switched the recorder off. 'So we *may* have our man.'

Kate didn't think that they did have their man but, at this juncture, did not think it politic to say so. 'Well, at least now you know that Miss Martinelli did not kill herself, and that the surgery are in no way to blame. I suppose that's progress of a sort.' She smiled sweetly in his direction.

Bill Robson did not react and, just then, Woody reappeared with a tray of coffee.

'I bet you're glad you retired,' Robson said, packing his briefcase.

'Damned right I am!' Woody said cheerfully. 'But let me tell you that Kate here is pretty good with her hunches about who did it, or who didn't do it. Am I right, Kate?'

Kate grinned. 'Well, I'm more inclined to know who *didn't* do it,' she said.

'So who *didn't* do it?' Robson asked without a trace of a smile.

Kate could see he was plainly without much sense of humour.

'Well, just for a start, I don't think Edgar Ellis poisoned Edina. I know it *looks* like it, but he was in love with her, you know.'

Bill Robson sniffed. 'Murder's not unknown where love is concerned,' he said, gulping his coffee.

'That's true but I still don't think it was him. I reckon he just didn't want to go on living without her.'

'How very romantic!' Robson said nastily. He was plainly not a great one for romance either. 'Well, I'm off to the hospital now to see our friend before he falls asleep again,' he said, draining his coffee.

'Good luck with that,' Woody said as he accompanied the detective inspector to the door.

When he came back into the room Kate said, 'I cannot *stand* that man. He's most likely a chauvinist; doesn't think women's opinions are worth anything.'

'He's OK, just a little out of his depth in a rural environment.' He glanced at his empty coffee mug. 'Do you think we need something a little stronger?'

'Yes, we definitely do. I'll find some brandy. And, before we go any further, don't tell me not to get involved because I am *already* involved!'

'So you are. Perhaps you and I should set up a detective agency!'

'Don't mock me!' Kate handed him a goblet of brandy. 'And besides, how could I work with a man who doesn't trust me?'

Woody looked aghast. 'What do you mean?'

'I don't even know your real name.'

'Oh – that…' Woody took a large gulp of his brandy.

'Yes, that! You have *never* told me your real name,' Kate said, 'the name you were christened with. I've asked you several times but you always make a joke of it and change the subject. I *know* you wouldn't have been baptised as Woody. Surely your real name can't be *that* bad?'

'Cheers!' he said, raising his glass.

'*Tell* me!' she yelled.

'OK then,' he said with a sigh. 'You're very persistent. It's just that it makes me feel a little idiotic.'

She waited.

'You'll laugh,' he said.

'I won't, I promise.'

'It's Abraham Lincoln Forrest.'

'You're joking!'

'I'm not! And you *promised* not to laugh.'

'Oh my God,' she said, smothering a giggle, 'how did that happen then?'

'It's like this,' Woody replied, 'my dad, although proud to be British, was even more proud to be American. He said it gave him the opportunities he'd never have got here. It gave him a beautiful, devoted wife, three kids and success in business. This was one way to show his allegiance. My brother is Theodore Roosevelt Forrest, known as Roose.'

'What about your sister?'

'Mom got her way that time. My sister's Silvia Virginia. Dad insisted on the Virginia, but fortunately it's also an Italian name.'

'You couldn't make it up,' Kate mused.

'My dad did.'

'OK, *Abraham Lincoln*, more brandy?'

'I should *never* have told you!'

CHAPTER TWENTY-ONE

Andrew Ross was standing on the doorstep having a crafty cigarette when Kate arrived at the medical centre the following day. It was normally another of Kate's days off but they were short-staffed and Kate was glad to accumulate a few days owing to her to add to her Christmas leave. She was also concerned about Edgar Ellis.

'I know, I know, doctors shouldn't smoke!' He grinned at Kate. 'Everyone lectures me!'

Kate laughed. 'I promise I won't.'

'Incidentally,' he went on, 'I know I don't have to tell you, but it's best that we say nothing to anyone about the old vicar trying to finish himself off. You know how word gets around and there are enough rumours circulating about Edina Martinelli already. But I think you should go up there and check him out when he's released from hospital which' – he consulted his watch – 'should be in about a couple of hours.'

'I'll keep checking,' Kate said.

It was early afternoon before Edgar Ellis was released, and collected from the hospital by Stan Starkey. Kate decided she'd let him settle in, visit him about four o'clock, and then she could go straight home afterwards.

As ever there was the usual gathering of residents in the hall at Seaview Grange, gossiping away, their voices tailing off as they saw Kate approach.

'He's home,' Ollie Pratt said, nodding upstairs.

'That's why I'm here,' Kate said, edging past them.

'Causin' everyone a lotta trouble,' added Gloria. 'What was the matter with him anyway? Any chance he was poisoned?'

She really is a most objectionable woman, Kate thought, as she made her way upstairs to Flat 6. The door was ajar.

Once again she found the vicar sprawled on the settee, but conscious this time.

He looked up. 'Oh, it's *you*, Nurse!'

'Yes, it's me. How are you feeling?'

He shrugged. 'My throat's sore with being sick and answering all these questions. The police won't leave me alone.'

'You can't really blame them,' Kate said, setting down her bag on the floor, 'after the note you left.'

'But they took it the *wrong* way,' he said petulantly.

'So what was the right way?' Kate asked, indicating that he roll his sleeve up so she could check his blood pressure.

'What I meant,' he said, 'when I said that if it wasn't for me she'd still be alive, was that I should have *checked* on her days earlier. If I had she might well be alive now. I can't live with myself for having been so remiss. I loved her, you know.'

'You are *not* to blame for her death,' Kate said firmly as she removed the cuff. His blood pressure was normal. 'So please don't do anything like this again.'

He sighed. 'I just don't see any point in living.'

'There are loads of reasons to be living,' Kate said as she drew up a chair next to him. 'Look, here's my card with my number on it and, if you ever feel like doing this again, please promise that you'll call me? *Please?*

He looked at her mournfully. 'I will, I promise. But my life is now completely without purpose.'

'That's an understandable reaction to your grief, but that feeling will pass. If necessary the doctor will prescribe you some medication to help you.'

'If you say so.'

'I do. Now, I suggest you get yourself into bed with a hot drink.'

He looked around. 'Do the others here all *know?*' he asked anxiously.

'Sharon promised she wouldn't say anything to anyone and I think we can trust her. She's the reason you survived. If it hadn't been for Sharon finding you, you probably wouldn't be here now. She was so upset and keen to help. The other residents only know that you passed out and had to be taken to hospital. They don't know why, so best leave it that way. And your medical details are confidential.'

'Thank you, that's a relief.' He thought for a moment. 'My poor wife died of food poisoning, you know, before I came here. It was traced to our local takeaway, which has since been closed down. She had a troublesome digestive system at the best of times. But I was stupid enough to mention this fact down in the residents' lounge, and now, of course, they associate *any* sort of poisoning with me. As if I would, or *could*, have done such a thing!'

'You mustn't let them bother you,' Kate said.

'If you ask me that stepson of hers had something to do with it,' Edgar went on. 'They were always arguing because he was after her money.'

'Hopefully the police will fit it all together before too long,' Kate soothed. 'Would you like me to make you a hot drink before I go?'

'That's kind of you, dear, but I'm fine. You go along home, and I'm sorry to have wasted everyone's time.' He turned his gaze skywards. 'The Lord will be my judge and salvation.'

'Call us if you have any problems.' *Because we're just that bit nearer than the Lord*, she thought.

He must have indeed been desperate, Kate thought. He was a vicar, after all; surely he believed that such an act would land him in Hell? She didn't know what to think. But, after her conversation with him, she was now convinced that Sharon should be taken off the list because, surely, if she had been the killer, Edgar Ellis would have been a convenient scapegoat.

When she got home she found Angie on the phone, making copious notes. She busied herself in the kitchen for several minutes before Angie walked in, still holding her phone.

'Maman is finally dead,' she announced, 'funeral at Essonne next Monday.'

'Are you going to go?' Kate asked.

'Yes, I'll have to. We've been checking out flights on the phone, Paul and I. I can fly from Exeter to Paris and arrive at much the same time as Paul's flight from Heathrow. And Jeremy's flying down from Stockholm, so it'll be lovely to see him. The plan is that I fly out Sunday and come back Wednesday or Thursday because, apparently, we all have to see her lawyer or whatever he's called. I expect I've been left a coffee pot or something.'

Kate considered a couple of nights in the house on her own with guilty pleasure. Perhaps Woody would share her bed here at Lavender Cottage instead of her always sharing his at On the Up, appropriately named due to it being halfway up to Penhallion cliff. She had only met Maman once, briefly, and hadn't much cared for her, so there was little point in attempting to appear too grief-stricken at the news. And, in spite of Angie's apparent indifference to her mother-in-law, Kate knew she'd been close to Maman before she returned to live in France. And Angie's late husband had been Maman's favourite son.

As Kate was considering Angie's in-laws, her own phone buzzed.

'It's me,' said Sharon Starkey. 'Just to let you know that I plan to pop in to see the old vicar a couple of times a day. None of the others, apart from the Potter sisters, have even bothered to ask how he is, or offered any help. Funny old lot they are!'

'They are,' Kate agreed. 'I'll look in soon though just to give him a final check-over.'

'If you have time,' Sharon said, 'I'll make you a coffee.'

The following morning Kate found Angie in the kitchen ironing a black dress.

'Do you think I should wear a hat?' she asked. 'Do you think women wear hats at French funerals?'

'I've no idea,' Kate replied.

Angie was to change her mind three times about what to wear for the funeral before finally setting off for Exeter Airport on Sunday morning. She'd unearthed a little black pillbox hat with a veil which she decided might make her look suitably mysterious in the face of possible fierce French competition. She decided on the black dress but not the check jacket she'd originally earmarked.

'I'll just have to be cold,' she said, 'but I can probably squeeze a T-shirt on underneath and hope that the church has some form of heating.'

Then she swapped her black kitten-heeled shoes for black stilettos, plainly out to make an impression. Fergal, apparently, had offered to accompany her but even Angie agreed it might not be a very brilliant idea to meet the French family of her late husband with a crazy Irishman in tow. And, Kate thought, particularly as Angie was likely to be footing the bill.

'I'll leave you to it,' Kate said, 'because I'm going out to lunch.'

Woody was going to take her out to lunch in Padstow. He'd phoned Rick Stein's tentatively at nine o'clock to be told that there had been a cancellation and a table for two was available.

'We're going to have a nice lunch,' he told Kate, 'and we are *not* going to talk about *anybody* at Seaview Grange. You OK with that?'

'I'm OK with that,' Kate agreed.

'You may talk about the weather, baseball, football, world politics, anything you like, but I do not want to hear a *word* about those people.'

As they drove towards Padstow Kate tried hard to clear her mind. Woody played some soothing music. Slowly, slowly, she began to relax. She glanced across at Woody and reminded herself how very lucky she was that this special man had become fond of her. She was no beauty, but she considered herself to be reasonably intelligent and she did care about people. She certainly cared about Woody. Very much.

When they were seated in The Seafood Restaurant and began studying the wonderful menu she realised that she had completely forgotten Seaview Grange and its residents for the moment. The food was amazing, the wine was marvellous, which Kate particularly appreciated since she drank three-quarters of the bottle because Woody was driving.

Padstow was busy as always, although the summer visitors had gone home. They wandered around the harbour and admired the boats, ate ice cream and visited a couple of shops and galleries. It wasn't until they were nearly home that Kate began to think about Seaview Grange and The List again.

She was obviously incapable of getting the place out of her mind for more than a few hours. The delicious fish she'd just eaten, infused with such lovely flavours, made her think again of the different kind of infusion that had been put into Edina's food. The syringe had to be the key to the mystery. The killer had to have access to syringes and, according to her research in the medical notes, the only resident of Seaview who had easy access to anything like a syringe was Gloria Pratt, but she used an insulin pen which was loaded with cartridges. Would it be possible to reload any empty cartridge with a solution of crushed-up digoxin? Possible, but very difficult. And probably irrelevant as it was possible these days for anyone to buy syringes online.

Where would the killer have hidden a syringe or syringes? He or she must have been wily to use such a method of killing so they could well have found some improbable spot to hide them. But where? Would they have just discarded them on the beach and hoped the sea would take them away? No, she thought, someone that cunning would be more careful. But where then would they hide them? And what opportunity could she have to take a look?

She decided to phone Sharon. Kate felt that she was the one person at Seaview that she could trust. And, on top of that, she did have access to everyone's apartment.

'Hi, Sharon, could I ask you to do something for me?'

'What sort of thing?'

'When you're cleaning the apartments can you keep your eyes peeled for anything unusual? Syringes, for example? Particularly syringes.'

'Syringes?' Sharon sounded mystified. 'I don't suppose the person's very likely to be leaving evidence like that around.'

'You're right, but have a look anyway.'

'I will,' Sharon said.

Reverend Edgar Ellis was pretty much back to normal health and looking considerably more cheerful when Kate popped in on Monday to check on him.

'I'm fine, really,' he assured Kate. 'And Sharon's been keeping any eye on me.'

'Good, I'll be off then,' Kate said, as she left him reading the *Tinworthy Gazette*. She wondered briefly about the organist up in

Little Barrington; had she given birth to Edgar's child? Was Edgar a father? Difficult to imagine.

As she descended the stairs she saw Sharon polishing the table in the hallway.

'He's made a really speedy recovery,' Sharon said.

'Yes, he has,' Kate agreed, 'but have *you* recovered? Recovered from the stress of finding these comatose residents?'

Sharon laughed. 'Yes, I have. I'm ready for the next one, whoever that may be!'

Kate grimaced. 'Dear God, don't say that!'

'Well, you never know! Fancy a coffee?'

Kate glanced at her watch. 'A quick one would be lovely.'

She followed Sharon back to The Stables, waving at Stan, who was digging a flower bed at the far end of the garden, on the way.

As Sharon topped up the water in her red kettle and settled it on the Aga she said, 'I'm *determined* to find out who's guilty of Edina's poisoning, if only to get them all to stop pointing at *me*. I have my suspicions but' – she tapped her lips – 'I'm sayin' nothin' yet.'

'I'll be in suspense for the next few days then,' Kate said truthfully, accepting a mug of coffee.

Sharon then chatted about her daughter in Canada, and Kate chatted about her sons in Scotland and Australia. And about becoming a grandmother for the first time.

'Calum Fraser Palmer,' she said proudly, then smiled to herself, thinking of Woody. At least they hadn't saddled the poor infant with a name like Winston Churchill Palmer or Benjamin Disraeli Palmer. Heaven forbid.

And as Kate headed home she wondered if Sharon would have any success in finding the syringe. Bearing in mind she had access to all their flats and all their lives, she just *might* come up with something.

CHAPTER TWENTY-TWO

Kate didn't have to wait long. The following day, at exactly eleven o'clock – she would forever have this time imprinted in her brain – Sharon phoned.

'How's your detective work going?' Kate asked.

'I can't talk for long. I'm at the top of the stairs in the middle of my cleaning. Listen, Kate' – Sharon sounded anxious – 'while I've been cleaning the flats and having a little snoop around, I've discovered a syringe and you won't *believe* whose flat I found it in.'

'Wow!' Kate took a deep breath. '*Tell* me whose flat it is!'

Sharon didn't reply.

'Sharon, *whose* is it?' Kate was having to stop herself from jumping up and down.

'I'm afraid I can't tell you that at the moment,' Sharon said, then added loudly, 'Yes, that'll be fine.'

Kate frowned. '*What?* You're not making sense; is the person there?'

'Yes, that's it,' Sharon continued in the loud voice.

'So you can't speak now?'

'Correct.'

'Sharon, I'll be up there as soon as I can. Get straight on to the police and text me the name of whoever it is. Stay safe.'

She heard the click then as Sharon ended her call.

Kate could hardly control her anxiety as she waited for news. But no text was forthcoming. She needed to get up there as quickly as possible and she sighed when she saw the next patient was old Sadie Thomson, famed for her gossip.

'I hear they've bin carryin' *another* body out from Seaview,' she said.

'No bodies have been carried out from Seaview,' Kate said firmly as she studied Sadie's rash. 'Have you been eating seafood again?'

Sadie sniffed. 'Our Bobby brought back a few muss—'

'Mussels?' Kate interrupted.

'Yeah, just a few,' Sadie admitted.

'You know you're allergic to seafood, Sadie, and that includes mussels. It's always going to bring you out in spots. Anyway, put some antiseptic cream on that rash and it'll disappear in a day or two.'

'And they say that the *second* body belonged to that old vicar,' Sadie went on, now completely disinterested in her rash. 'But I expect they'd have sent for you and *you'll* know all about it.' She smiled hopefully at Kate.

Kate sighed. She needed to get out of here. Was this woman ever going to go? 'The vicar had a bad turn,' she explained patiently, 'but he was allowed home after a night in hospital. Nothing to get excited about.'

'And then there's that foreign woman what got killed.' Sadie was like a dog with a bone which she had no intention of giving up.

'What about her?' Kate asked, looking at her watch.

'Well, it seems funny that it's not so long ago since *she* was carried out on a stretcher, dead as a dodo.'

'She was *not* dead,' Kate said, 'but she died in hospital later. Now, is there anything else I can help you with *health*-wise?'

'I suppose I'd better be off,' said Sadie without moving.

'Yes,' Kate agreed, 'because I have a lot of patients waiting out there.'

'All right, all right,' Sadie grumbled as she grudgingly heaved herself off the chair. 'Probably old Larry's first in the queue. He's always got somethin' wrong with him, so he has. Too much beer's his problem.'

As Kate ushered her out and consulted her patient list, she saw that it was indeed old Larry next. While she waited for him she checked her phone; no text message.

He hobbled in, collapsed onto the chair that Sadie had just vacated, and said, 'I hear they tried to poison the old vicar up at Seaview. Was it *you* that phoned for the ambulance?'

Kate, now desperate, said, 'Can you wait a little longer and see Sue? There's somewhere I have to be urgently.' She didn't wait to hear his grumbles but rushed to Denise to ask her to reschedule her appointments because there was an emergency at Seaview Grange. Denise looked puzzled. 'Nobody rang here,' she said.

'Take my word for it,' Kate said as she rushed towards the door.

It was unbelievable. Kate blinked and blinked again. Once more there was an ambulance parked in front of the door of Seaview Grange, lights flashing. A couple of people stood round the gate, as well as the residents in the doorway, the women weeping openly.

Feeling sick in the pit of her stomach, Kate rushed in the door and pushed her way in. All she could see was Sharon lying at the foot of the stairs, her head against the stone step, Stan in tears beside her. Two paramedics were standing talking in low voices.

Ollie came forward. 'I found her,' he told Kate, 'and she was a goner.'

'What happened?' Kate asked, feeling weak with shock as she bent over Sharon's lifeless body. Stan was unable to speak.

'We heard the thump while we were cooking our lunch, didn't we, Ollie?' Gloria said. 'We thought maybe the postman had left a big package or somethin' so we carried on with our recipe for a while before Ollie went out to investigate and there she was. You shouted, didn't you, Ollie?'

'When I came down to see what the commotion was about,' said Cornelius Crow, 'all I could see was the flex of the vacuum cleaner stretched across the top of the stairs, just like when Edina tripped.' He hesitated and shuddered. 'Then I looked *down*.'

'She probably left the flex across the top of the stairs again, like she did before,' said little Hetty, 'and she must have tripped over it by accident.'

Stan, with tears streaming down his cheeks, said angrily, 'Sharon wouldn't have tied the flex across like that. Someone did it on *purpose*. Most likely whoever did it tied the flex across to make it "look" like an accident.'

Kate turned to the Pratts. 'Did you hear her shout out?' she asked.

'No, we didn't hear anythin' except the bump, did we, Ollie?' Gloria said.

Ollie nodded in agreement.

'Then she could have been unconscious before she fell.' Kate felt sick as she looked at the pool of blood beneath Sharon's head and wondered if the injury might have been caused before the fall, by the fall or even after the fall.

There was a moment's silence.

Then Kate said, 'Has anyone rung the police? They should have been here by now. Have they not been yet?'

Everyone looked in her direction until one of the paramedics said, 'I just did.'

'Thank God,' said Kate.

'Why do the *police* have to be involved?' asked Cornelius.

'Because someone's killed her, that's why,' Kate replied with feeling. 'Someone *here*. And the police need to see Sharon before she's moved.'

There was an appalled silence again.

Then the paramedic said, 'We were here within ten minutes of getting the call, but she was dead when we arrived. Nothing we could do.'

Kate looked up to the top of the stairs but couldn't see any flex.

'I disconnected the cord,' said Edgar Ellis as he slowly descended, 'in case Cornelius or David tripped over it. Should I have left it in position?'

'Just tell the police when they get here,' Kate said, realising for the first time that David Courtney was there as well. 'Were *you* here when it happened?' she asked him.

'I was sorting out some of Edina's things,' David Courtney said defensively, 'and, like everyone else, I knew nothing about it until I heard Ollie's cry. I thought it seemed odd that she didn't scream or something.' He looked horrified, or else he was a damned good actor, Kate thought.

Everyone was looking at everyone else except Stan, who was still weeping over Sharon's body. Somebody *here killed her*, Kate thought. And wasn't it very strange that this should have happened at the exact time David Courtney was in Edina's flat? Sharon had phoned from the landing upstairs when she called Kate. Was it David Courtney who had overheard Sharon and prevented her from telling Kate what she'd found?

Kate was only too conscious of the fact that Sharon had been doing what Kate had asked her to do. She felt wracked with guilt and desperately sad. But somehow or the other she needed to struggle to keep it all together and preserve some sort of professional demeanour. To prevent herself from breaking down she turned her attention to the two Potter ladies and Hetty Patterson, who were grouped together in a state of shock.

'We were just watching television, weren't we, Daisy?' said Violet. 'Lovely programme about someone buying a house…'

'Yes, and we didn't hear a thing until we heard everyone talking out in the hall,' added Daisy.

'And I'd been on the phone to my poor sister,' said Hetty, 'and I didn't hear a thing either.'

'I don't feel safe here any more,' wailed Daisy.

'We must all try to be sensible, Daisy,' said her sister.

'And watch you don't trip if you go upstairs,' added Hetty, wiping her eyes.

'Well,' said Violet, 'if it was Sharon who was positioning that flex at the top of the stairs, it's not likely to happen now, is it?'

'Of *course* it was her! She's got her just deserts,' Hetty snapped.

Kate was appalled at Hetty's remark. 'She'd hardly trip *herself* up, would she?'

Hetty snorted, then asked Kate, 'Do you think the police will protect us, Nurse? I shan't feel safe in my bed at night now.'

'You'll have to ask them,' Kate said shortly.

Five minutes later they could hear the police siren and Bill Robson dashed in, followed by two uniformed officers.

'Mrs Palmer,' he said, 'well, well, well, fancy seeing *you* here!'

'It's *Nurse* Palmer today,' Kate said through gritted teeth. She wished fervently that it was Woody who was there, and not Robson. Then again, had it been Woody, she'd probably not have been able to resist falling into his arms and bursting into tears. Then, for sure, her professional credibility in the village would be lost.

She stood back as he bent over Sharon's body. He said something to the two officers, who promptly began to photograph the body from every angle.

'She tripped over the flex upstairs,' Gloria supplied.

'Where have I heard *that* before?' Robson looked around. 'Nobody leaves here until they've been questioned. Is there somewhere you can all wait?'

'There's a residents' lounge,' Kate said.

'OK, everyone, into the lounge please. You too, *Nurse* Palmer.' Kate was glad that he plainly intended to remain on formal terms.

'I have something I must tell you,' Kate said to him as the others shuffled into the lounge. 'Sharon phoned me a couple of hours ago to say she thought she'd found some evidence, and was about to say whose flat she found it in.'

Robson stood stock still. 'She did?'

'Yes, she did. I told her to phone you immediately and to text me, but the person concerned must have appeared and obviously overheard her because she had to change the conversation rapidly before the call ended.'

'What time was that?'

'Eleven o'clock.'

'We didn't get any call. Why did she phone you first and not us?'

'I don't know.' *But I can guess*, Kate thought. 'But she seemed convinced that she knew who the killer was. And that person has to be one of the residents, or David Courtney, who was here at the time. He or she must have been listening.' Kate sighed. 'If only she'd had a chance to tell me who it was.'

'So where's her phone?' Robson asked. 'If she'd been talking on it shortly beforehand then she obviously had it with her. Was it found on the landing, the stairs, the hallway?'

He marched into the lounge and called out, 'Has anyone got Sharon Starkey's phone? Has anyone *seen* the phone?'

There was silence while everyone looked at everyone else and shook their heads sadly.

Then Kate remembered. 'It shouldn't be difficult to find,' she said, 'because it was bright pink. But let me ring her number and see if we can hear it anywhere in the building.'

Kate clicked on Sharon's number and let it ring, and ring. After a minute she shook her head sadly. 'Couldn't hear anything anywhere, not even an answering service.'

'I'm going to need a detailed statement from you all,' Bill Robson said, making a note. He thought for a moment before turning to Kate. 'I suppose it stands to reason that she *could* have tripped over the flex which, I'm told, was stretched across the top of the stairs. *Again.*'

'But I *told* you that was how Edina broke her ankle, and she was convinced that someone wanted to kill her, which they eventually did. And now, poor Sharon.' Kate felt her eyes fill up again.

'Sharon was the cleaner, right?'

'Yes, and that's her husband there, being comforted by the paramedic. Poor Sharon – everyone pointed the finger at her, but she was hardly likely to do it to herself, for God's sake!'

Kate made a vow to herself that she would do everything in her power to bring Sharon's killer to justice. And whoever it was *must* have her phone, otherwise where was it? It was the least Kate felt she could do and nobody – not Woody or this wretched man or anyone else – was going to stand in her way.

Violet Potter touched her arm lightly. 'Come into the lounge, dear. There's a kettle and some mugs in there and there *should* be some teabags.'

Kate hesitated. She saw Stan, almost in a state of collapse, being shepherded into the residents' lounge along with everyone else. Feeling desperately sorry for him, Kate entered, crossed the room and sat down next to him.

'I can't believe this,' he moaned. 'I can't believe it. *My Sharon!*'

'I'm so sorry, Stan, but we'll find out who did this.' Kate squeezed his arm and hoped she sounded more confident than she felt.

'*Who* would do this?' Stan wiped his eyes. 'And they won't let me go with her.'

'You'll be able to see her later,' Kate consoled, 'but they'll first need to establish exactly how she died.'

'She died cos she fell down the bloody stairs!' Stan's voice rose to a crescendo. 'And what I want to know is, who bloody well *pushed* her?'

'Oh, apparently she tripped over the cord of the vacuum cleaner,' said Violet Potter, who had positioned herself on Stan's other side.

'My *arse!*' shouted Stan. Violet flinched. 'As if Sharon would leave the cord stretched across the bloody staircase just so she could trip over it! For God's sake!' He turned to Kate. 'We've been married more than thirty years.' Stan put his head in his hands. 'How am I going to live without her?'

Afternoon became evening and Bill Robson was still taking statements from every single resident. Kate glanced across at David Courtney, seated beside a uniformed policeman, and still waiting to be questioned. If there was ever any doubt that this man was a suspect, there surely couldn't be now.

It was half past seven before Bill Robson got all the statements he wanted. He wound up the session by saying that he would be producing warrants to search all the flats. This resulted in a chorus of outrage. He also wanted to know how to contact the grange's management team, and the details of everyone there. Ollie Pratt was happy to oblige, dashing in and out of his flat with folders and sheaves of paper.

'Absolutely ridiculous!' Cornelius Crow was sitting immediately behind Kate. 'That David Courtney's been in and out of Edina's flat ever since she died so they're not going to find any incriminating evidence *now*, are they?'

David Courtney must have overheard, but he remained impassive. Kate was inclined to agree with Cornelius but, right now, she just wanted to go home, have a good cry and be comforted by Woody.

CHAPTER TWENTY-THREE

'I need to get out of here,' Kate told Woody later, 'after the day I've had.'

'Come right on over,' Woody said. 'Tonight's the night the fish-and-chip van comes down to the village, so why don't I get us some dinner?'

'Can I bring Barney with me?'

'Of course you can.'

'You and I are going visiting,' Kate informed Barney as she attached the lead to his collar.

'I've already heard,' Woody said thirty minutes later, hugging Kate. 'Bill Robson's been on the phone. It must have been awful for you.'

'Not as awful as it was for poor Stan Starkey,' Kate said. 'They'd been married thirty years, he told me.'

'First thing – you need to eat.' He passed her a package of fish and chips and sat down at the kitchen table.

Kate realised she hadn't eaten anything since breakfast-time and was extremely hungry. 'Can we eat out of the paper?' she asked.

'Is there any *other* way?' He grinned at her. 'We don't want to wash plates, do we?' He handed Barney a couple of chips.

'I don't want to do anything,' Kate admitted. 'I'm feeling absolutely shattered.'

Woody sighed. 'Well, I had Bill on the phone for the best part of half an hour, so think I've got the gist of what's happened. We can talk about it, if you want, *apres* fish and chips. I've put salt and vinegar on them, by the way.'

'Thanks,' Kate said. She took a mouthful of the flakes of white haddock encased in a crisp batter, which she knew were delicious, but she could hardly taste it.

After three mouthfuls she put down her fork, picked up her wine, and emptied the glass.

'What's wrong?' Woody asked. 'Is your fish no good? Mine's delicious.'

'No, I'm sure it's lovely but I'm just finding it difficult to swallow.'

'Well, you're drinking that wine fast enough! You're drinking like your sister!'

'I feel so responsible for Sharon's death. I was the one who asked her to snoop around in all the flats to see if she could find evidence of some kind.'

'She didn't *have* to do it,' Woody said gently.

'She did it because I *asked* her,' Kate said.

Woody shook his head. 'I can't work out why on earth she would stand at the top of the stairs and make that phone call, so that everyone could hear. Why didn't she wait until she got home or text at the very least?'

'She was speaking very quietly,' Kate said. 'She must have thought she was safe.'

'Remind me, *who* lives upstairs?'

'Well, there's Cornelius Crow with his crime books and his obsession with murder. There's Edgar Ellis, the retired vicar, who was supposedly in love with Edina, whose wife died of food poisoning and who recently tried to commit suicide. And there's David Courtney, Edina's stepson, who just *happened* to be "sorting out Edina's stuff", as he put it. Quite a coincidence that he should be there, don't you think?'

'Hmm, maybe,' said Woody. 'And was everyone else where they should have been, in their own flats?'

'Apparently. Therefore, it stands to reason that one of the three upstairs must have pushed her down. Because I do believe Sharon was hit on the head or stunned and then she was pushed because, one way or the other, she didn't shout or scream when she got to the bottom. And she was hardly likely to stretch the cord across the top in order to trip herself, was she?'

'But the flex wasn't found to be there afterwards?'

'Yes, because Edgar Ellis disconnected it in case anyone *else* tripped over it. Both he and Cornelius saw it though. But I agree with what Stan thought – I think it could have been placed there *after* she was pushed to make it look as if she tripped over it accidentally.'

'That would be my guess,' Woody agreed. 'Or it's possible that she was killed at the foot of the stairs and *before* the flex was stretched across the top to make it look like she'd fallen.'

Kate was relieved to know they'd been thinking along the same lines. 'I was always certain it wasn't Sharon that poisoned Edina, and I think now this definitely proves it,' she said.

'Well, let's wait to see what the medical reports come up with.'

Kate sniffed. 'Would they be able to tell whether the injury that killed her was caused before she fell or afterwards?'

'Most likely,' Woody replied.

'I expect they'll just say that death was caused by falling down a long flight of stone stairs and bashing her head on the lowest one.' Kate recalled the patch of blood on the bottom step and the way that Bill Robson had that measured and photographed, along with everything else. 'How would they know if she was pushed or not? And where did Sharon's phone go to? Whoever killed Sharon must have her phone.'

'You'd be surprised with what they can come up with,' Woody said, 'and they're searching all the flats right now so hopefully they'll find the phone.'

'But whoever took it has had time to get rid of it, or hide it,' Kate said, 'although it was bright pink so it should be relatively easy to find.'

Woody nodded. 'I'm afraid you're right. But, for now, try to put it out of your mind. This is now a double murder inquiry and I'm going to be back at the police station most of the time.'

Kate couldn't sleep a wink. Afraid of disturbing Woody, Kate eased herself out of bed and went into his kitchen to make herself a hot drink. The dog, who'd been asleep on Woody's sofa, looked up hopefully.

'No, we're not going out for a walk in the middle of the night,' she said.

Did Woody have hot chocolate? No, apparently not, but he did have instant coffee, so that would have to do.

She'd been tempted again and again to delete the Potters and Hetty from The List. But something made her hesitate. She kept thinking about the twins' resentment because Edina had got the flat *they* wanted. They obviously *still* wanted it, but would that have been enough of a motive to poison her? Then there was Hetty. She didn't like the way Hetty had spoken just after Sharon had died. But Hetty was Edina's great friend.

She'd left a question mark next to Gloria's name, only because she was such an objectionable character. But there was little means or opportunity for her to have committed the crime. But Kate still felt that Gloria was unlikely to be the killer although she left her on The List, mainly because she didn't like her.

She was now fairly certain it had to be David Courtney, but that didn't answer the question as to which flat Sharon had found the proof in. Edina's flat couldn't be ruled out because David Courtney could have been there specifically to remove any evidence he might have left behind.

That left Cornelius and Edgar. Cornelius was weird, and he seemed almost to be enjoying the current drama. He certainly didn't seem concerned.

As for Edgar, well... He'd apparently idolised Edina, so why on earth would he have wanted to kill her? And *had* he poisoned his late wife? Kate considered his recent suicide attempt; was that some sort of cry for help or had he really wanted to kill himself? Either because he couldn't bear the thought of life without Edina, as his note suggested, or because he'd actually killed her? *Could* it be possible that he was the killer?

Kate's thoughts moved downstairs. If someone had bashed Sharon on the head at the *foot* of the stairs and then rushed up to stretch the vacuum flex across the top to make it look like an accident, they'd have had to move pretty quickly. This made the Pratts in Flat 3 unlikely suspects, as she doubted either of this bulky couple could move that fast. Surely someone would have seen one or the other of them if they'd ventured upstairs today? And, since it was Ollie who apparently found the body, he'd have had to rush downstairs in time to 'find' her and let everyone know.

What about Stan? Kate couldn't believe that he could have murdered Sharon but you never really know what goes on in a marriage, they say. Could his grief have been feigned? But how could he be a suspect when he'd been at the far end of the grounds, pruning a tree, when Sharon met her fate? Hetty had had to rush out to find him and break the awful news. But why would he have wanted to kill Edina in the first place?

Kate got back into bed, then tossed and turned. She tried hard not to think of Seaview Grange or any of its inhabitants, but concentrate instead on the prospect of a trip to California, and meeting some of Woody's family. She was certainly going to be ready for a change of scenery.

CHAPTER TWENTY-FOUR

Kate and Barney got home about eight o'clock in the morning. In spite of having the dog for company Kate felt strangely alone all day. She was unable to distract her thoughts from the horrifying scenes of yesterday, and the blood pooled around Sharon's shattered skull.

The house seemed unusually empty without Angie, which Kate thought was odd since Angie spent much of her time in her so-called 'studio' and the rest either with Fergal or at The Greedy Gull. It wasn't the first time Angie had been absent either, because back in July she'd flown up to Sweden for her annual ten-day pilgrimage to see Jeremy and his Swedish wife and two boys. Angie and Ingrid did not get on terribly well, mainly because Ingrid strongly disapproved of her mother-in-law's fondness for gin, and so Angie was forced to considerably limit her intake while she was there. She was not over-enthusiastic about Ingrid either, particularly her passion for healthy outdoor living. Jeremy, of course, made it all worthwhile but, nevertheless, Angie was always relieved to get home. At least now she'd have the opportunity to see her son on his own for a couple of days.

Angie phoned late that evening. 'We finally have *chère* Maman pushing up the daisies,' she informed Kate. 'Tomorrow morning we must all present ourselves at the solicitor's office to find out what she's left us. Not much, I suppose, but it should be interesting. From there I'll go straight to Charles de Gaulle and I should be home by the evening. Anyone else been poisoned or booted down the stairs in my absence?'

Kate still felt too emotional after Sharon's death to tell her sister the latest news over the phone. Furthermore, the police had done a thorough search of all the flats in Seaview Grange and found nothing.

Angie arrived home at about ten o'clock on Thursday evening. As she dragged her overnight case through the door and flung her coat onto a peg, she said, 'You'll *never* guess what!'

As Kate hugged her sister, she asked, 'What?'

Angie headed into the kitchen. 'I'll just pour myself a gin and then I'll tell you. Can I pour one for you?'

'Might as well,' Kate said, preparing herself for a detailed account of who was who at the funeral.

As Angie deposited two gin and tonics on the coffee table she said, 'We saw the solicitor this morning. And he read out the will.'

'Did you get the coffee pot?'

'No, I got two hundred and fifty thousand euros!'

'*What?*'

'I'm not too sure of the official exchange rate at the moment,' Angie went on, sipping her gin, 'but it's well over two hundred thousand pounds.'

'It certainly is!' Kate agreed. 'Wow, that's amazing! And unexpected!' *And it could buy a lot of gin*, she thought. 'She must have loved you more than you thought.'

'She loved George,' Angie said, referring to her late husband, 'and so she left the same amount to Jeremy and to each of his boys, and to each of Paul's family too, of course.'

'She wasn't exactly poor then?'

'No, she wasn't.'

'Have you had any thoughts on what you might do with the money?' Kate asked, imagining Fergal would probably get his holiday paid for after all.

Angie took another sip. 'I've been thinking about that. Kate, you don't have to work any more! I'm going to pay off all those bloody bills!'

'Angie, you don't have to do that…'

'Look, you took this job to pay for everything and I appreciate that – I really do!'

'I'm sure you do, Angie, but—'

'Kate, I'm rich! *We're* rich!'

Kate was moved by Angie's generosity but at the same time she wondered why she wasn't feeling over the moon at the prospect of becoming a lady of leisure. What had begun as a financial necessity had now become her way of life. And she *liked* it.

As if guessing her thoughts, Angie said, 'Well, I'm going to pay everything off anyway. And you can go out to Australia too – how about that? It's entirely up to you if you want to carry on working or not.' She wrinkled her nose. 'It wouldn't be my scene working with all those unhealthy people and their germs.'

'No,' Kate agreed, 'it wouldn't be your scene.' *But it is mine.*

'But I have got another idea. Did you know The Locker's closing down?' Angie referred to the little coffee shop close to the beach, which could be seen from their window.

'The Locker Café?' Kate asked, puzzled.

'Yes, Polly Lock told me she'd had enough of tourists and teas and she is planning to close permanently now the season's over. I'm interested in buying it.'

'Buying it? *You?* What the hell would you do with it? And, if Polly can't make the place pay, why do you think you could?'

'I have ideas,' Angie replied loftily. 'I've always liked that little place. It would make a lovely bar.'

'A *bar?*'

'You're beginning to sound like a bloody parrot, repeating everything I say. Yes, a *bar*! Somewhere you could get a *drink*, right?'

Kate took a deep breath. 'But The Greedy Gull's just down the lane!'

'I *know* where The Gull is! But it's a *pub*! This would be a nice little *bar*, continental style, selling alcohol, of course, but also coffee and snacks.'

'Angie, you'd be your own best customer!'

'Don't talk rubbish! OK, so I'd probably have a little drink now and then but that place, given a bit of character, could be a gold mine! A few yards from the beach; not just booze, but ice cream, sandwiches, cakes.'

'And you'd dispense all this single-handed?' Kate asked. 'Because for sure *I'm* not getting involved!'

'I haven't asked you to. No, I'll take Fergal in with me.'

'*Fergal?* But he hasn't got two pennies to rub together!'

'I'll *employ* him, stupid! He could give up most of his jobs except, maybe, the postcards.'

'And he'd commute from Plymouth every day?'

'Well, no, because there's a tiny two-roomed flat above the café.'

'*What?* Kate stared at her sister in amazement. 'You seem to know an awful lot about the place, considering it's not even on the market yet.'

'Well, I've got quite friendly with Polly Lock,' Angie said. 'I had a long chat with her at The Gull the other night and she told me all about it. And, given this unexpected inheritance, it almost seems like it was meant to be.'

'And now you're going to tell me that Fergal will take up residence in this two-roomed flat? Not rent free, I hope?'

'Of course not,' Angie replied. 'He's paying now for the caravan, so he could pay me rent instead. And I'll be paying him anyway for working behind the bar.'

'You've got it all worked out in a very short time,' Kate remarked drily.

'I've been thinking about it all day,' Angie said. 'I just need to check it all out.' She paused. 'Anyway, why are you looking so glum?'

'There's been another death at Seaview Grange,' Kate said.

'Oh my God! Who is it *this* time?'

'Sharon, the cleaner.'

Angie sniffed. 'So what was *she* up to? And how did she meet her end?'

Kate told her. 'What makes it worse is that she was on the phone to me just seconds before, telling me that she knew where the evidence was and who the killer might be. But the person concerned must have overheard because the next thing we know is that Sharon's at the foot of the stairs, dead. And her phone's disappeared.'

'Oh dear,' said Angie, stifling a yawn, 'but it's not as if she was a *friend* of yours.'

'We *had* become friendly,' Kate snapped, 'and it was on account of me asking her to look for evidence in the flats that this tragedy happened, so I feel responsible.'

Angie stopped in her tracks and glared at her sister. 'Why do you *always* have to get involved? Try to forget this Karen.'

'*Sharon!* Kate corrected. 'And this is quite different. I've been involved right from the start when Edina Martinelli broke her ankle by falling down the same stairs. And I'm going to do my damnedest to find out who the killer is because it's the *least* I can do!'

'OK, OK,' Angie said. 'Look, we're both tired, and you're upset. We'll both feel better in the morning I feel sure.'

'Yes, you're right.' Kate hugged her sister. 'Sleep well!'

After Angie had gone to bed Kate worried that she'd been a bit grumpy with her sister. After all, apart from the trip to the funeral in France, Angie was probably quite stressed about Fergal and about the purchase of The Locker. She had a lot on her plate; buying any kind of property was always stressful. Talking of property… Kate got The List out again and looked at her column for the Potter twins. They too had owned a shop that had changed hands, now Demelza's Boutique. Could that be a lead? She decided to pay it a visit tomorrow.

CHAPTER TWENTY-FIVE

As Kate walked up the main street in Middle Tinworthy, she wondered whether Demelza might have any knickers left over from the reign of the Potter sisters. She should really have bought some last time she went to Exeter but it wasn't worth the long drive again.

There appeared to be a great deal of pink, both inside and outside the shop. A couple of faceless models in the window wore very glittery mini-dresses, which Demelza had pronounced as 'perfect for the Christmas season'. Kate studied the thigh-high hemlines on the ultra-thin models and giggled at the thought of Woody's reaction if she were to wear something similar to the police ball. Always assuming he asked her, of course!

Inside the girl sitting at the pink-painted desk was chewing vigorously while clicking frantically on her phone with sparkly purple nails. She had a forest of eyelashes and some bright pink streaks in her long dark hair. She also displayed an impressive front with a rose tattooed on one of her magnificent bosoms, and 'Alan' tattooed on the other. *Whoever Alan is, she's got him for life*, Kate thought.

'Can I help?' The girl moved what appeared to be chewing gum to one side of her mouth. Kate saw her staring at the nurse's uniform. 'We don't do much for older ladies,' she added.

'I guessed that,' Kate said. 'Are you Demelza?'

'Yeah, that's me.' She stood up reluctantly and laid her phone on the table.

'I don't expect you can help me,' Kate said, 'but I wondered if you stocked ladies' underwear, knickers, or whatever you call them these days?'

'Well, we got a few. Is it for your daughter – or *you*?' Demelza indicated a shelf at the rear of the shop.

'For me,' Kate confirmed.

'We've not got much in the way of sixteens, though,' Demelza said sadly.

'Well, I sometimes fit into a fourteen,' Kate said, already doubting her wisdom at coming over the doorstep. 'But I believe this shop used to be an old-fashioned draper's? Have you anything left over from then?'

Demelza sighed. 'I suppose there might be something right at the back of the stockroom.'

'Would you mind having a look?' Kate asked.

Demelza shrugged and disappeared into the back of the shop, giving Kate an opportunity to have a look around. There were no drawers with folded-up items, only a few mini-dresses hanging round the walls and the blare of some pop music. She doubted if Daisy and Violet had ever crossed the door since they sold the place to Demelza.

Demelza returned. 'No, we've got nothing.'

'It's just that I know the two old ladies who used to own this shop,' Kate said.

'A couple of tight-fisted old biddies,' Demelza snorted.

'Really?' Kate was genuinely surprised. This was the first bad word she'd heard about the sisters.

'Yeah, really,' Demelza said. 'Mean as muck they were! They wanted top price for this place and wouldn't take a penny less. Apparently, they didn't get the flat they wanted up at Seaview so they weren't in the best of moods. They got quite nasty when I tried to talk them down. I pity anyone who got on the wrong side of them!'

'Oh, you do surprise me,' Kate said truthfully.

'So would you consider a thong then?' Demelza asked, coming up behind her. 'I gotta lotta thongs. They're ever so popular, you know.' She looked at Kate. 'Not so much with old people though.'

'No, I really hadn't considered a thong.' Kate suppressed the desire to laugh. What *would* Woody say? Should she buy one just for the sheer hell of it? To see Woody's reaction? She looked at Demelza's bored face. 'But I see no reason why not!'

'What? A *thong*?' Demelza's eyes widened and her mouth fell open.

'Yes, a thong.' Kate was beginning to enjoy herself. 'I gather you don't have any waist-high, tummy-reducing, sensible-type pants?'

Demelza appeared to be speechless.

'So, I'll have a thong. Something a little naughty and fun, something my boyfriend might like. What would you recommend?'

It took Demelza a few moments to regain her composure. 'Yes, of course, size sixteen?'

The next day Kate was pleased when Woody arrived mid-afternoon.

'Can we have some coffee?' he asked, kissing the top of Kate's head.

He followed her into the kitchen. 'I've had a hell of a day with Robson. He seems to think I'm a local expert and know *everyone*. Where's the silly sister?'

'Trying to do a deal on The Locker,' Kate said with a sigh as she put a pod in the coffee machine.

'The *Locker*?'

'Yup, The Locker. She has fancy ideas about turning it into a bar. She's more than two hundred thousand pounds richer than she was when you last set eyes on her, thanks to the French mother-in-law who's just died.'

'Wow!' Woody rolled his eyes. 'It'll take even her a while to drink *that* much gin!'

Kate sighed. 'I have to presume she knows what she's doing. After all she's older than me, you know. And I'm fed up of trying to keep her on the straight and narrow, and now she's met this Fergal…'

'He's still on the scene?'

'Not only is he still on the scene but she's planning to involve him in this crazy business venture of hers, and have him live in the flat upstairs.'

'Maybe, just maybe, it might be the making of her,' Woody said. 'But a *bar*! I mean she's likely to drink away all the profits, isn't she?'

'Very probably,' said Kate. 'Let's talk about something else.'

'OK, I was at Launceston Police Station when the news came through.'

Kate stopped in her tracks. 'You did? What news?'

'Sharon Starkey was killed by having the back of her head smashed in. It's unclear if she was still alive or not when, and *if*, she was pushed downstairs, but her head injury and her death were *not* caused by any fall.'

'Oh my God, so my theory was right then. I can't believe this,' Kate said. 'So, did the killer pound her head against the step or something?'

'No, but we do know exactly what was used: one of the ornaments that was displayed on the hall table.'

'What, the lovely serpentine lighthouse and tin-mine?'

'The lighthouse, to be exact. Bill took them back to the station for forensics because whoever used it didn't have time to clean the damn thing afterwards.'

Kate poured the coffee. Shocked beyond belief, she sat down shakily on one of the kitchen chairs.

'Alas, no fingerprints,' Woody continued. 'Only Sharon's, and I guess that's because she dusted the things every day.'

'So the killer wore gloves?'

'It would appear so.'

Kate blinked away a tear as she took a sip of coffee. 'Poor, poor Sharon! This is horrendous!'

'Yeah,' Woody agreed, 'someone was making sure that she died. What beats me is that no one in that whole building actually came out, or heard anything, while the killer was *there*.'

Kate thought for a moment. 'Well, they're all elderly and hard of hearing I suppose. But yes, it does seem incredible, and makes me think she didn't fall down the stairs at all, but was just killed instantly with the lighthouse.'

'It's now a full-scale double-murder inquiry,' Woody said. 'None of the residents are allowed to leave the area, and that includes David Courtney.'

David Courtney. Kate's thoughts kept returning to David Courtney. The very fact that he'd been there, in Edina's flat, at that exact time, was surely far too much of a coincidence. He'd had the motive to kill his stepmother and presumably inherit the money, and he just *happened* to be there when Sharon was making the phone call. It would have been relatively easy to follow her down the stairs and hit her on the head when she was least expecting it, then attach the cord across the top to make it look like it was an accident.

Kate shuddered.

'Bill's very thorough, he'll find the killer,' Woody said firmly. 'He knew straight away that it wasn't the fall that killed Sharon, which is why the forensic guys took the carvings back to the station.'

'It's so horrible,' Kate said. 'Who could do such a thing? My money's on David Courtney.'

Woody put his hand over Kate's. 'It's time now for you to quit this sleuthing, Kate. I mean it. We have a killer in our midst and they likely know you're involved. You are in danger. Please, Kate, leave it to the police.'

'But—'

'No buts. You can have as many theories as you like, but keep clear of Seaview.'

'I can't refuse to go to Seaview if I'm needed. It's part of my job, OK? I just have to accept that they're all suspects but it's hard to imagine any *woman* being so brutal,' Kate said, refilling their cups.

'Believe me, women can be mighty evil,' Woody said, 'but when you question them, butter wouldn't melt in their mouths. Present company excepted, of course.'

'Of course,' Kate agreed. She still couldn't rule out the Potters or Hetty Patterson, unlikely though that might be. She could foresee another sleepless night ahead. And, if she did manage to snatch a few minutes' sleep, chances were that she'd have nightmares about who could be responsible for such heinous crimes.

Later, they went to bed at Lavender Cottage because Angie was with Fergal at The Locker Café.

'Let me have a couple of minutes to get undressed,' Kate said, heading for the bathroom.

'What's with the modesty?' Woody asked, sitting up in bed in his Mickey Mouse T-shirt with the *Police Gazette*.

Kate took a few minutes to remove her clothes and wrestle the thong into position, with the minimum discomfort to her crotch. Then she sashayed into the bedroom.

Half-asleep, Woody looked up from the *Police Gazette*.

'Holy moley!' he exclaimed.

CHAPTER TWENTY-SIX

The rest of the weekend was calm because Woody flatly refused to discuss the murders any further. They walked the dog, they went to the cinema, they ate Chinese. By Monday Kate was feeling almost normal again. Until she arrived at work to be told that Cornelius Crow had developed a worrying rash and, as he was forbidden to leave Seaview Grange for any reason, could he please be visited? Kate wondered at this; surely he was allowed to move around in the area?

She drove up to Higher Tinworthy and parked alongside a police car outside the Grange. The police officer got out of his car as he saw Kate get out of hers.

He studied Kate for a moment. 'Who are you visiting?'

'Cornelius Crow, Flat 5,' Kate replied.

He drew himself up to his full height, which couldn't have been more than five feet, seven inches. Policemen were not only getting younger, but shorter, Kate decided. When had they stopped recruiting tall people?

She shuddered involuntarily as she made her way upstairs, averting her eyes from the lower step. It appeared to have been thoroughly cleaned, and Kate wondered who was doing the cleaning now as she rang Cornelius Crow's doorbell.

'Come in, Nurse,' he droned as he opened the door and led her into a large, dimly lit room, mainly due to the heavy claret-coloured curtains pulled across the windows. In one corner was a long desk on which an old anglepoise lamp illuminated a laptop computer, which was surrounded by a sea of paperwork.

He drew back the curtain on one window and indicated a black leather sofa which faced the most enormous wall-mounted television screen that Kate had ever seen. 'Do sit down, Nurse.'

'You've got a rash, I understand?' Kate said as she sat down and opened the bag on her knee. She observed her patient, who was wearing what could only be called a smoking jacket, in black and silver brocade, with black jeans. It was a strange combination on a strange man who was studying her with his very strange, intense black eyes. 'Shall I have a look at it?'

She then caught sight of the enormous collection of framed movie posters which adorned the walls: *Paranormal Activity*, *The Exorcist*, *The Texas Chain Saw Massacre*, *The Shining*, *Halloween*, *The Silence of the Lambs*, *The Blair Witch Project*...

Kate shivered.

He watched her intently. 'I'm a movie fan,' he said.

'A *horror* movie fan,' Kate corrected. 'Don't tell me you enjoy watching stuff like this?'

'My dear woman, I *love* watching stuff like this! It gives me inspiration for the tales I tell, the books I write, the nice little twists of horror I can insert into my writing if it looks like it's becoming dull – little shocks to wake up the reader.'

For a moment Kate recalled childhood memories of herself and Angie hiding behind the sofa, one or the other peeping out from time to time to see if 'the scary bit' was over. In retrospect, and in comparison to this collection, these 'bits' were hardly scary at all.

'What about your rash?' Kate asked again.

He smiled. 'I must say I rang the surgery at a rather *rash* moment, my dear.' He gave a little laugh. 'I really wanted to ask you a few questions.'

'Are you telling me you *don't* have a rash, Mr Crow?'

'Oh, please, call me Cornelius.' He frowned. 'But never, *ever* call me Corny.'

'I wouldn't dream of it,' Kate said.

'In reply to your question: no, I don't have a rash. But I wondered if you could tell me a little more about the final moments of Edina's life? Did she hallucinate? Go into a coma? Have fits?'

Kate stared at him in horrified amazement. 'I've no idea. She died in hospital and, as you must be aware, she left here in a coma. Why do you ask?'

'Purely research for my next book. I fancy a poisoning for a change. I've been concentrating too much on stabbing and garrotting lately.'

'And *that's* why you wanted me to come up here?' Kate asked, annoyed. 'Surely you can do your research online?'

'Ah, but that was not the only reason,' Cornelius said. 'I'll confess I find you rather attractive. Like me, you seem to be drawn to crime. Fascinating, don't you think?'

Kate gulped. She needed to get out of here. 'Drawn to crime?'

'Yes, earlier this year you found a body on the beach, you then met the murderer and almost got killed, you were there when Edina was close to death and you arrived shortly after Sharon Starkey was killed. Why is that?'

'Pure coincidence,' Kate stuttered. For a brief moment she thought of Bill Robson who'd said much the same thing.

'I don't think so,' he said firmly. 'I think you gravitate towards crime without realising it. Would you like some coffee?'

'No thank you,' said Kate, looking towards the door.

'I'm sorry if I got you here on false pretences,' he droned on, 'but it seemed the only way to have an opportunity to see you on your own. And I wondered if I might invite you to dinner?'

'Dinner?' Kate echoed stupidly.

'I am a reasonable cook. I've never married, always had to look after myself.'

Kate's head was in a whirl. This strange man was asking her to dinner, here. She took a few moments to find her voice. 'It's most kind of you, Mr, er, Cornelius, but—'

'I realise you know nothing about me,' he interrupted, sitting down at the far end of the sofa, 'so I'll give you a little background. I was born in India where my father was in the Diplomatic Service and highly respected. I was the result of his dalliance with one of the Indian housemaids, and was brought up along with my three blond half-brothers. The strange thing is that their mother appeared not to notice, or at least not to mind my presence, but then again she was a remote figure to us all. She was a social animal and rarely in the house and I'm not at all sure she knew which children were hers anyway. We were all sent off to boarding school in Devon when we were five, and only allowed home for the long summer holidays. I was mostly ignored by my half-brothers and I never saw my natural mother again. She probably was sent to work elsewhere, but I've no idea why I was kept in the family.'

Kate couldn't help but feel moved. Here was a lonely man who most likely had never fitted in anywhere, who'd immersed himself in his writing, and who was offering to cook dinner for her.

She cleared her throat. 'I'm truly sorry, Cornelius, but I'm in a relationship so I don't feel I can accept your kind offer. But I am very flattered that you should ask me. Perhaps we can have a coffee together occasionally when I visit here?'

He shook his head. 'I *thought* you'd refuse. Never mind, I shan't detain you any longer. I'm sure you have many patients awaiting your attention.'

As Kate stood up and headed towards the door she tried hard to think of something else to say, to lighten the mood. But, before she had the opportunity to say anything, he'd opened the door and was ushering her out, saying loudly, 'Thank you for calling in, Nurse. I'll take your advice.'

And with that he shut the door firmly behind her.

For a moment Kate stood still, trying to digest what had just occurred. He had *actually* asked her to dinner, which he himself was presumably going to cook! Then he'd taken no for an answer and rapidly shown her the door. As she walked down the stairs Kate had already begun to worry. Had she offended him? But surely he must have known that she was in a relationship with Woody Forrest, since everyone else on the planet seemed to know.

As she crossed the deserted hallway she checked the table, where only a few letters lay on the undusted surface. The table looked empty without the two serpentine carvings, which were still presumably in police custody.

Should she have accepted his invitation? Kate then had another thought; perhaps he intended to poison her! Did he think she suspected *him*? Had he, in fact, poisoned Edina's ready meals? And had he killed Sharon?

Her head buzzing, Kate returned to the medical centre. Cornelius Crow's fathomless dark eyes haunted her for the rest of the day. Did he really fancy her or was he merely intending to finish her off? In which case was he guilty of the two killings? She'd been so convinced it had to be David Courtney. And now *this*.

Woody appeared later in the evening and suggested a drink at The Greedy Gull. As they seated themselves at a corner table Kate told him about her visit to Cornelius.

'First of all, he got me there on false pretences by saying he'd got a rash,' Kate told him, 'and I don't know what he'd have done if Elaine went instead of me.'

'Perhaps he's just got some sort of fetish about nurses,' Woody suggested.

She described the dark, gloomy room and the horror-film posters decorating the walls. Then she told him about Cornelius's invitation to dinner.

Woody took a hefty swig of his pint. 'Let's face it, you're not a bad-looking old broad!'

'*Old broad!*' Kate spluttered. 'Rinse your mouth out, *Abe!*' She knew how much he hated to be reminded of his real name. 'Just watch who you're calling an old broad!'

'Less of the *Abe*!' he instructed. 'Anyway, I like old broads and you're probably the best old broad around here. And seems like our friend Cornelius reckons that too.'

'Do you think he planned to poison me?' Kate asked.

'Possibly,' Woody said with a grin. 'We can't rule it out. On the other hand he might have cooked you a cordon bleu meal and completely won you over. Just be flattered, my love!' He peered at her over the rim of his glass. 'Not everything the residents say up there makes them killers. But, on that subject, what about the Pratts? After all, he was the person who supposedly "found" Sharon Starkey at the foot of the stairs.'

'But *he* was never a suspect. Gloria Pratt was the suspect.'

'They're *all* suspects,' Woody said, 'every single one of them, including the three old girls downstairs, not to mention Stan Starkey himself.'

'But Stan, according to Hetty, was at the far end of the garden at the time Sharon was killed,' Kate pointed out.

'Stan was at the far end of the garden *after* Sharon was killed,' Woody corrected. 'He could have had time to get out there before all the dozy oldies emerged from their apartments.'

'But why on earth would he have wanted to kill his own wife?' Kate asked. 'He was distraught when her body was found.'

'That could have been an act, Kate.' Then Woody, seeing Kate's horrified expression, added, 'I'm not saying it *was*. I'm just saying that some of the killers I've met over the years would have earned Oscars for their performances, for the weeping and the wailing. You're too trusting.'

'I just don't think Stan would have done it,' Kate said firmly. 'They were a nice ordinary couple.'

Woody shook his head. 'That's what I mean when I say you're too trusting. But that's one of the things I like about you.'

'Now you're being patronising,' Kate snapped. 'And don't forget, I'm a pretty good judge of character.'

'Yes, you are. Believe me, I want this thing done and dusted just as much as you do. If we don't get it sorted out soon I'm in danger of having to cancel my trip to California. I'm supposed to have retired but I'm up there every damned day at the moment. OK, can we change the subject now? How's that sister of yours making out with her business project?'

Kate sighed. 'She's obsessed with the idea of this bar. And of course Fergal is over the moon, but why wouldn't he be when he's going to be ensconced in a nice little flat? Anyway, the transaction appears to be going through and Angie has swapped being an artist and is going to be a landlady instead. She's planning some sort of Cornish theme, she says, and calling the place something like The Pirates' Cabin or The Smugglers' Den.'

'That means she'll be robbing unsuspecting tourists all summer, but what's she going to do in the winter?'

Kate shrugged. 'I've no idea. If I question her in any way she accuses me of being a pessimist, or having no faith in my own sister.'

'And *do* you have faith in your own sister?' Woody asked.

Kate visualised Angie's failure to get any decent acting roles and, more recently, the summerhouse bulging at the seams with unsaleable art.

'Not a lot,' she said.

'You never think I can do *anything*!' a petulant Angie shouted at Kate the following afternoon.

'Not true!' Kate replied. 'But I just want you to think this thing through properly before you go signing on the dotted line. Just remember that from November to March there are very few visitors here. Maybe a few at Christmas, that's all. You won't make money in the winter, will you?'

Angie rolled her eyes heavenwards. 'We'll attract *local* custom. We'll advertise and do special offers. We'll be *different*.'

'Des won't be too pleased,' Kate said, 'because he won't like competition and he has the backing of the brewery and all the local trade to see him through the winter.'

'Yes, but we'll have a *theme*,' Angie said in the patient voice of someone talking to a young child. 'Smugglers, pirates, shipwrecks – that sort of thing. Not just a tatty old seagull painted on each side of the fireplace!' She referred to Des Pardoe's artistic efforts at The Greedy Gull.

'Tourists might like your theme,' Kate said, 'but the locals are going to go to where the beer is cheap. I'm not being pessimistic, I'm being *realistic*. And don't go telling me that you're going to tog Fergal up as a *pirate* or something!' Kate snorted at the very idea.

There was a stony silence.

Kate looked at Angie in disbelief. 'You were *never* planning to tie a scarf round his head and make him wear an eye-patch, were you? A parrot on his shoulder, perhaps? Or a tricorn hat like Poldark? And you, with red curls, like a sixty-year-old Demelza? Mind you, you'd certainly be a sensation!'

Angie glared at her sister. 'Don't be ridiculous! I might have known you'd take that attitude! You haven't got an adventurous bone in your body!'

'I'm just trying to be practical, Angie, because these are not very practical ideas. The locals are Cornish, they've seen it all before, and they're not going to get excited by Fergal swanning around in a pirate's costume when they can go up to the pub. Most are beer and cider drinkers and Des has countless beers and ciders on tap. Get real!'

'Then we'll get by on our summer trade,' Angie said, 'because, after all, The Locker didn't do much trade in the winter, did it? And they've been going for years.'

Kate sighed. 'I'm not trying to be a killjoy, Angie, but I honestly don't want to see you lose money on this venture.'

'You just concentrate on nursing all those geriatrics of yours, and doing your detective work,' Angie retorted, 'and I'll concentrate on my proposed venture.'

CHAPTER TWENTY-SEVEN

The opportunity to tend to some geriatrics and do some detective work presented itself next day.

'You're not going to believe this,' Denise said. 'Ollie Pratt asked if you could call as he has some sort of sickness bug and he doesn't want to chance coming down to the surgery and spreading it around. I can't believe how many calls we're getting from the Grange! It was never like this when Elaine was doing it!'

'To be honest, I think they all need a bit of reassurance since the murders,' Kate said, 'and you can't really blame them.'

Kate got into her car and made that oh-so-familiar journey up to Seaview Grange again.

'Come in, come in, dear,' said a completely healthy-looking Ollie Pratt a short time later. 'I expect you could do with a nice cup of tea, couldn't you?'

'Well—'

'Gloria's got the kettle on,' he interrupted firmly as he shepherded her in the door.

The Pratts' living room was cluttered with newspapers, magazines, large jigsaw puzzles, shopping baskets, several packets of Mr Kipling's cakes, and two large Persian cats, who regarded her with disdain. There was an enormous hi-fi system in one corner, with innumerable CDs and DVDs everywhere, including the floor.

Kate stepped carefully over three CDs and one cat before lowering herself carefully onto the black vinyl settee. 'What seems to be the trouble, Mr Pratt?'

'I'll tell you in a minute,' he whispered. 'It's not me, you see, it's *Gloria*.' He pushed his finger to his lips just as Gloria waddled in.

'You might've done a bit of tidyin' up before you go askin' the nurse in here,' she said to her husband, who was frantically picking up the CDs and a couple of stray biscuits, one of which had been crushed into the multicoloured carpet. 'Sorry about this, Nurse, but I didn't know we was havin' a visitor.'

Gloria was fully made up, her blonde hair tied back in a ponytail, adorned with a pink scrunchie, and displaying several inches of grey roots.

There didn't appear to be anything wrong with either of them, and Kate wondered how to make her escape.

'Never mind, I got the kettle on,' Gloria said, fanning herself with a dog-eared copy of *Hello!* magazine. She was clad in a voluminous pink top, which reached almost to her knees, below which two chunky calves strained to be released from some leopard-skin-patterned leggings. Her other half, still frantically removing stuff from the floor, was displaying an indecent amount of builders' crack each time he bent down, as his jogging bottoms parted company with his T-shirt.

Mugs of tea were produced, along with assorted packets of cakes and biscuits.

'A Bakewell slice?' Gloria offered.

'No, thank you,' Kate replied, 'I'll just have the tea.'

'A country slice?' Ollie was holding out one of the Mr Kipling boxes in her direction. When Kate refused he jammed one into his mouth and said, 'They're my favourites, they are.'

Why on earth was she here? Kate wondered. Surely *they* weren't going to be inviting her to dinner? As if reading her thoughts, Ollie was making faces to the effect that he couldn't say what he wanted to say in front of Gloria, who seemed completely unaware that he'd contacted the medical centre. Several minutes later after discussing the weather, Gloria heaved herself out of the chair she'd been sitting on and said, 'The buns must be nearly ready and I promised to take some in to Violet and Daisy.'

'Gloria's a wonderful baker,' Ollie informed Kate as his wife made her way into the kitchen, which was partitioned off from the rest of the room. A few minutes later Gloria reappeared with a Tupperware box and announced she was taking some buns to the Potters. And would Kate like to take some home? Kate politely declined.

When she'd gone out and he reckoned she was out of earshot he murmured, 'I think she's tryin' to kill me.'

Kate almost dropped her cup. '*What?*'

He patted his huge belly, then spoke quietly with one eye on the door. 'I've been havin' a lot of problems with my digestion lately, and I got a feelin' she's puttin' somethin' in my food.'

'Why on earth would she want to do that?' Kate asked, refusing his further offer of a country slice with a shake of her head.

Ollie stuffed another one in his mouth. 'At least I know Mr Kiplin' ain't plannin' to finish me off!' He laughed, and a passing crumb missed Kate by inches.

'So what would she be putting in your food?' Kate asked, wondering if this could be the source of the digoxin.

'I dunno. But me food tastes funny and she's actin' funny. Jealous like. Always *was* jealous of Edina, of course.'

'But Edina is no longer with us, so why now?'

'Well, it wouldn't surprise me if she saw off Edina, and now she's got it in for me!'

'Ollie, don't you think your imagination might be running away with you?'

Ollie shook his head, still glancing towards the door. 'She likes to help a bit in the garden, you know, and Stan keeps a load of weed killer in his shed.' He narrowed his eyes and nodded as if to confirm. 'Now, how much weed killer would it take to kill someone, eh?' He leaned forward and lowered his voice some more. 'She's not the full shilling, you know – hasn't been for years.'

'She seems perfectly sensible to me,' Kate said quietly.

'But she *ain't*. I just wanted you to know, see, so that if you find me dead one of these days you'll know why. More tea?'

'No thank you, that was very nice,' Kate said, hurriedly draining her cup. 'I think perhaps you might be a little oversensitive at the moment, Ollie. I think everyone here is. Why don't you help Gloria with the cooking and the baking and then you can see exactly what she's putting in the food?'

He glanced back towards the door. 'She wants a divorce.'

'She *does*?'

'Yeah, she's been on about it for months. But she don't want to leave here, see and, if we divorced, we'd have to sell this and go our separate ways. But, if she was a *widow*, well…' He paused and grimaced. 'She'd be laughin', wouldn't she?'

At that moment Gloria came back in.

'Sure you don't wanna try one of me buns?' she asked Kate.

'Most kind, but I won't, thank you,' Kate replied, getting hastily to her feet. 'I must be going. But thanks very much for the tea.'

'Don't forget what I told you,' Ollie said quietly as he escorted her to the door. 'I reckon she's got it in for me.'

Kate didn't feel she could take Ollie's fears seriously. She decided not to mention the strange visit to Woody. And then she wondered who the management had sent to replace Sharon. She should have asked Ollie and Gloria.

Sharon had not only cleaned their flats and the communal areas, she had carried their shopping upstairs, delivered the post from where it was left on the hall table to the incapacitated, and generally kept an eye on them.

How was Stan coping? He had plenty of jobs to do outside so couldn't possibly give the residents much individual attention. And he was only recently widowed and undoubtedly bereft so probably didn't fancy doing much of anything. Kate wondered if she should contact him to see how he was doing, although she wasn't altogether sure how she could offer to help. Nevertheless, as she left the Pratts' flat, she decided to have a walk round outside to see if she could see him. She found Stan at the top of a ladder repairing some stonework on one of the chimney stacks.

He waved and began to descend.

'Don't let me stop you,' Kate said, 'I know you're busy.'

'No, I've been tryin' to keep myself occupied so I can stop myself from thinkin' about Sharon,' he said as he reached ground level. 'It's on my mind all the time unless I'm doin' something. But it's time for a cup of tea.'

She followed him into the old stable building and watched as he filled up the red kettle and set it on the Aga.

'How are you feeling?' Kate asked, looking at his sad face. 'Or is that a stupid question?'

'It ain't a stupid question, Kate. The truth is I'm feelin' bloody awful. But I was hopin' you'd get in touch because I know Sharon thought a lot of you and valued your opinion.'

'Oh, I wouldn't say that,' Kate murmured guiltily.

'She did. And she'd want you to help me now.'

Kate wondered what was coming. 'How can I help you?'

'You can help me to find out who killed my lovely Sharon,' he said as he located a couple of mugs. 'The police have gone through everything thoroughly and admit they've found nothin', but I still think they might have missed somethin'. It's got to be one of the residents and I want to know who it is and why they killed her. It's the least I can do.' He sniffed. 'The keys to all them flats were in the pocket of Sharon's apron but the police have given them back to me. I think you owe it to Sharon cos, after all, it was you that asked her. I'm not blamin' you and I know Sharon was as keen as anybody to find out who it was, ever since that Martinelli woman accused her of trying to trip her down the stairs. Sharon told me that you'd asked for her help to find some evidence, so somebody needs to have a good old scout around because Sharon must have been on to something after she'd done the rounds that mornin'.'

'Yes, you're right,' Kate said. 'She called me.'

'There you are then! We *know* she found somethin' in someone's flat, but *whose*?'

'Do you have any idea which flats she'd cleaned and which she hadn't that morning?' Kate asked.

'No I don't.'

Kate thought for a moment. 'But would we find anything *now*? Surely the police did a search? And what about her phone?'

'They took enough time goin' through everythin',' he said as he poured the tea and handed her the Princess Diana mug, 'but they haven't found her phone and they should be able to see Sharon's bright pink phone a mile off. If we could find that phone we'd know who the killer is. Now *where* would you have disposed of somethin' if you'd used it to kill someone? Sharon said somethin' about a syringe?'

'That's right,' Kate said. 'She phoned me from upstairs, and that would indicate that whoever killed her lived up there.'

'But why would she risk phonin' from up there if she didn't think it was safe?' Stan pulled out a couple of chairs from under the kitchen table and signalled Kate to sit down. 'So she must have thought it wasn't any of them upstairs, mustn't she?'

Kate wasn't so sure. 'So, in that case, who else could it be?'

'The Pratts,' he said.

And they were the ones who said they had heard something but didn't go out to see what was happening.'

'And then there's them women of course,' Stan said.

'What – the Potters and Hetty? Why would any of the old ladies *want* to kill Sharon?'

He tapped his nose. 'There's no tellin'. There's somethin' a bit funny with that Hetty, and the Potters are desperate to move into Edina's flat, and keep nagging me about it. It's nought to do with me. But I'm goin' to ask you a favour; I was goin' to phone and ask you anyway. Them flats need searchin' thoroughly to see if the police might have missed somethin' and I need your help for that. Because whoever killed my Sharon has her phone hidden somewhere.'

'What could I possibly do to help you search the flats?' Kate felt a mixture of excitement and trepidation at the idea.

'We're goin' to be needin' a new cleaner and you could say you were helpin' me out in the meantime,' he replied.

'All right,' she said, realising it was too good an opportunity to miss. 'But I am a witness as far as the police are concerned so let's hope they don't find out.'

Then, almost at once, Kate began to doubt her wisdom at agreeing to help. The thought of snooping around in other people's flats was a somewhat frightening idea. What if she got caught? And surely the police would already have discovered any incriminating evidence? And what would Woody say? How often had he told her to 'not get involved'!

'Now,' he continued, 'they're all goin' on a day's outing to Cothele tomorrow because I'm drivin' the bus and I'm goin' with them, see? Ten quid a head, light lunch included. The damned thing was booked a month ago although I don't much feel like goin' now. Still, at least they've all got to stay together and I've got to make damned sure they do. We'll be out all day.'

'And…' Kate said tremulously.

'And I'll give you the keys before we set off.'

Oh Lord, Kate thought. 'Are they *all* going?'

'I'm tryin' to persuade them all to go, that's for sure,' Stan said. 'At the moment the only doubtful is Cornelius Crow, who likes to be cooped up in that gloomy flat of his all day. But I'm workin' on him.'

'Tomorrow?' Kate asked.

'Tomorrow, dear. We'll be leavin' here around nine o'clock and I don't reckon we'll be back much before five, so plenty of time for you to have a good nosy around.'

Kate gulped. Then again this was her golden opportunity to do something constructive.

'Stan, I'm not too happy with this idea, you know.'

'You'd be doin' it for my Sharon,' he said, 'not for me.'

'And you could guarantee that all the flats would be empty for hours on end?'

'Of course I can. How else are they goin' to get back if not on the bus?'

'What about David Courtney?'

'He comes and goes. No tellin'.' Stan shrugged. 'But unlikely he'll be around. He's got a garage to run, such as it is.'

'So, do you want me to do some actual cleaning then?' Kate asked, visualising all the cobwebby corners in Lavender Cottage, not to mention the less-than-pristine oven, the messy fridge and the salt-sprayed windows that required washing and polishing.

'No, just pick up a duster or somethin' if anyone sees you. Not that they *will*,' he added hastily.

Kate was being pulled in two directions. As well as having to get past the policeman who was normally parked outside, she'd almost certainly be breaking the law if she were to be discovered, uninvited, looking through drawers and cupboards. On the other hand she just *might* be able to find some tiny detail that the police had overlooked. Something that might even solve the case! Unlikely, but just possible. Sometimes you had to stretch the law the tiniest bit.

'OK,' Kate said after a few minutes' contemplation, 'but perhaps you should tell them in advance that I might be dashing around with a duster and a mop?'

'No,' he said firmly. 'If they get wind of the fact that anyone's goin' to be in their flats they'll all have a massive tidy-up, and we don't want that, do we? If they've become slap-happy since the police looked around, then we want them to stay that way. One of them might have got careless.'

'Hmm,' Kate said. Then, after a minute, 'All right, I'll do it. Leave the keys for me somewhere when you leave in the morning and make sure they all have a sticker or something on them indicating which flat they're for. I don't want to be jingling keys around, trying various ones in the doors, when David Courtney could be around.'

'No problem,' he said. 'In the residents' lounge there's a little table in front of the window with a drawer in the top. I'll leave the keys in there and the outside door will be open.'

CHAPTER TWENTY-EIGHT

With every passing hour Kate was regretting more and more her decision to snoop. Five flats full of drawers, cupboards and goodness-knows-what. How thorough could she be?

In the evening Stan phoned. 'We're all set for the outin' tomorrow,' he said. 'I've even been able to persuade bloody Cornelius to come as well.'

'What about David Courtney?' Kate asked. 'Do you think he's likely to show up?'

'Well, he's back in Exeter most of the time although I think the cops are keepin' an eye on him. He's very unlikely to be puttin' in an appearance but I've had a good nosey round Edina's flat anyway, so you just concentrate on Cornelius's, Edgar's and the ones downstairs.'

'And what about the policeman who's normally on duty at the gate?'

'Oh, he comes and goes. Now I come to think of it, he's not normally there on a Thursday. They've a weekly meetin' at the station or somethin'.'

Five flats, Kate thought. *Spend an hour and a bit in each; start at ten, finish at four, allow an hour after they leave and before they come back…*

She was feeling increasingly nervous about this whole thing, aware that she was stepping into very dangerous territory here. She'd be very glad when it was all over.

*

On Thursday morning, having ensured the policeman was not on duty, Kate found the keys in the drawer and made her way nervously upstairs, brandishing a duster and a mop. She closed Edgar's door quietly behind her.

The place was a lot tidier than it had been on her first visit, but where to start? There was a bureau in front of the window which was probably as good a place as any. In the first drawer she found a collection of what appeared to be old sermons, along with a couple of Bibles and hymn books. There was a drawer of photographs, all higgledy-piggledy: Edgar with presumably his wife at some sort of official function. She appeared satin-clad, with a corrugated-iron-type perm and didn't look at all pleased at being there. There were dozens of photos, all featuring the same lady. *He should put them in an album*, she thought, then remembered her own random snaps lying around in boxes and drawers. Funny how you never got round to putting the things in order.

Another drawer full of more sermons, hymn sheets, letters from grateful parishioners: '*Dear Reverend, Thank you so much for the beautiful service you conducted for my husband last Tuesday…*'; '*Dear Rev., Thanks for doing my daughter Kaitlin's wedding last Saturday. It was lovely…*'

Notepaper, envelopes, paperclips, elastic bands – the Reverend had the lot.

Kate made her way to the kitchen. A recipe book lay on the table top, *Cooking for One*. Poor Edgar. There was also the usual quota of cutlery and crockery, nothing sinister there. Edgar appeared to have a penchant for spaghetti hoops in tomato sauce, these outnumbering baked beans by two to one. He was keen on tinned sardines too. And tinned custard, rice, prunes. The fridge was no more exciting: two Fernfield Farm meals – one cottage pie, one shepherd's pie – both intact, no pinpricks. He liked cheese, bacon and sausages. The bedroom was next. Edgar did not appear to have many clothes; those he owned were well worn: jackets patched at the elbows, shirts with frayed cuffs, scuffed shoes. Were vicars paid so badly? How come he could afford to live here? And then she recalled that he'd told her that his wife had bought the flat.

A drawer full of vests and Y-fronts, another full of dog-collars, socks (mainly black), a few cufflinks. Few personal possessions compared to most people she knew.

Kate took a deep breath. This whole exercise was ridiculous! No one in their right mind would leave any evidence lying around after five weeks. Rubbish would have been collected at least twice and, according to Woody, that would have been searched anyway. So, where else would someone hide a phone and a syringe?

Kate closed Edgar's door quietly behind her and headed across to Cornelius's flat. She had, of course, already been in this creepy abode once before, and was not relishing the prospect of visiting again.

As before, the heavy curtains were drawn across the windows, dimming the interior. She pulled them open, reminding herself to close them again when she left. The effect was instantly brighter but scarcely more cheerful; the posters on the walls looked more lurid than ever and the clutter more apparent. There was a shelf housing hundreds of DVDs which she'd not noticed before. No surprises there; they were practically all horror films. And another shelf with all his books. She hadn't realised he'd written so many. What a disturbing world this man existed in!

Kate hadn't noticed the metal filing cabinet before either. It was next to the table where the laptop and the anglepoise lamp were. Inside were files packed with correspondence (mainly with his publisher), insurance documents, brochures, computer supplies and all the normal paraphernalia of everyday living. Only one piece of paper, with very little written on it, caught her eye, and she lifted it out.

If you don't stop that noise I'm going to find a way to silence you.

Edina had been right; it had been Cornelius who'd posted the note in her letterbox. Kate studied the copy carefully. She wondered if the print was different because perhaps he'd practised a few times to get the font right.

It didn't, of course, necessarily make him the killer, but he was rapidly heading to the top of The List again. And it made it imperative that she searched this flat very thoroughly.

The kitchen was relatively tidy with nothing suspicious residing amongst the cutlery and crockery. Cornelius had a lot of tins in his cupboard and very little in his fridge other than some milk and a half-eaten loaf. He did like a drink though; Kate found two bottles of Scotch and three of gin, plus several packs of tonics and sodas.

The bathroom was very untidy, with discarded damp towels strewn across the floor, shaving things balanced on the handbasin, shampoo and bath-oil bottles teetering precariously on the edge of the bath. The cabinet only contained some expensive aftershave, mouthwash and several packets of Alka-Seltzer – probably to counteract his consumption of the Scotch and gin.

The bedroom was, in contrast, almost minimalist. Cornelius had a king-size bed with a black satin cover. There were no other adornments: no cushions on the bed or rugs on the highly polished floor. There was a dressing-table with a couple of small drawers containing scissors, nail clippers, odd tissues and the like – all very mundane. He had an extensive wardrobe with a great many smart suits, tuxedos and smoking jackets. Why? Where did he go? She went through the pockets and checked inside his shoes which, she reckoned, would make an ideal hiding place for a phone. Then she burrowed among his silk boxer shorts, neatly folded socks, expensive ties and monogrammed handkerchiefs, but found no phone or anything whatsoever that could be used to inject poison into Edina's meal.

Sighing with frustration and not a little disappointed, Kate was almost out the door before she glanced back and remembered she had to draw the curtains across again. Then she headed downstairs to check on the Pratts' possessions.

Inside Flat 3 she had never seen so many packets of cakes and biscuits, a freezer full of oven chips, ice cream, desserts. You could almost gain half a stone just looking at this stuff. Kate headed straight for the bathroom cupboard.

'Beachcomber Blonde' proclaimed the packet of home-dye, alongside the leg-waxing kit, the eyelash dye and a set of false nails. Was any of this woman real? And was all this beautification just for Ollie? Or competing with Edina perhaps? There were syringes but they were pen syringes, which Kate knew could not be used for anything other than insulin. Well, that would appear to rule out any possibilities there.

Both the lounge and the bedroom were messy: cheap magazines scattered everywhere, one cat sitting on the coffee table alongside a packet of shortbread, another on the windowsill washing its face. The bedside cabinets yielded only pills, packets of peppermints and tissues.

Kate replaced everything carefully. She looked out at the two pots on their patio, both crammed with straggling end-of-summer geraniums and well-established weeds. No one had been digging in there for months. So much for Ollie's theory that Gloria liked gardening, so perhaps she really did help Stan so she could get her hands on the weedkiller! Poor Ollie!

The Potter twins' flat was next.

She tiptoed across the hall and let herself in. Not a sound anywhere. The silence was a little eerie.

The twins had left their lounge very tidy with cushions plumped up and a neat pile of *Woman's Weekly* magazines on the coffee table. The drawers in their sideboard yielded lace doilies, tablecloths, napkins and napkin rings, and bundles of photographs. Two identical little girls in knitted bathing-suits on a pebbly beach somewhere, both brandishing buckets and spades. More and more photos of the two of them; this one, side by side, in gymslips and wrinkly stockings, probably lisle. Another one in their liberty bodices and navy school knickers, a hankie peeping coquettishly out of a pocket. Kate wished she had time to study them all in detail in this forties time warp.

The kitchen was predictable and Kate found nothing untoward. The twins favoured doing their own cooking with a cupboard full of all manner of flour, baking soda, rice, split peas, lentils, not many tins and no sign whatsoever of any instant meals, Fernfield Farm or otherwise.

The bathroom shelves were full of talcum powders, Steradent and boxes of pills. Anything sinister could only be in the bedroom, which was pink. There were twin beds with frilled white covers tidily in place. The bedside cabinets contained some Mills & Boon paperbacks and more pills, countless pills, for anything and everything: headaches, sore throats, coughs, indigestions, constipation and diarrhoea, to name but a few. These ladies were taking no chances. No digoxin, though, and no syringes. The wardrobes contained sensible coats and tweed skirts, the drawers (all with lavender sachets) filled with neatly folded blouses and jumpers. There was a drawer containing knickers and vests, and more lavender sachets. A photograph of a stern-looking lady with tight lips and a tight perm dominated the top of one of the bedside cabinets. It had to be Mother. No sign of Father, though. No sign of a pink phone or anything else.

Kate glanced at her watch. Three o'clock. Time to move on to Hetty's flat, not that she expected to find much there. This really was a wild goose chase.

Hetty's flat was equally predictable except that her reading matter was more sophisticated. She had lots of classics on her shelves, plus

Tolstoy, Joyce and, glory of glories, Hilary Mantel! Lying on her coffee table was a neatly folded copy of the *Guardian*. Who would have thought it! Kate had been convinced Hetty was a *Telegraph* reader. You never did know with people!

Hetty appeared to do her own cooking too, with no microwaveable meals or instant anythings. She seemed very keen on tomato juice, Camembert, and vanilla yoghurts. In the bathroom was talcum powder again (*somebody* was still buying the stuff), more Steradent, mouthwash, aspirin. No digoxin, no syringes. In the bedroom, alongside the neat and tidy single bed, was a collection of hardback library books next to a large alarm clock and a covered jug of water. The top book was an Agatha Christie.

Kate looked idly out of the window at Hetty's flowerpots. Whatever bedding plants had been growing in there had been removed and the soil weeded and turned over. Well, at least one of the residents appeared to do some gardening.

As she turned back into the room she stumbled on the edge of a sheepskin rug and went flying into a pink bedroom chair which crashed to the floor, Kate with it. She picked herself up slowly, feeling very foolish. She straightened the rug, replaced the chair and headed back to the dressing-table to double-check the jewellery drawer when she heard a door opening somewhere. She froze for a second. Was it Hetty's outside door?

Just as she turned back to examine the jewellery drawer, the bedroom door opened.

'What the hell are you doing in here?' David Courtney asked.

CHAPTER TWENTY-NINE

Kate gulped and pushed the drawer in hurriedly.

'Dusting,' she replied. 'That's what I'm doing in here.' But, as she was speaking she noticed she'd left the duster hanging on the doorknob, right beside where he was standing. She hoped he hadn't noticed, but he had.

He picked up the cloth and held it at arm's length. '*Dusting?* Long-range dusting? Remote-control dusting?'

Kate struggled to compose herself because she realised that only a show of confidence now could get her out of this mess.

'Dusting,' she repeated as she pushed the drawer back in. 'Stan asked me to do some cleaning while everyone was out. So that's precisely what I'm doing.'

'Last I heard you were a nurse,' he said sarcastically.

'I *am* a nurse,' Kate replied, 'but I'm just helping out. And even *you* must have noticed that they've lost their cleaner.'

He crossed the room and pulled open the drawer she had hastily shut. 'What exactly are you doing in Hetty's jewellery drawer?' he asked.

'I was about to dust it, but it had stuck. I've just managed to loosen it.' Kate knew that sounded feeble. She pushed the drawer shut again. 'And I could ask you the same question: what are *you* doing in Hetty's flat?'

'Hetty is a friend of mine and was a very close friend of my stepmother's. I've got a key to this flat in case she needs help of some sort.' His eyes narrowed. 'What exactly are you looking for?'

'Dust,' Kate replied, grabbing the duster from him.

'I don't believe you.' He came towards her and pulled open the drawer again. 'Were you planning to help yourself to some jewellery, perhaps? Sell it on? Supplement your lowly income?'

'I *told* you. I'm here to do some light cleaning. And, come to that, why *exactly* are *you* here?'

'To see who was in Hetty's flat when I knew she would be out. I heard a crashing sound as I came down the stairs from my stepmother's flat.'

Kate cursed her clumsiness that had resulted in her tripping and the accompanying noise. In any case she plainly couldn't now examine the contents of the jewellery drawer, but at least she'd examined everything else. Time to go. She wished he'd disappear.

'I shall have to tell Hetty that you were in here,' David Courtney said sanctimoniously.

'Tell her whatever you like,' Kate snapped, 'because Stan will confirm that he asked me to clean.'

'In the jewellery drawer?'

Kate sighed. 'OK, so I'm nosy. Just wanted to have a look, that's all. I am *not* a thief.'

'I shall ask Hetty to check everything,' he said, 'and there'd better not be anything missing.'

'Nothing *is* missing,' Kate snapped, 'but not everyone is as honest as Sharon was so I'd suggest you tell her to lock away her valuables before a new cleaner arrives.'

'I'd like you to leave this flat right now,' he commanded.

'I've finished anyway,' she said as she walked towards the door.

He glared at her but said nothing as Kate swanned past him and let herself out into the hallway. She stood there for a moment, thoroughly shaken. What on earth would happen now? Would David Courtney make a complaint? And say that he found her looking in the jewellery drawer? She should *never* have agreed to this mad idea of Stan Starkey's, never. What if Bill Robson got to hear about this little incident? And what on earth would Woody say?

Feeling sick to her stomach, Kate replaced the duster and mop in the cupboard and headed to her car. She'd like to wait to see if he left as well. As she saw him appear in the doorway she waited for a moment and was then relieved to see him get into his own car and drive away. Would he come back? Why had he come there in the first place? Hopefully, he hadn't seen her sitting in her car. Would he have remembered their conversation in Exeter when she told him she had a Punto?

Kate waited five minutes, then got out of her car and walked round to where she knew Stan kept his gardening stuff in the search for a trowel, because she'd had a sudden idea.

Fortunately, Stan's gardening shed was unlocked and inside Kate found everything arranged in orderly fashion with trowels, forks and other short-handled tools arranged tidily on a shelf. She had precisely one hour to do some digging before the residents returned. She looked round the corner to the front of the building again to ensure that David Courtney had not returned while she was in the shed, and fortunately there was no sign of him.

Armed with a trowel and a plastic pail, Kate began to remove some of the compost from the first of Hetty's pots. She realised she could well be wasting her time because who was to say that Hetty hadn't been forking over her pots before planting winter pansies or something?

As she dug deep into the pot she heard the sound of a car approaching up the drive. Kate peered nervously round the edge of the building, horrified to see David Courtney had returned. She quickly emptied the soil from the pail back into the pot, spilling some in her haste, but that couldn't be helped. She had to get away from here; digging in Hetty's flower pots could hardly be classed under the heading of cleaning. She'd have some explaining to do – *further* explaining to do if David Courtney reported her.

Kate dashed back to the shed and replaced the trowel and the pail. She waited in there, heart pounding, until she reckoned he was safely inside and hopefully *not* looking out the window. Then she edged round from the back of the house and, keeping close to the wall, tiptoed round to the front. She only wished she hadn't left Hetty's patio in such a mess.

Kate switched on the ignition, started up the motor and drove a short distance away to where she knew there was sheltered layby. It was only then she realised she still had the keys to the flats in her pocket. She didn't dare go back in case the bus got there at the same time as she did. She decided to wait there, hidden, until she saw the bus return and then she'd seek out Stan Starkey, hand back the keys, and tell him what had happened. She didn't want to be seen by any of the residents at the Grange again this evening.

It was quarter past five before the bus came back and its passengers disembarked slowly and wearily. Kate then wondered if Stan would have to return the bus to wherever he'd hired it from, but instead he parked it round the side of the house. She waited a few minutes to give him time to get into the old stables again before she walked back to the Grange.

Stan was just filling up the kettle as she peered in the open door.

'Ah, Kate!' He came forward and closed the door behind her. 'Any luck?'

Kate shook her head as she handed back the keys. 'Not only did I not find anything, but I managed to upset David Courtney as well.'

She told him about her search in all the flats, ending in Hetty's, and how she'd tripped, sent a chair flying, and attracted David's attention.

'He had a key to her flat, he told me, so he could help her in an emergency. And I was just about to search the drawer which contained her jewels,' Kate said, 'so he couldn't have come in at a worse moment. He virtually accused me of not only trespassing but also being about to rob Hetty of her jewellery.'

'Well, you had a good excuse, hadn't you?' Stan suggested hopefully.

'Not good enough, I suspect. And it must have looked suspicious, I suppose. He'll certainly inform Hetty of all this, but what if he reports me to the police?'

Stan patted her shoulder. 'Listen, if there's nothin' missin' from that drawer then why would the bugger report anythin' to anyone?'

'You don't suppose he might deliberately remove something just to get me in trouble, do you?' Kate asked anxiously.

'Why the hell would he do *that*?' Stan looked genuinely surprised.

'Well, just to get me off his back, perhaps. Oh, I don't know… And that's not all, Stan. I wanted to have a look in Hetty's flowerpots on the patio.'

'*Flowerpots?* What do you mean?'

'Well, the soil had been dug over recently by the look of it. And, if you wanted to get rid of something like a phone, and you knew that the general rubbish was likely to be examined, where would be an unlikely place to hide it?'

'Never thought of that,' said Stan. 'So, did you manage to have a look?'

'I only got halfway down the first one,' Kate replied, 'when I heard David Courtney coming back again, so I had to quickly replace the soil and I spilt an awful lot of it. I'm really sorry.'

'Don't worry,' Stan said after a moment. 'If she says anything to me I'll just say that a bird must've been lookin' for a worm or somethin' in there.'

'It would have had to be a pretty big bird,' Kate said, grinning at him ruefully.

*

Feeling deflated and worried, Kate got home at quarter to six. She'd found nothing incriminating, she'd managed to antagonise David Courtney – who was now as suspicious of her as she was of him – and she'd made a mess on Hetty's patio. Would the old lady notice when she got back and looked out of her sitting-room window?

As she made herself a cup of coffee, Kate tried to justify to herself what she'd done. What if David Courtney had reported her to the police, saying he'd caught her red-handed in Hetty's jewellery drawer? That could cost her her job and would most certainly not endear her to Bill Robson.

Perhaps Angie and Woody were right about her not getting involved; it should all be left to the police. But she'd so badly wanted to help Stan find Sharon's – and Edina's – killer.

Kate's mind was in a complete whirl when Woody phoned half an hour later.

'Hi!' he said.

'Hi,' she replied.

There was a pause. 'Are you OK?' he asked. 'You sound a little down.'

'No, I'm fine,' she lied.

'OK then, shall we have a drink in The Gull later?'

Kate hesitated. He'd know something was amiss if she refused his invitation.

'Or would you prefer to come over here?' he asked.

Well, if they were going to have an almighty row it would probably be better to have it in private.

'I'll come over about half past seven,' Kate replied without enthusiasm.

This could be the proverbial straw that broke the camel's back, she reckoned as she ended the call. And he was now almost certainly aware that all was not well.

*

Woody had lit the woodburner and switched on all the table lamps, which provided a cosy, intimate atmosphere.

'Wine?' he asked as Kate sat down on the sofa.

'Gin, please,' Kate replied, 'and tonic.'

After a few minutes he reappeared with two glasses containing hefty measures of gin, plus cans of tonic and slices of lemon.

As Kate helped herself Woody said, 'You look like you need that.'

'I do,' Kate confirmed. It was no good; she'd have to tell him.

He leaned forwards and they clinked glasses. 'What's up?' he asked.

'Well,' Kate said, 'where do I begin?' She took a long gulp of her drink and then gave him a detailed account of what had happened.

Woody sighed. 'Honestly, Kate, how often have I told you not to get involved? Don't you care that I'm worried? After all, I've every reason to be.'

Kate could hear the disappointment in his voice. 'I'm sorry, Woody, and I do care – very much – that you worry about me. And I know that, perhaps, I shouldn't have agreed to do this, but I might just have found *something*. And, if I'd had more time, I'm sure I would have found something in Hetty's flowerpots.'

'Hetty's *flowerpots?*'

'Yes, her flowerpots were the only ones that had recently been disturbed. *Think* about it, Woody! If you wanted to get rid of a phone or a syringe or something, where would be an unlikely place to hide it?'

'So, is Hetty now top of your list?'

'Well, no, because *anybody* could have hidden something in the flowerpot.'

Woody groaned.

'Are you going to shout at me?' she asked.

Woody sighed. 'Why would I do that?'

'Because David Courtney might report me to Bill Robson,' Kate said, 'and *he's* not my biggest fan.'

'That's true,' said Woody. He looked out the window for a moment. 'But surely you had every right to be in there if Stan had asked you to do some cleaning?'

'Yes, and it was pure coincidence that I was just about to start examining Hetty's jewellery drawer when he came in. I mean, it must have looked a bit dodgy, don't you think?'

Woody nodded. 'Yeah, that would take some explaining, I guess. OK, try not to worry about it, Kate.'

'And let's get this straight,' Kate said, sitting bolt upright, 'I did *not* remove a thing from that damned drawer! I hadn't even had a chance to look inside it.'

'I believe you, my love,' he said. 'You've no need to convince me. Another gin? Incidentally, I have to go up to London tomorrow for a police reunion thing, but I'm back Saturday evening and I'll call you then. Just try, will you, not to get into any more trouble while I'm gone?'

'As if,' Kate replied.

CHAPTER THIRTY

Kate had only just finished washing off the salt and sand which was stuck to the front windows of Lavender Cottage due to the previous night's Atlantic gale, when she heard the ping from her phone which heralded the arrival of a message.

The message was from Sharon. *What?* How *could* it be from Sharon?

It's me – Stan. I've found Sharon's phone, the message read, *and I think I know who killed her and Edina. I've found something interesting. Meet me at the garden shed at 5 o'clock. Be careful, don't be seen, park the car somewhere else.*

Wow! Kate stood transfixed by the screen for a moment. At last…! She wondered if good old Stan had managed to find something incriminating somewhere as well as the phone. She wondered why he was texting her on Sharon's phone but of course he wouldn't have her number on his own phone. Come to think of it, she'd never seen Stan with a phone. Perhaps he didn't have one himself. Perhaps he'd had an opportunity to go through Hetty's pots and her own hunch had been correct. She wondered at the secrecy; perhaps the killer was aware that he or she had been rumbled and was on the lookout? As regards hiding the car, all the residents of Seaview Grange – and everyone else for that matter – must know by now that she drove a red Fiat Punto, which would look far too conspicuous parked in front of the house. She rang Sharon's number but there was no reply, so there was no way she could contact him to check that he had in fact sent the message. She knew she really should phone the police, but what if David Courtney had reported her for being in Hetty's flat?

Kate consulted her watch: 4 p.m. She wished Woody was around; she always felt safer when he was nearby. He would, of course, tell her it was some sort of trap and not to get involved. After all, Stan could well be the killer and she'd be walking into trouble. *Could* Stan be the killer? And, if not, was he in danger too?

In the meantime she decided she should tell her sister she was going out. She went up to the summerhouse to tell Angie and found her sister burrowing amongst her canvases and in a state of high excitement.

'I've just had a phone call from Luke down at The Gallery,' she said, 'and he's sold my "Indian Sunset" painting!'

'Hey, that's terrific news!' Kate said. 'Many congratulations!'

Angie's abstract art didn't do an awful lot for Kate but nevertheless she was truly delighted for her sister. Even if 'Indian Sunset' had been languishing in The Gallery for six months.

'Do you know who's bought it?' Kate asked.

'A tourist,' Angie replied. 'A tourist with great taste, obviously. And I'm now looking around for another one in the hope that Luke can sell that too. After that I'm meeting up with Fergal in Launceston, after I've been into the estate agent and signed the contract for buying The Locker Café.'

'Wow!' Kate exclaimed. 'You're having quite a day, aren't you? I'm off to Seaview Grange to see someone, so I'll see you later.'

'No,' Angie said, 'I won't be back tonight. We're staying in Plymouth, Fergal and I.'

'What, in the caravan?'

'Not likely!' Angie replied. 'We're going to celebrate my good fortune at a restaurant and then a club in the Barbican after which I've booked us into a nice hotel. We may even stay for a couple of nights.'

'Well, good for you!' Kate said. 'See you whenever!'

*

Thirty minutes later Kate parked her car in the layby. It was a quarter to five. She'd sit in the car for five minutes and then make her way along to Seaview Grange and the garden shed.

She'd deliberately worn a dark blue anorak with a hood, which she now pulled up over her head because not only had it begun to drizzle but her still-auburn hair could be a giveaway and she'd surmised, from the tone of Stan's message – if it was from Stan – that it was imperative she should not be seen.

Luckily, no one was around. She skirted the building, her head down, becoming equally nervous and increasingly excited at the revelation to come. It *must* be David Courtney, surely! Or Edgar maybe? Or…? *No*, she scolded herself, *stop this futile guessing! Very shortly you will* know*!*

Kate made her way back towards the garden shed. It was dark early because of the weather and the only sound that could be heard was the drumming of the rain on the roof of the shed. The door wasn't locked. She peered inside, but no one was there. She'd never been round to the back of the shed before and it seemed as if nobody else had either, apart from Stan obviously, because the uneven ground was littered with undisturbed stones and weeds.

Now Kate could see, lying on the ground, a large iron cover, larger than a normal manhole cover, which had been removed to expose a gaping void. Stan was certainly taking no chances! She looked warily down into the hole and saw stone steps descending into its depths.

'Stan?' she called loudly. No reply. Was he down there? 'Stan – it's me!'

Still no reply. She looked around and could see no one anywhere. She wondered if the light on her mobile phone could penetrate into the darkness of what was plainly a cellar.

'I'm on my way, Stan,' she called out as she cautiously made her way down a couple of steps, still looking anxiously around. He didn't appear to be there. The light only illuminated the next few steps and, as she turned to climb out, she was pushed roughly from behind, lost her balance, and the next thing she knew she was lying on a cold stone floor with aches and pains in every limb. Had she broken something?

Kate managed to sit up, relieved at least that her back wasn't broken, and gingerly felt her arms. She'd certainly sprained her wrist and her left elbow was badly grazed from what she could make out in the gloom. She tried to stand and, as she wobbled to her feet, felt her legs buckle. She put out her hand and supported herself against what was presumably a wall, although her eyes hadn't yet adapted to the darkness. She looked around in the near darkness at the empty cellar – it was probably around nine feet square, with stone walls and a stone floor. As her eyes became accustomed to the gloom she realised that the place was completely empty and very cold. Who had pushed her?

Just then she heard someone coming down the steps behind her. She tried to turn round. 'Is that you, Stan?'

All she remembered afterwards was the deafening crash on the side of her head before she passed out. And then – oblivion.

Blackness. Then grey mist and everything a blur.

Kate struggled to see, to wake up from this nightmare. She wanted to lift her hand to feel the side of her head where the pain was, but she couldn't.

Slowly the blur diminished and Kate could just decipher three stone walls and a stone floor, on which she was sitting with her back against the fourth wall. She tried to move her feet but couldn't. Then she tried to move her arms, but couldn't do that either. It took Kate a few minutes to realise that her hands were tied behind her back and her ankles were roped together. She tried to shout, then, exhausted, closed her eyes again. Surely she'd wake up from this nightmare in a minute?

'No point in shouting,' said a voice, which was definitely not Stan's. 'No one can hear you down here.'

CHAPTER THIRTY-ONE

Kate, her head thumping, turned with difficulty towards the sound. Every bone in her body was thumping.

Hetty Patterson smiled.

'What the—?' Kate stared in horror at the little woman.

'Make yourself comfortable, Nurse,' Hetty said, 'because you aren't going anywhere. Ever.' She smiled again. 'You've meddled once too often,' she went on, 'so this is entirely your own fault. I had to hit you, I'm afraid,' Hetty added politely, 'because otherwise I wouldn't have been able to tie you up.'

Kate was still staring at her in total disbelief. 'What have I ever done to *you*?' she asked, desperate to rub her head. Was she suffering from concussion perhaps and was this really happening at all?

'What have you done to *me*?' Hetty snapped. 'I hear you got as far as my jewellery drawer, not that you'd have found anything there. And then you chose the *wrong* pot, Nurse!'

Kate was still desperately trying to gather her thoughts together. This tiny woman *had* hidden evidence in a flowerpot then and she, Kate, had chosen the wrong damned one! But... none of this was making any sense. Why had she been so stupid as to think that Stan might have sent that text? Oh, God.

'You killed Sharon?' she asked after a moment. She was beginning to feel a wave of terror invading her body.

Hetty leaned down and looked straight into Kate's eyes. 'Needs must, Nurse. She found my syringe, damn her! The silly woman thought I'd gone out but I'd gone upstairs to help David sort out

Edina's things. It was as I was coming out that I heard her talking on the phone – presumably to *you*?' She didn't wait for an answer. 'I couldn't be having *that*, Nurse.'

'So how did you kill her?'

'She was caught off-guard at the foot of the stairs. One whack with the lighthouse and down she went!' Hetty said cheerfully.

Kate shuddered. 'So you bludgeoned her to death?'

Kate was staggered beyond belief to think that this tiny woman was capable of such evil. Why? And was she, too, about to be bludgeoned to death? She tried desperately to move her limbs; there was slightly more leeway with her wrists than with her ankles. If she had time she might be able to loosen them eventually, but she doubted time was on her side. In spite of being tied up she realised she was shaking. Terror had replaced pain and curiosity.

'But,' Kate said, staring at her and desperately playing for time, 'that means you must have killed *Edina*! Your *friend*, Edina!' Even if she was about to be bludgeoned to death, she needed to know. She needed to keep her talking too because, when the conversation ended, who knew what could happen?

'She took everything that was mine,' Hetty spat. '*Everything*. I spent years trying to find her, you know.'

In spite of her continuing headache Kate was frantically trying to make sense of the conversation. Again, she wondered if she was having some sort of prolonged nightmare. *Please, God, let me wake up in a minute!*

'I don't understand,' Kate said. That was most definitely an understatement.

'Why should you? It's none of your business,' Hetty snapped.

That much was true, Kate supposed. She stared at Hetty, who seemed to be in some sort of trance.

'He was *so* beautiful,' she said at last.

'Who was?' Kate asked quietly. *Keep her talking, for goodness' sake.*

'My son,' Hetty replied. 'So beautiful. Perfect.'

Hetty had had a *son*? *Keep her talking.* 'I'm sure he was,' Kate said.

'He should have grown up to study medicine, or law,' Hetty continued. 'But it wasn't possible.'

'What wasn't possible, Hetty?' Her mouth was so dry she was having difficulty speaking.

'For him to grow up with me.'

'But why not?'

Hetty sighed deeply. 'It was my first teaching job, and they sacked me. I was a disgrace, they said. You didn't go having babies back in the sixties if you weren't married.'

'Ah,' said Kate, aware of the scandal this would have caused then.

'I tried to keep him,' Hetty said, 'I tried. But I couldn't go back home and I couldn't get a job...' Her voice tailed off.

Hetty had had to give up her baby, that much was obvious. Perhaps it had affected her mind? Kate needed to know.

'Hetty,' she asked, 'couldn't the father have helped you?'

'I loved him, you know,' Hetty said. 'I loved Roger. He was my one and only love. *Ever.*'

'What happened to Roger, Hetty?'

'He left me before I had his baby. He'd fallen in love with someone else.'

'That's *awful*!' Kate said. *Keep her talking, for God's sake!*

'And I couldn't afford to keep my baby.'

'So you had him adopted?' In spite of her situation Kate found herself feeling some sympathy for anyone who had to part with their baby.

'No, his father wanted him. He'd married the woman he left me for and his new wife couldn't have children. And they could give him the sort of life that I couldn't. He persuaded me it was the right thing to do, and I let him. More fool me!'

'Oh, Hetty, I'm so sorry. Did you ever see your son again?' She had to empathise with this woman, keep her talking...

'I waited,' Hetty replied. 'I waited and I waited until I heard that Roger had died. Then I went in search of the woman he'd left me for, the stepmother to my son. She was never kind to him, you know.'

Slowly, slowly everything was slotting into place. There was silence for a moment.

'Does David Courtney know he's your son?' Kate asked then.

'No,' Hetty replied. 'He has no idea. He thinks his mother died when he was very small. But, as you can see, I didn't.'

'You certainly didn't,' Kate muttered.

'Then Roger left all his money to Edina, with the proviso that it had to go to David after her death. And all David wanted was some of that money earlier when he really needed it.'

'And she wasn't parting with it?'

Hetty shook her head. 'That woman took my lover, and then my son. I've waited a long time to get my revenge.'

There was a further silence. Kate tried hard to think how she herself would have felt in those dire circumstances. As a mother, she could only imagine the agony of having to hand over your child. Hetty must have thought it preferable to hand him over to his natural father than the anonymity of a formal adoption. Perhaps, in her youthful innocence, she'd thought he'd keep in touch and let her see her boy from time to time. Plainly he hadn't.

'I'm so sorry, Hetty,' Kate said sincerely. 'But did you ever tell Edina that you were David's mother?'

Hetty shook her head. 'No, I did not. And it took me years to track them down because they'd lived abroad for some time. Australia. But apparently, she wanted to come back to Europe and to her opera. She was a good singer in her day, you know.'

'So I've been told,' Kate said. Hetty seemed to be still deeply ensconced in the past and Kate wondered what was going to happen when she returned to the present. She couldn't see anything that could be used as a weapon but who could know what this woman was likely to do next? Kate tried to control her shaking but she continued to feel pure terror permeating every inch of her body.

'But she was a lousy mother,' Hetty added. 'So when I heard she was buying a flat here, I decided to buy a flat here too. Then I had to wait some more for a good opportunity to kill her.'

'Did you always plan to kill her?' Kate asked.

'Oh yes, I had to bide my time. But David needs that money. It'll be his now.'

In spite of her terror Kate decided she had little to lose by asking some more questions.

'So you injected digoxin into Edina's meals?'

'Wasn't that a *brilliant* idea!' Hetty's face lit up. 'And wasn't I *lucky* that those meals were delivered on the morning of the very day when I was leaving for Bournemouth? I took them into my kitchen so I could take them up to Edina before I left. And, by the time I did what was necessary, I was sure she would not be around when I got back!' Hetty laughed.

'But how did you come by the digoxin, and the syringe?' Kate asked, suddenly aware that she might be about to be injected herself.

'All from my dear sister's bathroom cabinet! She stopped taking her digoxin when she started her cancer treatment and she's certainly not going to be needing it now, poor thing.' She was staring fixedly at Kate. 'And now it's *your* turn! Your *own* fault, Nurse, because you shouldn't have been meddling in my affairs. And now I'm off to see my dear sister again, for two or three weeks and probably for the last time. You're really lucky, you know, because I've run out of digoxin. If I'd known I wouldn't have injected *all* of Edina's meals because a couple would have done it, and then I'd have some left for you. I could bludgeon you, of course, but I've sprained my wrist rather badly after Sharon Starkey, so I'll just have to leave you to it.

'When I get back you should be dead. Because you can't get out of here and, believe me, you can't be heard. Nobody, not even your friend Stan Starkey, has been down here for years. It was an ice cellar, you know. Completely sealed. Very useful for those big houses in the days before refrigeration, I'm told. And I'll replace the iron cover when I go up and, let me tell you, there's a bar that goes over the top and keeps the cover down. It's unlikely anyone will remember this is underneath and you certainly won't be able to lift it up from the inside, even if you manage to free yourself.'

She stopped speaking and smiled to herself. 'When I first came here I heard there was an old ice cellar somewhere in the grounds and it's taken me some time to find it. I've had to check every inch. I'd thought of killing Edina down here, but the digoxin did the trick.' She glared at Kate. 'Someone, I suppose, *may* find you eventually, but you'll be long gone, and they certainly won't suspect me.' She waved a plastic-gloved hand in Kate's direction. 'I'm only doing what's necessary, Nurse. I'm not having David's life messed up any further.'

Was this the act of a woman consumed with love for the son she had had to give up, or was she mad? Probably both. Kate knew she had to have one last try to save her own life.

'I'm sorry, Hetty. I had no idea of the misery you must have suffered. But your secret's safe with me.' Not true, of course, and unlikely Hetty would fall for it.

Hetty shook her head. 'I don't blame you for trying to get out of here, Nurse.' She bent down so her face was only inches from Kate's and smiled. 'But I'm afraid I don't believe you.'

'Hetty, I—'

'Shut up!' Hetty roared. 'It's getting dark, so go to sleep. It'll pass the time.' With that she stood up straight and then headed towards the steps. 'Farewell.'

The last sound Kate heard was the heavy clang of the cover being replaced at the top of the stairs and then the rolling of something over the top, which was presumably the iron bar being set in position.

Then silence. Total silence.

CHAPTER THIRTY-TWO

Blackness, complete blackness.

Kate found herself blind in the dark, sealed in an underground cell. It was dank and cold. *I have to get loose*, she told herself, *there's got to be a way out of here*.

There was no light and she could feel no incoming air. How long could she survive? The relief she'd felt at not being bludgeoned or injected was now being replaced by a new terror: to die alone, gasping for air and water, down here in this horrendous place.

Kate fiddled with her wrists. Was it her imagination or had the rope loosened very slightly? Hetty had said she'd sprained her wrist so perhaps the knot was not as tight as she'd intended it to be. She shuffled around some more on her bottom on the cold stone floor. She had to get free because she had to get out of here. Kate pulled her wrists apart as much as she could bear with the rope burning into her skin. Then she waited for the pain to subside before pulling again. One more pull and surely she could slide one hand out?

It took two more attempts and then, sighing with relief, Kate was able to wriggle one hand out and then the other. Now she needed to feel for the knot that tied her ankles together. She drew her feet up and searched tentatively with her fingers. For such a tiny woman with a sprained wrist, Hetty Patterson had somehow succeeded in tying a strong, tight knot round her ankles. It would take time, but Kate reckoned she probably had plenty of that. Or had she? How long would the air last in a sealed cellar? And how long could she survive without water?

Then she suddenly remembered – her phone! She dug into the right-hand pocket of her anorak, and then the left. No phone. Not in her jeans either. Of course Hetty would have removed it! Even if she hadn't, Kate reckoned there would be no signal down here.

For the first time since she'd stupidly fallen for that text and voluntarily walked down into what was rapidly becoming her tomb, Kate wept. How could she have been so damned stupid? She wept not only for her own stupidity but also for the fact that she now had to face a slow and probably agonising death.

She must not panic. *Someone* would find her. She was *not* going to die. No way – not Kate Palmer! And certainly not at the hands of that evil little woman. Kate felt a fingernail tear, with a shot of pain. She automatically put the finger into her mouth and tasted blood. She couldn't let that stop her. But the knot was beginning to unravel. She'd have to be patient and probably lose all her nails in the process. She needed to be able to stand up and feel her way round the walls, then she could climb the staircase and at least *try* to remove the cover above. And she could shout.

Kate felt a tiny glimmer of hope. She wasn't dead yet and she could have been if Hetty had followed her usual methods of disposing of people.

Another fingernail snapped. She tried in vain to pull her ankles apart but the rope was far too tight. She worked on the knot some more. And, as she did so, she suddenly remembered the dog. Oh God, poor Barney! She'd shut him in the kitchen before she set out for Seaview Grange and she tried hard to remember if she'd filled up his food bowl or his water bowl. If only Angie decided to stay in Plymouth for one night instead of two, it wouldn't be too bad. There'd be puddles on the floor, of course, but that wouldn't matter. Oh, the poor, poor dog! He'd never spent much time without one or the other of them ever since they'd rescued him from the dogs' home three years before. He'd wonder what was going on and he'd most likely howl, but would anyone hear him?

At last Kate was having some success. She felt part of the knot loosen and dug her fingers into the next curl of rope. It was going to take time, but she could do this. She had to be able to move, to stand, to walk around in this dank dark prison, to find an escape. She shivered, chilled already.

Relieved that she had luminous numbers on her watch at least, Kate noted that it was almost seven o'clock, and she'd been in this hell-hole for nearly two hours.

And then she *did* it! The knot loosened and Kate was finally able to lift her feet out of their prison. The rope had scorched her right ankle but she couldn't feel any blood so hopefully it hadn't penetrated the skin. She wiggled her toes to combat the beginnings of pins and needles.

Slowly Kate attempted to get to her feet, staggering as she did so, and automatically stretching out her hand to steady herself against the invisible wall. For a moment she thought her legs might buckle under, and then she found the wall and rested against it until she got her balance back. Her head still ached but the pain had diminished slightly.

Kate set off, feeling her way round the walls inch by inch. On the fourth wall she stumbled on something, then realised it was the bottom tread of the steps. She hesitated for a moment before slowly ascending, terrified of losing her balance and falling in the absence of any type of handrail. When she felt her head brush against something solid she realised that she'd reached the top and the iron cover. Flexing her muscles, she raised both hands above her head and pushed hard. Nothing. No movement, no give at all. But perhaps she could be heard?

Kate shouted. She shouted, 'Help!' and 'I'm in the ice cellar!' and, finally, '*Please*, somebody help me!' Then silence. Was it still raining? She listened for a minute and realised she could hear the muffled pattering of the rain on the iron overhead. So, everyone would be indoors and who was going to be around to hear her? Stan was her only hope. He just might be pottering around in the garden somewhere, although highly unlikely on such a murky evening.

She sat down at the top of the steps and considered her plight. No one was likely to miss her until tomorrow at the earliest, and no one was likely to be wandering around the grounds of Seaview Grange until tomorrow morning, if then. Somehow or the other it looked as if she was going to have to survive the night in here and save her strength for hammering and shouting tomorrow. But what could she hammer with other than her bare knuckles? Kate felt in her pockets. A couple of tissues, three Polo mints, a clothes-peg! Where had *that* come from? And a scrap of paper. Was there anything written on it? She had no idea. And tapping a clothes-peg against a heavy iron cover was not going to get her very far.

Kate leaned forward with her head in her hands and considered the hopelessness of her situation. Someone *might* find her eventually but how long could she survive without air and water? A day? Two days? She mustn't get thirsty and she must conserve oxygen by not moving around too much.

Comfort was not an option. She had the choice of a cold, hard step, or a cold, hard floor. She checked her watch again: nearly eight o'clock. No one was likely to be around for at least twelve hours. And tomorrow was Saturday. Did Stan work on a Saturday? Would anyone be anywhere near the garden shed area? And could they hear her if they were?

Kate made her way carefully down the steps and felt for the wall again. She'd sit down with her back against it and do some thinking. She wished she could take off her anorak and roll it up to make a cushion for herself, but she felt far too cold. Shivering, she sat down and rested against the wall, trying not to cry. Crying might give her some relief but it solved nothing and she'd only got a couple of tissues.

What if she was never found? A skeleton in the ice cellar. They'd find her car parked in the layby and wonder why on earth it was there. Surely Woody would come looking? He was due home tomorrow evening and he was bound to phone her when he did. Perhaps if he didn't get any reply on her mobile or the landline he might begin to worry. Her mobile – where had Hetty dumped her mobile? She'd probably stamped on it, broken it in a million pieces and then dumped it into a bin somewhere on her way to bloody Bournemouth.

Kate felt her chances of escape diminishing again. But maybe they'd start to comb the area on Sunday? Could she survive that long? Kate looked around. There wasn't a glimmer of light anywhere, so this hole was well and truly sealed off, which it would be of course, due to its original purpose as an ice cellar. She suddenly thought how awful it must be to be blind. They did say though, didn't they, that if you were blind, your other senses became sharpened: hearing, feeling, smelling, tasting. Nothing here to listen to, apart from the patter of the rain, nothing to smell – apart from mould and damp – or feel, apart from cold, hard stone.

How had one tiny, eighty-something-year-old woman got the better of her like this? Would she ever see her boys again? Or the lovely little grandson? She tried to imagine how they'd receive the news. 'We regret to inform you that your mother, Katherine Elizabeth Palmer, aged 58, was found dead in a cellar belonging to a large house in Cornwall.' They'd be horrified. *What the hell was she doing in a cellar?* they'd ask.

Woody would know she'd been investigating. 'You shouldn't have got involved,' he'd shout at her lifeless body. 'I *told* you not to get involved!' And, of course, no one would ever suspect dear little Hetty. Dear little Hetty with the dying sister. The mystery of who killed Edina Martinelli, Sharon Starkey and Kate Palmer would never be solved. All evidence would long ago have disappeared and no one would point a finger at a tiny old lady. Would she ever tell David Courtney that she was his mother? Probably not. She'd look on fondly while he spent the money on reviving his business, and he'd never know what she'd done.

Were her actions that of a mother sent mad by grief, or had she always been a psychopath?

Kate awoke with a start and a crick in her neck. Her head had fallen forwards while she dozed. It took a few seconds to work out where she was and then she remembered and the nightmare returned. She rubbed her neck and her bottom which had become numb on the hard, cold floor. It was 22.25, and there was a long night ahead.

She staggered to her feet and began to walk up and down. It took five normal paces, she discovered, to walk from one wall to the opposite one. Perhaps she'd try walking round the four of them, her right hand against the wall to guide her. Kate walked and walked, being careful when she got to the steps which broke up the fourth wall. She wondered if she might become dizzy walking round and round in such a confined space.

She was thirsty. She'd ration herself to one Polo mint and hoped that might help. If only she'd thought to bring a bottle of water with her, like she did when she walked the dog. The dog! How *was* poor Barney? Kate sat on a step and tried not to cry. No amount of crying was going to get her out of this hell-hole. And no amount of shouting was going to be heard by anyone at this late hour, so she'd conserve her strength in an effort to survive as long as possible.

Then Kate prayed again that Angie might decide to stay only one night in Plymouth. She prayed too that Woody would try to phone her and then wonder where on earth she'd got to. Kate was not a religious woman but, like most people, was not above begging for some divine help when needed. And, God, did she need it now!

She resumed walking round the walls. Five or six paces, turn, another five or six paces… How did people survive in solitary confinement in dungeons and places, sometimes for years? At least they must have had some inflow of air and water. Aware that she had neither, Kate reckoned again that perhaps the diminishing oxygen supply could be maximised if she didn't use up too much of it exercising. But exercising, such as it was, was preferable to sitting on that hard floor again, her back against the wall. She considered lying down; perhaps if she got herself into some sort of foetal position she might be able to doze. Anything was worth a try.

Kate lowered herself gingerly onto the floor. If she folded up the hood of her anorak into a ball, it might serve as some sort of pillow. She was never *ever* going to complain about hard mattresses or lumpy pillows again! Never!

She closed her eyes and prayed for sleep.

Kate woke after half an hour, then dozed for a few minutes and then woke up again. This pattern repeated itself until quarter past three, when she decided she was too cold and too uncomfortable to contemplate any proper sleep. She walked round the four walls again, realising she was coming to know them quite well. There was some protruding stone on wall number two, and a row of little dents in wall number three. Number four featured the steps, and number one was relatively smooth. Then she sat on the second-to-bottom step again, and realised, with a shock of terror, that she was beginning to find it difficult to breathe. She looked at her watch again; it was 7 a.m. She realised she needed to conserve the oxygen as much as she could and, feeling cold and exhausted, stumbled back to the corner and lay down again. Feeling nauseous and light-headed and terribly thirsty, she began to drift in and out of consciousness.

She was in Queensland with Jack and Eva, swimming in the warm sea at the Gold Coast, visiting the koala sanctuary, with the barbecue to look forward to later. A world away with constant sunshine, and her deeply tanned son saying earnestly, over and over again, 'You should move out here, Mum!' Oh, how she wished she had!

Now she was up in Edinburgh with Tom and Jane, in their grey stone house, the cold east wind rattling its ill-fitting sash windows. 'We're going to get them double-glazed, Mum, but it's expensive because we don't want to lose the character.' The house was warm and cosy inside though, with its pale-yellow painted nursery because, at first, anyway, they hadn't wanted to know the sex of the baby. Best to be safe with yellow. Then the angelic little bundle that was Calum Fraser Palmer arrived, two days after her own birthday. 'You should come up more often, Mum,' said Tom, and Jane nodded in agreement.

Next Kate saw Calum as a bigger boy, wanting to know about his Granny Palmer. 'Granny Palmer died in a cellar when you were a baby, Calum,' they said. 'Why?' he asked. 'What was she doing in a cellar?' 'You may well ask!' roared Woody, who was there as well. 'Because she got *involved*! How often I told her not to get involved!' And Angie said, 'Well, at least Fergal can move in now!'

Kate woke with a start. Back to the waking nightmare, the blackness and the silence and the cold. She saw with some horror that she'd slept throughout the day, that it was now eleven at night. Her thoughts were becoming jumbled and fuzzy. Was it still Saturday? How much longer would she be able to breathe this air? She was already struggling. It was taking all her energy to force her lungs to get the oxygen out of the air. And she had a raging thirst.

She wouldn't be able to shout now even if she had the energy because her mouth was so dry that her lips were sticking to her teeth and she couldn't form the words properly. She'd eaten the other two Polo mints. She'd read somewhere that you could drink your own urine which, although not an attractive proposition, wasn't even possible without some sort of container to catch it in.

Kate finally wept and then wondered if she could drink her salty tears. She felt incredibly tired. Time ceased to matter. She was in Hell, and Hell was supposed to be hot. This hell was freezing cold. Nobody had missed her. She was going to die down here, and soon. She looked at her watch. Now it was 11.25.

Kate lay down on the floor and waited.

CHAPTER THIRTY-THREE

Somewhere, deep in the nightmare, a dog was barking hysterically. She knew that sound, that bark, but she was too exhausted to open her eyes, or care for that matter. Even through her closed eyelids there seemed to be light. If this was Heaven it was OK because they obviously allowed dogs. A near-death experience they called it, but this was surely a *real*-death experience – all light and air and nothing to be afraid of any more. If she had the energy she'd open her eyes and look down on her crumpled body in the cellar. *Who needs a body anyway?* This was much, much nicer, this floating on air.

Now she was moving towards the light in the tunnel that everyone spoke about. And there were voices. Male voices. She'd really have preferred a choir of angels.

CHAPTER THIRTY-FOUR

Kate had no idea where she was when – at around four in the afternoon, she later discovered – she opened her eyes to a blur of daylight and lots of white everywhere. Where had all this white come from? What was this thing stuck in her arm? Who was calling her name? 'Kate, Kate,' someone was saying. *Yes, that's me, I'm Kate*, she thought. She felt warm and comfortable, so she'd probably died and gone to Heaven.

'Kate, Kate, darling…'

Darling? She hadn't been called 'darling' in years! Who would be calling her 'darling'?

Things began to take shape through the blur. Why was there a drip in her arm? And someone was holding her hand. Who? Kate focussed her attention toward the direction of the voice.

'Woody?'

'Oh, thank God,' said Woody, squeezing her hand.

'Where am I?' Kate had always wondered if people *really* said that, and now here she was saying it herself! She wanted to giggle; she'd say it again. 'Where am I?'

'You're in hospital, Kate, recovering from your ordeal.'

'Ordeal?'

'Remember, in the cellar? Kate, tell me, who shut you in down there?'

The cellar! The cold; the damp; the thirst. She hadn't died then?

'I thought I was going to die,' she said.

'You damned well nearly did, Kate. *Please*, can you tell me who shut you in that cellar?'

Everything was coming back now. 'How did you find me?'

'Barney found you, Kate. But who—?'

'Hetty,' Kate said, struggling to sit up. 'It was Hetty.'

'*Hetty? Hetty Patterson?*'

'That's her.'

'Dear God, *why?*'

A nurse had appeared, looking stern. 'Take it easy,' she admonished Woody, 'you're not to tire her.'

'No, no,' Woody agreed. He released Kate's hand. 'I'll be back in a minute.'

Kate could hear him talking outside the door. 'Who's he talking to?' she asked the nurse.

'Probably to the policeman who's been on watch outside,' the nurse replied.

'Oh,' said Kate, 'good.'

And she dozed off to sleep again.

When she awoke Woody was there again.

'What are you doing here?' she asked sleepily.

'Well, that's a fine welcome from your knight in shining armour! Not that I can take all the credit; it was Barney who led us to you.'

'Barney?' Kate opened her eyes fully.

'Your dog. *He* found you really,' Woody said.

'He did? How… why…?' Kate struggled to sit up. She felt pain in every bone in her body. 'Woody, I'm so sorry for ignoring your warnings. You must have gone through hell. Can you forgive me?'

'Of course I can! But don't worry about that now; I'm just so glad you're alive.

Can you please confirm – you did say it was *Hetty* who did this to you?'

'That's right. Hetty Patterson. She killed Edina and Sharon.'

'Unbelievable!' He adjusted her pillow. '*Hetty Patterson?* Edina Martinelli's friend?'

'She had her reasons, believe me! *Ouch!*'

'You're lucky, nothing is broken,' Woody said, 'but you're a mass of sprains and bruises. Now, tell me what happened.'

'I will, but first tell me how you found me?'

'OK,' Woody said. 'First of all I didn't get back from London until nearly midnight, thanks to an accident on the 303, just this side of Stonehenge, on the single carriageway. Hours and hours it took to clear; no escape route; no phone signal. Bloody awful! I decided it was far too late to phone you when I got home, but now I wish I had.'

'There was no signal in the cellar,' Kate whispered. 'Besides, Hetty took my phone.'

'No, but I'd have wondered why you weren't available, particularly if I couldn't get you on the landline either, and I'd have gone straight across to your place to see what was going on. It was around seven thirty this morning before I strolled over there, hoping you'd be up so I could cadge a cup of coffee.'

Kate was beginning to feel weepy. 'But I wasn't there.'

'No, you weren't there, and Angie wasn't there, and your car wasn't there. I couldn't work it out, and then I heard Barney howling.'

'Oh my God! Did you have a key with you?'

'Fortunately I did, and found a frantic Barney in the kitchen.'

Kate wiped a tear away with a tissue. 'The poor dog! He must have been shut in there since Friday.'

'He was pleased to see me, I can tell you! So I cleared up the mess, gave him some food and water—'

'Oh, *Woody!*'

'And then I phoned Angie, who was in Plymouth. What the hell was she doing *there*? She said something about seeing you on Friday before she left, and you were heading for Seaview. So then I tried to lock Barney back in the house again but he wasn't having any of it and started this awful howling, so I took him with me, running all the way from your place to mine and then we drove up to Seaview.'

'And then Barney found me?'

'First, I found your car in the layby. What was it doing there?'

'It's a long story…'

'And then,' Woody continued, 'I went to see Stan Starkey but he hadn't seen you and knew nothing at all about any visit, like Angie had told me. But, all the time, Barney was straining on the lead. I guess he was trying to tell us something and it took a few minutes to sink in. Then I let him lead us across the grounds and round to the rear of the garden shed. At first we couldn't see anything because the cellar door had been cleverly covered over with leaves and stones and was hardly visible. But Barney was pawing away at the cover and Stan remembered it was there, so that's how we found it. And you.'

'What a great dog he is!' Kate wiped away some fresh tears. 'And thank you so much for bringing him with you when you went up there. I'm so sorry…'

Woody took her hand. 'Hey, don't get upset! Anyhow, Stan said the old ice cellar hadn't been used for years but it was still mighty airtight, so I guess we got to you just in time.'

'Oh Woody!' The tears were flowing freely now. 'I'm so sorry for what I've put you through! I thought I'd died!'

'You damned nearly did! Now, tell me everything.'

CHAPTER THIRTY-FIVE

Kate arrived home the following morning, accompanied by Woody, welcomed by a relieved Angie and an ecstatic Barney. The dog had spent the previous evening being praised and thoroughly spoilt with an enormous steak dinner.

Bill Robson, of course, had wasted no time in making an appearance, complete with voice recorder.

'I've been told not to tire you,' he said. 'But I thought you'd like to know that Miss Patterson has been arrested in Bournemouth.'

Kate nodded. 'She killed them both, you know, and she had a bloody good try at killing me. How did you know where to find her?'

'Fortunately, David Courtney had the sister's address, although he couldn't understand why anyone would want to question *dear little Hetty*,' Bill Robson said drily. 'We'd have found her eventually anyway.'

Kate felt a sudden surge of pity for David Courtney. It was inevitable that Hetty's motive for killing Edina would eventually come out. He'd discover his real mother, and then lose her to what would almost certainly be a life sentence…

'He's got some shocks coming to him,' she said sadly.

'He has indeed,' said the detective inspector, 'but now, in your own words, can you tell me exactly what happened?'

And so she did.

'I've been given two weeks' leave over Christmas!' a beaming Kate informed Woody a few days later. 'They said they couldn't possibly refuse me after what I've been through!'

'Thank God some good's come out of it all,' Woody said, 'and I'm delighted. Do you think we can get to California and back without you getting involved in some murder or other?'

Kate grinned. 'I can't of course *promise* because you just never know! I shall have to start watching more American crime programmes!'

Woody sighed. 'I'm not going to let you out of my sight when you get over there because, God knows, there's plenty of crime in LA.'

'I'm only feeling a little nervous at meeting your mother,' Kate confessed, 'although I'm sure she's lovely.'

'She is lovely and she's going to love you. Now, I'm booking my ticket for December 6th and I'll book yours for the 20th, which will give us two weeks together over Christmas and then we can fly back in early January after New Year. Say around the 5th or 6th?'

Kate felt a surge of happiness and excitement. 'Will it be sunny over there?' she asked.

'Of course it'll be sunny,' Woody replied. 'It's always sunny in California.'

A LETTER FROM DEE

Dear Reader,

Thank you for reading *A Body in Seaview Grange* and I hope you enjoyed meeting Kate Palmer, amateur sleuth, again. She's not finished yet so if you'd like to keep up with her further escapades, or any of my other books, you can sign up on the following link:

www.bookouture.com/dee-macdonald

Your email address will never be shared and you can unsubscribe at any time.

And, if you enjoyed this book, I would appreciate it if you could write a review because I love to know what my readers think and your feedback is invaluable.

And you can get in touch via Facebook and Twitter.

Dee x

AuthorDeeMacDonald

@DMacDonaldAuth

ACKNOWLEDGEMENTS

This book would not have taken shape without the invaluable help of my editor, Lucy Dauman, whose expertise and encouragement have shaped my ramblings into a credible plot. Many thanks to Lucy for everything she's done.

My thanks too to my very supportive agent, Amanda Preston at LBA Books, and a special thanks to my friend and mentor, Rosemary Brown, who knocks my plots into shape and without whom you'd probably have guessed the killer's identity by page 2!

I must thank Stan Noakes, my husband, for his support and patience, and my son, Daniel, and family, who keep me up to date on reviews.

And, as ever, a huge thank you to the expert, dedicated Bookouture team who all contribute to the publication of this book: Kim Nash, Noelle Holten, Sarah Hardy, Alex Crow, Hannah Deuce, Hannah Bond, Alexandra Holmes and my cover designer, Tash Mountford. What a fantastic team they are and, also as usual, a thousand apologies to anyone I've unwittingly omitted.

Made in United States
Orlando, FL
04 April 2023

31742368R00138

Practice nurse Kate Palmer is ready for so
quiet in her little Cornish village, but there
a murder on her doorstep...

Kate's retirement in Cornwall hasn't qu
planned – Lavender Cottage is in need o
repairs and her sister Angie's fondness f
rather stretch the purse-string

So when Kate is asked to do some nursing
retirement flats in Seaview Grange, she j
chance. The old Victorian house has stun
the sea and the retirees are a peaceful bu
until Edina Martinelli, a glamorous ex-o
is found poisoned in her hom

Edina's death is ruled an overdose by Digo
medication she had been on for years. But
woman she met was not suicidal, and with
of her practice on the line, she decides to do
Luckily she's got the newly retired Detect
Woody Forrest to help her...

It's not long before Kate discovers evidenc
and there's no shortage of suspects. Was
vicar? The ill-tempered stepson? Or per
neighbour finally had enough of her cons
It seems everyone had a motive, but who
had the stomach for murder? And will th

ℬ www.bookouture.com

ISBN 978-1-83888-214-3

90000

9 781838 882143